Louise Burfitt-Dons is an author and a screenwriter of TV
movies shown on television networks worldwide. She was
born in Kuwait and has lived in the UK, Australia and France.
Louise is married with two daughters and one granddaughter.
Her home is now London with her husband Donald.

Stay up-to-date with Louise at:

www.louiseburfittdons.com

Twitter @LouiseBurfDons

Facebook /LouiseBurfittDons

'The world of British Jihadi brides and internal bullying of political parties. Domestic violence, trafficking, sharia law... a terrific book for our times.' Harriet Khataba, *Her Story Matters*

'Ambitious, fun and chillingly real.' LBC

'Jihadi Terrorists and Tory Party politics combine in a thriller written by an insider.' Goodreads.

'The complexity of the terrorist threat undermining British society today ... Original, compelling.' RSA

'Great political story built around politicians, radicals, Muslims and Islamists --- who want to become martyrs.' *Crime Reader*

'A wonderfully written fast-paced political thriller! Brilliantly constructed plot and fascinating look inside the villain's mind.' Ellie Midwood, *Girl from Berlin*

'I was really desperate to get to the last few chapters of this book to find out how everything tied together! Intense and teasing.' Vine Voice Reviewer

I was gripped from the beginning! I had been reading in the news about the Jihadi bride trying to return to the UK and enjoyed watching the Bodyguard series and suddenly I was in the middle of Louise's story. I was enthralled by Zinah, her influence over women and the terrorist threat she presented. A very real story of modern day Britain. A great read. I can't wait for the next Karen Anderson book.' Amazon Customer

A fascinating behind the scenes of politics, feminism, jihadi recruits which grips from the start.' Waterstones reviewer

'Contemporary Britain, portrayed with as much vivid setting and attention to detail that Christie gifted to her Marple books. A convoluted and clever plot. An exceptional read.' Goodreads.

'A well-written insightful thriller with several threads that fairly hums along. The author's description of the inner workings of the Conservative Party is an education in itself. Add to this the view of life in post-Brexit Referendum Britain from the viewpoint of a private investigator, a born-again jihadist and the numerous other protagonists and you've got a recipe for thrills that reaches a climax at the Party Conference. Looking forward to another Karen Anderson novel.' Amazon Customer

'A current, relevant read. Karen a private detective, finds herself caught up amongst ISIS extremists as well as corrupt politicians. A read that was close to home literally as I reside in a London Borough. The author embraced the relevant issues and created an interesting page turner.' Amazon Customer

Also by Louise Burfitt-Dons

<u>FICTION</u>

The Missing Activist
The Killing of the Cherrywood MP

<u>NON-FICTION</u>

Moderating Feminism

<u>PLAYS AND SCREENPLAYS</u>

Kidnapped to the Island
Mother of All Secrets
Your Husband Is Mine
The Ex Next Door
Christmas in the Highlands
Aka Christmas at the Castle
The Counsellor
A Christmas Riddle
Act Against Bullying Monologues
The Valentine Card
Painkillers

THE
SECRET
WAR

LOUISE BURFITT-DONS

Published by NEW CENTURY

nc

A Paperback Original 2021
Copyright © Louise Burfitt-Dons 2021
The right of Louise Burfitt-Dons to be identified as the
author of this work has been asserted by her in
accordance with the Copyright, Designs and Patents Act
1988.

A CIP catalogue record for this book
is available from the British Library

ISBN: 978 1 91 644915 2

New Century
Duke Road
London W4 2DE

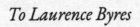

To Laurence Byres

Part One

THE LIVERPOOL CONNECTION

Chapter One

Ms Fong's front room filled with the pleasant aroma of vanilla and coffee beans. It was approaching ten o'clock and her favourite time of the day. The Chinese tutor had decided that morning in March she would resurrect Chairman Mao in her online classroom for the Liverpool High School students.

Lizzy Fong was trendy, trim and a stimulating teacher. Internet learning was no longer a big deal, but Zoom classes counted as a new thing. She was running much later than usual because she'd done the neighbourly deed and dropped off food to a pensioner under lockdown, unable to shop for himself. There was plenty still to gather before lessons began. Notes, quotes, pen, pad, props, and a tin of butter cookies.

Since her arrival in Liverpool from Beijing eighteen months ago, Elizabeth Fong had been an enormous hit. Her sessions never bored because they were always stimulating and unpredictable. The number studying Mandarin to GCSEs was double that of the previous year. She sometimes screamed, often swore, and even danced to music during her classes. The teacher was never subtle. But it was all to get the sleepy kids engaged in the learning process.

Lizzy Fong liked Zoom more now she was familiar with the software. Coming together face to face using the meeting app was as simple as wiping your nose. She'd sent the links with a password the night before, as per schedule. The pupils came online like ghosts appearing from the dark.

'Hiya, everybody.' The popular instructor greeted her early birds with open arms and a cheery wave. 'How are you?'

'Good morning,' they chorused back. She expected full attendance, and that's what she had got. Almost.

'Tony! Where are you, Mr Anthony? Tell your fans why you have no clothes on?' Lizzy Fong feigned alarm at the sight of the student's naked chest. Very Sarah Bernhardt.

'What?' The student leapt to his feet to show off the raspberry-print chinos and made a quick pirouette. As he circled, laughter rippled around the internet classroom followed by loud applause and whistles. Tony Gee, the know-it-all who liked to be the centre of attention working off his iPhone at a local sports ground, played to his public willingly.

'Tony, why are you in the damn park?' The students loved her street slang. She made squinty eyes and crossed her arms.

Another profile lit up. Lizzy Fong counted fifteen participants now amongst her audience who were mostly Chinese, British-born and clever as hell. Come the summer, this lot will smash the exams. Well, they would have aced every single one of them if it hadn't been for Covid-19 and the bloody government who'd gone and cancelled the GCSEs.

They'd sure beat the academic crap out of the rest of the slackers in the city, which meant big jobs and big bucks in the future.

Lizzy Fong sometimes dressed up as Mao Zedong when she covered this subject. She was a talented actress and did an excellent job too of Lao Zu, Confucius, Sun Tzu, Deng Ziaoping, and Aladdin. But today she'd run out of time to dress up and wore black slacks and a plain red shirt.

'Maoism is a philosophy Chairman Mao developed himself. Its emphasis is on the military line to capture power. He called it the Protracted People's War. The Leader liked to fight to get his way. What do you think of that?'

'All war is bad.' One of the younger students asserted.

'I agree,' said another.

'So, smarty pants. You don't want to take direct action? So this morning we will talk about ways of getting along with people who fail to share your views. Who has heard of International Relations? Explain why Chinese born in the UK always get top grades in the subject?'

'Do we have to answer in Mandarin?' Mrs Fong got this question every hour of the day.

'Do we have to answer in Mandarin?' she mimicked. 'Yes, stupid. You do. What do you kids think this is? A cookery class?'

Two of the girls covered their faces with their palms, while another dropped her lip.

'You bloody respond in English if you have to. It's up to you at this stage,'

'You ask in Mandarin,' said Tony. 'We will answer in English.'

All agreed on the compromise.

'How many of you are aware that Leslie Charteris was from Singapore? Does that name mean anything to you?' Ms Fong noticed her students shifting uneasily in their seats, in their bedrooms or in their kitchens. 'Come on. Am I that old? Don't you all know he wrote The Saint?'

They grinned into cameras and onto the communal screen, headphones on, full makeup applied.

'Roger Moore. Didn't he play James Bond?' Eric Yue suggested.

Tony jumped up and took aim at his laptop with an imaginary gun. 'De de de dee, de de dee.' He hummed the famous 007 theme.

'You want to take this class, Tony?' An eruption of nervous laughter followed.

'Leslie Charteris? Chinese? I never knew that,' one of the slower students chipped in.

'When the author arrived in the You Ess, what happened?' Lizzy Fong made a dark and menacing face. 'He couldn't become resident because of the what?'

'The Chinese Exclusion Act?' someone suggested.

'Yes. Very good. Now you are on the ball. At last you are awake. What did they call us? Orientals.'

'Nooo.'

'You could not live legally in the States. None of you. Not even if you had one parent who was full blood American.'

A latecomer joined the group, but out of shot. But they'd at least logged in to enter the class. Who was it? Still five students unaccounted for. It could be any of them. And she didn't have time to check every Johnny-come-lately.

'It's on the television,' said someone.

'What is?'

'My mum watches The Saint over and over.'

'Britain is definitely not like that,' another student declared. She had the habit of pissing off the teacher whenever she could.

'What?' Ms Fong shook her head from side to side. 'You don't believe this country is racist then? Where have you been all your life?'

'No. I do not.'

This prompted more tutting and pen tapping from the meeting. Lizzy encouraged this kind of intellectual conflict.

'Let me hear one student at a time, please. Jennifer Cheung, you go first.'

'You can't miss Chinese celebrities in the UK. They're everywhere. They wouldn't have become famous if there was racism.'

'Give one example, Jenny?'

'Gok Wan.'

'Is that the best you can do?' The teacher from Guangzhou pulled her red shirt down low on her hips. They talked like brainwashed puppets. 'Who told you there is no discrimination? Boris Johnson?'

'But there are many other examples.' Jennifer stressed her point. 'Michael Chow is famous for his restaurants.'

Other suggestions came forward rapid fire. Mostly young kids Ms Fong hadn't heard of.

'KT Tunstall. She played the piano from four years old.'

'Our community is the oldest in Western Europe, so of course we have made progress. But name me one minister in government who is ethnic Chinese.' *Did she need to drum it in?* 'Things must change here. And they will.'

'Have you marked our essays yet, Ms Fong?'

'Who asked that?' Lizzy Fong's assignment had been a thousand words in written Mandarin, on the formation and origins of the national Communist Party. Preparation for this class. 'Of course. I'll email your marks back to you soon.'

It'd been a good homework to set. The CCP considered students potential recruits. These kids would never refuse an offer from the party unless they needed a brain transplant. Only the top ranks qualified for 'ideological training and observation'. And those who trusted members like Lizzie Fong recommended. But she'd not broadcast that sort of insider info about.

'Who is that? Who is our late student? Why don't you show yourself, our latecomer?'

The blank screen filled with a black and white sign. It read 'Kill all Chinese before they kill us.'

A second message followed in hand scrawled letters. 'They started the virus.' Finally, a Nazi flag appeared.

Lizzie Fong steadied herself, dizzy with shock, and fumbled for her keyboard. The intruder began a racist rant in Scouse English.

Why couldn't she cut the creep off? In her panic, she'd forgotten how to do it.

She kept an eye on the dumbfounded Zoom class. One by one, their lights switched off.

'What, what, what, what?' Someone screamed back. 'Lock him out. Shut him down.'

The interruption had blind-sided her. How'd it happened?

'Find the controls, Miss Fong. At the bottom.'

She located the right icon next to Share Screen under Advanced Sharing Options.

Under the section entitled 'Who can share?' She'd allowed 'All participants'. She clicked the button 'Only Host' and closed the window.

Faint and frazzled, the teacher ran the computer mouse over the list of names to find and remove the hacker. But he'd checked out. And after all the dithering she was too late to stop the in-meeting file transfer of scenes showing Chinese atrocities, memes, sexual abuse images. She shut down the lesson with, 'I will message you.'

The unexpected AI assault floored her. The full fury of it left her trembling and mad with herself. It was *her* fault. She'd not taken adequate precautions against a cyber attack. It was an oversight waiting to happen.

Mistakes occur through haste, never through doing a thing at leisure, she thought. But crisis brings opportunity.

She must not waste it for the sake of the Party.

Chapter Two

On the morning of 28 March 2020, Karen Andersen switched off the TV in the Chiswick flat, which doubled as an office. Silence reigned supreme as she pondered her options.

Covid-19 had spread across the continents one by one. The global pandemic dominated the news networks. A statement from the Prime Minister detailed the very latest on lockdown restrictions. These only allowed you to leave home for food and medical supplies, travel to work, and daily exercise. It certainly didn't include having overnight sex sessions with people you don't live with.

So when her boyfriend, Haruto Fraser, called hands free on his mobile, she'd expected an answer to the what-time-will-you-be-here question. The plan was for him to move in with her at Devonshire Road that day and her prepared lamb dish was on slow cook ready for his arrival. But, unknown to her he was driving away from London to visit a sick relative, so that outcome now seemed highly unlikely.

'It's my uncle, whom I've barely heard of before today. My mother rang and insisted I do it. She does not understand lockdown rules at all.' The delay was almost welcome news. It gave Karen time to sort the place. If Haruto brought all his earthly possessions with him, they'd be tight on space. His new start-up enterprise in cyber surveillance meant that trunk-loads of lenses, batteries and weirdly shaped drones would all have to squash into the small two-bedroom flat.

'Where are you headed?' The screeching of car tyres over the Bluetooth confirmed that wherever it was, his driving skills hadn't improved.

'The M1 first. Then who knows? I don't even have a street. Just the name of a village near Liverpool called Tarbock Green. I've got a landline number, but of course he's not answering, is he?'

'That's enough for me to trace him.' Karen Andersen was a private investigator. The title might conjure up images of Lisbeth Salander from *The Girl With The Dragon Tattoo*, but mostly the work was quite pedestrian, involving CV checks or internet fraud. People also got in touch over stolen pets and missing relatives. So locating addresses was her thing, and she found out the address using reverse phone look-up tools.

'That is so helpful,' said Haruto. 'Thank you. I'll call you when I'm there.'

Her iPhone lit up next with the name, Quacker. If she got research work from his firm Partridge Securities, it'd be a different matter altogether. His cases included serious stuff for the Home Office. These gigs were anything but run-of-the-mill paper affairs. However, times had changed. Since Covid, with the possibility that a quarter of a million Brits might die from it, the most taxing task close to going undercover was contact tracing.

'I wanted to make you aware I'm down in Sussex. Chris told me not to come home. It's because of the virus thing.'

Quacker's wife worked for the NHS as a nursing sister and was at the sharp end of the fight against the speeding illness.

'OK.' Karen continued decontaminating the top of the piano. 'Has something happened between you?'

'I made the mistake of coughing over the phone and now she's told me to stay at our holiday place. Very pleasant it is too, despite the lack of some usual amenities.'

Karen thought it perhaps an excuse on Chris's part to keep her demanding husband at a distance while she did back-to-back nursing shifts.

'But I read in the papers they'd ordered all camps to close.'

'Well, this one is shut, officially. I'm lucky to get in. They've been turning campers away. But under Covid circumstances, it's a yes for now. Official government advice states sites can stay open, I quote, "Where people live in these as interim abodes whilst their primary residence is unavailable". I assume that means us. Chris, quite rightly, doesn't want me to go back to Acton. Pass corona on to her. She's in so much demand at the hospital.'

'But are you positive it's the virus?' Karen peered out the window at the unusually empty street below.

'No. I've got a high temperature. But I'm only assuming it. I'm not sure without a thermometer.' He started a fit of coughing. 'Other than the sensation of being kicked by a cart horse, I feel fine.'

'You don't sound too well.'

'One good thing, though. This place is excellent for Wi-Fi. It's only about fifty metres from an antenna. And now that they've cleared out the weekenders, there's nobody much using it. Might even fit a bit of video streaming in. Fourteen days in here and I'll need something to occupy myself.'

'Lucky that you snuck in when you did.'

'Britain's quite different to Holland in this. I've just learnt they are allowing all of their caravan parks to stay open as a herd immunity experiment. The theory is, spread the virus amongst the public. It'll either kill them off or they'll survive and be resistant to the strain forever more,' Quacker spluttered. 'I don't know that's too smart, though.'

'So what happens if they close your camp site?'

'Then I'm forced to leave because of the £1000 pound fine. And Chris has to move into a hotel, being frontline. I thought she'd go for that idea, but her immediate response was, "Only if it's five star", which I very much doubt.' He coughed several times.

'Is there anything I can do?'

'Yes, there is, actually.' Quacker lacked his usual confident tone. 'Why I called you was because Yorkshire rang.' He was referring to a one-man band up north which passed work to

Partridge Securities and vice versa. 'They've heard from the local MP, a constituent's daughter is missing.'

'When did this happen?'

'I should elaborate. She's not so much missing as put herself into self isolation. And not told her family where. And the mother's worried. With social distancing, no one can roam about the country like before.'

'No trains, no non-essential car travel.'

'And they reckon she may be in West London somewhere. So I suggested to them you would chase it up for them.'

'Consider it done,' said Karen Andersen.

'I'll send you over what I have, shall I?' Quacker signed off with a ghastly, choking gasp.

Within seconds, his email flashed up on Karen's screen with a photo attachment. An eighteen-year-old UCL student with friends living in a side street somewhere off Turnham Green Terrace.

It was a blessed relief to have the excuse to scout the neighbourhood. She circumvented the local vicinity. While quieter than usual, the Chiswick High Road was still busy despite the new restrictions. Hadn't anyone heard of social distancing?

At least six groups huddled close together on the green opposite the tube station, not a face covering between them. They included someone who fitted the description enough for Karen to take a punt and introduce herself.

15

The girl was sitting with a much older male student, a half-interested Lothario she'd hooked up with.

'I can't believe I'm on a search list!' The girl pulled her baseball cap down low and muttered under her breath, 'Sod off back to whoever you work for and say you didn't find me.'

'No,' Karen mumbled from behind her tight black mask.

'You're the bloody Covidstasi, aren't you?' she blurted out, curling her toes up in front of her on the grass. 'Tell tale tit.'

Karen Andersen hated busybodies who timed their neighbour's daily jogs least they exceeded the one-hour limit. Or bit your head off in the shop if you strayed two centimetres beyond the on-floor markings. She shied clear of snoops. But with corpses piling up from the corona, she'd willingly become one herself.

'Your mother deserves to know where you are. She is worried about you.'

'I thought you'd told her,' said her male companion.

'If I go back home, I'll be locked up there for bloody months,' she protested. 'I don't see the enormous deal with this staying-in thing.' She stared down at her phone, battling tears. 'Everyone overreacts.'

The boyfriend crossed his arms and shook his head in disapproval.

Karen left them to their private murmurings. When she returned to the flat, she washed her hands for twenty seconds, took off her shoes and jacket and disinfected them with antiseptic wipes. Then her keys and wallet. The kitchen, which doubled as a purification station, no longer smelt of garlic and coriander.

She was deep in the dumps over springing the girl who'd been trying to cling on to a one-sided relationship. It muddied her mood. Is that how Haruto felt? Why would he want to live with her? A pain in the backside sometimes.

A dismal thought to sour a sunny Friday afternoon in March.

17

Chapter Three

Friday would be tough for Helen Rogers. But the hospital was an opportunity to escape the hellhole. The grunge pad. The suicide flat, which smelt of bad drainage made worse by poor ventilation.

Time to move. This place is a prison.

She'd rather have hopped on a cheap flight and flown to Ibiza. Paradise compared to a bus ride for her shift. But it was lockdown and there were no planes leaving to party island. Plus, there was a fancy car at her disposal.

Helen had been awake since dawn. The dread and mood of apprehension hadn't yet abated. Somewhere she read that if you moved the hands of a watch anti-clockwise in your mind, you could reverse time. Wasn't that an old Cher number?

She found the song on her iPhone and played it through a Bluetooth speaker.

How Helen wished she could do that. *Rewind the clock to yesterday.* Way before the sex game which went so horribly wrong. Why had she suggested it? Anything to hold on to Paul Honey. Stop him making up with his greedy, money-grabbing wife. You won't be able to come round here any more, he'd told her. And you might give me corona too.

He was the one with the cough.

Putting on makeup, she daydreamed of being rich and loved. In the mirror she saw herself as pretty, alert, radiant. The music stopped.

She made coffee from the dregs of an old packet, so stale the aroma of nuts and wet cardboard filled her nose. The dark thoughts returned and flipped her into depression. She was sunk. No idea what to do next.

She'd twisted and lied for him, hadn't she? But the cover-ups and money laundering had counted for nothing. Not a dickie bird. He'd got her to under-invoice property deals, syphon funds through her own personal account and into his. All for zero. Zilch. Looking back, she would never have seen the cash, anyway. Not a penny.

The urge to call his number was almost overwhelming. In case the events of yesterday were just a blurred, confused dream. Her heart leapt at the thought.

Resist picking up the phone.

Act as if the whole incident never happened. She had to, had to, had to. It sapped her of any desire to get dressed.

She applied another coat of mascara to distract herself.

Turn a negative into a positive. His words.

Helen Rogers, valiant volunteer, was due at the Northwick Park Hospital. But today she didn't feel like it. So what would happen if she failed to show? Her non-appearance might attract unnecessary attention, that's what. The last thing she needed was scrutiny of her movements.

Carry on with the same routine. Act normal. Get on with it.

Anyway, Helen loved the Florence Nightingale role. Kind, efficient and unflappable was how she wanted to see herself one day. She deserved an MBE for her dedication during the crisis, didn't she? But her good-hearted gesture to help on a ward after the property office closed down hadn't worked on Paul Honey. She'd expected her selflessness to impress him and make him love her more.

'Great for your CV going forward to show you're doing something!' is how he'd responded. Patronising prick.

The memory stirred her into action, and she left the flat with a determined stride. It was a fresh spring morning as she slid into the driver's seat of Paul Honey's black Mercedes, which was wider than double her hallway.

This is the company vehicle he promised me. It's rightfully mine.

Helen belted out an Abba hit as she sped away, inhaling the new car smell which still lingered even two months on.

The law was clear. Essential workers only can leave their homes and travel to their place of employment. But the roads were busy. They couldn't all be frontline staff like her, she reckoned.

Get out of my way!

She streaked passed traffic, ignoring the angry blasts of horns as she cut across the lanes.

Helen reached the Tyburn Lane and parked in the adjacent side street. The red 182 bus was completely empty for the final hop, apart from a solitary relief driver heading to work.

Chapter Four

A t four in the afternoon, Liverpool University Hospital rang Haruto Fraser to let him know that Professor Tomio Nakamura, the seventy-two-year-old retiree, a former biochemical lecturer, had tested positive for Covid-19.

The drawing room of the professor's 1970s bungalow smelt of damp, unwashed laundry. The news did nothing to make him breathe easier either. His uncle who he'd packed off in an ambulance could die from the coronavirus.

It was a shock. Haruto had found him bent double on the front step, gasping for air. He still hadn't expected such a bleak prognosis.

He needed a drink. Or food. Or both. He checked out the limited stocks in the kitchen. A hoard of dried beans, canned apricots and bottled water. None of it turned him on. The fridge where most of the edible stuff lived was nearly empty.

He retrieved his rucksack from the back seat of the car. Packed solid with non-essentials, there were three cans of beer. But it was a stark choice. Flick the top off a warm Asahi or break open a bottle of Tomio's whiskey, which he usually only drank under protest. But at least something with which to fill his grumbling stomach. Neat Scotch would have to do.

Considering the unfavourable circumstances, he remained upbeat, if restless. He had planned to call his mother in Japan hours ago. But he'd become absorbed in his books. Tomio's front room was a mini library. Mostly science and engineering, it was also a mecca for maps, charts, atlases, and travel brochures from a past era.

A police car pulled up in the driveway and parked behind Haruto's Toyota. Two officers got out, a white female and an Asian male. Haruto preempted the knock and opened the door.

'Professor Naka - moo -?' The lady officer spoke first.

'Nakamura.'

'Oh yes. So, is he here now?'

'No. He's in hospital in Liverpool.'

There was none of the usual 'Can we step inside, sir?' Today police positioned themselves some distance from the front door to avoid the risk of contagion. It meant the officers were ankle deep in the overgrown grass.

'Sorry to hear that. Not coronavirus, is it?'

'Yes, it is.'

'Really?' The officer's eyes widened with astonishment.

'He caught it, unfortunately.'

'Wow.'

'Yup.'

'Well, I hope he'll soon be OK. I'm Kylie Brown. And this is Raj.'

'Right.'

'So, how's he doing?' Forgetting social distancing momentarily, she moved in closer to catch every word.

'Not good. I had a call from the doctor. They tried him on a ventilator, but he's not responding.'

'Oh, that's bad. And you can't visit him or anything, can you?'

'No. And it's only been an hour. I phoned the ambulance as soon as I got here.'

'As well you came when you did.'

Came when I did?

Several times, he'd thought, where were the neighbours? Why didn't they step in?

The condition of the house said worlds. Run down. In need of serious attention. But more than that. It screamed out, 'The black sheep of the community lives here.' Someone had thrown a stone, smashing a pane in the window and daubed graffiti on an outside wall, telling the paedo to move on.

'I'm not from here. My mother asked me to drive up and look in on him.'

'So, where are you from?'

'London.'

'But you'll be staying here for a while now, won't you?' Kylie stared at him with her suspicious police eyes.

'No.'

The officer glanced at the generous amount of Scotch in the tiny glass Haruto held in his hand and raised her eyebrows. *Drink driving?* 'He's rather reclusive, isn't he?'

'It seems so.'

'Doesn't get on famously with his neighbours. People in the street.' She jangled her car keys. 'We'll be on our way then.'

'What was it you wanted him for?'

The side-kick officer crossed his arms. 'The break in? You knew about that, did you?'

'I know nothing about it. I only drove in a few hours ago.'

Kylie took over. 'From what we understand, someone heard a commotion from the house. A week back? Didn't he tell you anything himself about the incident?'

'No.'

'Oh.'

'By the time I arrived, he'd collapsed. He wasn't up to saying a word.'

'A lady living nearby rang to say she'd seen a young man leaving this property bleeding profusely. But she wouldn't give us her name, so we can't verify the facts, can we? Thank you for nothing,' she said, cupping a hand to her cheek. 'No idea why they do that. Ring the police, then hide when we come.'

Her partner grinned. He clearly enjoyed his boss's dry irony.

She continued, 'So that's why we came round to see Mr - your relative.'

'Professor Nakamura.'

'He didn't want to open the door to talk to us.'

'Well, he likes to be left alone.'

She gave a half smile. 'We traced the young... shall we say... *person* only because he arrived at the hospital with significant stab wounds straight after the attack. They discharged him, but only after they'd checked him for the virus. We've since had a call that he tested positive. And they asked us to notify the professor so he could self-isolate.'

'He was already. He was a loner.' Haruto didn't think this required pointing out a second time.

'Look, we're just doing our job.'

'Who was the idiot who broke in?'

The police officer raised her eyebrows and shrugged. 'The gentleman in question?'

'The idiot in question.'

'A university student. And he claims he wasn't breaking in. He went no further than the garden gate, apparently. And your relative was the aggressor. Rushed him with a knife. We have a signed statement from the student to that effect.'

Haruto tried to picture the scene. Something didn't fit. 'You believed that?'

'Pressed on the reason for the visit? He was a concerned citizen.'

'Really?'

'He'd heard there was an elderly gentleman living alone. He wanted to help him. An unlikely story, perhaps. But that's what we were told.'

'How could he have passed on the coronavirus to my uncle unless he physically got inside?'

'As I said, the professor didn't want to speak to us about it. So we haven't his statement to go on. Can't understand why. But if you'd rather we delve further, we can do so.'

Haruto forced himself not to tighten his jaw and show his mounting frustration. 'He was minding his own business and trying to keep safe. Speaks for itself. And why rob a place like this?'

'I don't think robbery was the motive. It was more likely connected with the Zoombombing.'

'The what?'

'Someone crashed an online high school class and put up racist posters. Anti-Chinese. Some people we spoke to thought your uncle could've been behind it.'

'Why would he do that?'

Kylie tapped herself on the chest. 'I'm not saying he did. Just trying to establish why neighbours have not stepped in.'

'Try lack of concern.'

'The community is very close, sir.'

Haruto's phone went off. 'It's the hospital.'

'Answer it, please. We'll wait.' They moved back away to give him some privacy.

'He didn't make it. Died half an hour ago apparently,' said Haruto, as he closed the call.

The sound of the police two-way radios broke the awkward silence which followed.

'So sorry for your loss.'

'I'm only a distant relative. But thank you. I'd better get on.' He resisted the urge to slam the door on them.

'Well, if you need us, we're here to help. I'll give you my number.' She took out her card. 'You'll be organising the funeral, I suppose?'

'Not me. I can't. I have to drive back to London.'

'I don't think you can though.'

'Why's that?'

'Government rules. As you've been inside the house and in close contact with your relative, you must self-isolate here for a fortnight. Sorry. But if you need us, we're not far away.'

Unable to leave for two weeks? Why hadn't he got the hell out of Tarbock Green hours ago?

'You drove up in the Toyota, didn't you?' She peered at the number plate. Made a mental note.

The other cop pointed to the broken window. 'That's fresh since last time, init?'

'Not the nicest place for you to stay.' Kylie rubbed her rubbery hands together. 'If you're out of groceries or loo rolls, you know what to do.' She held her phone to her ear. 'We're a peaceful community round here, mostly.'

'I'll be fine.'

'And if we learn any more on the break in, we will drop in on you again.' Coded language for, 'Now we've got your number plate, we'll be keeping an eye on you.'

Great. Stuck there for fourteen days. Up the proverbial creek without a paddle.

Chapter Five

Social isolation and loneliness were rising, and not just because of coronavirus. In Japan, lonely people had resorted to renting fake family members because they had no one to visit them. Lying about relationships was now a thriving business.

False dads. Bogus uncles. It seemed you could hire anyone for a price.

That Friday night Haruto Fraser, twice removed nephew of a deceased misfit, skilled with a knife and a potential Zoombomber, would have paid big money for a phoney to take his responsibilities away.

But this was Britain 2020 and when he suggested that in fun to his mother over FaceTime, she didn't laugh.

'You should have visited him or something. Showed some family loyalty. You could have gone on a cruise with him.'

The stain on the carpet was not black mould but dried blood, he told her. It was clear the fight occurred inside the bungalow and the intruder had come off worst. But the tables had turned, and poor Tomio had caught the guy's Covid and died.

Why would anyone want to break into the modest single-storey house?

'I know you'll do the honourable thing by our family.' His mother drew attention to his obligations under Japanese tradition. 'You do the funeral. Nobody else will.'

'Sure.'

'Dealing with the death of a relative is part of growing up.'

'I'm twenty eight.'

'Exactly.'

'You can donate his books to the university. But for the rest, just order a house clearance. Unless you want something for yourself.'

'I doubt it.'

'And you stay safe, eh?'

You stay safe?

Haruto was pretty relaxed about the virus. He assumed if he got it, he'd shake it off in no time. But what to do for two weeks? The tip was closed, the hardware stores shut, and anyway he couldn't leave the house. He was in complete social isolation.

Mouse droppings lay everywhere and exuded a stale, unpleasant odour. The place needed fumigating and a major sort out. The back room had experienced a landslide of paper, old science magazines, and empty Amazon book packages.

He found more food in a Sainsbury's plastic bag from a recent home delivery, amongst which lay a tin of ravioli. It smelt vaguely of tomato and not much else, but spooned it down cold anyway before finishing his whiskey.

His mother was right. Haruto would have to learn something about Tomio and quick. Traditional funeral services had given way to live-streamed events via social media. But even if he organised Professor Nakamura's online send off, would anyone bother to check in?

How did his uncle fall so fast and far from respected lecturer at a leading university to community bum? No idea. But maybe leave the analysis until later and instead get rotten on the Scotch.

Haruto had been desperate to return to London and move in with Karen. But what was going on there? He'd attempted to call, but she didn't pick up until close to ten that night.

Chapter Six

By seven thirty Helen Rogers had joined the barely spaced-apart staff, amid the doom and gloom following the overnight deaths on the ward from Coronavirus.

The Senior Ward Sister arrived for the daily briefing: new admissions, bed capacity, and the skill mix of the nurses. 'Did anybody here make it outside for the Clap For Carers?' she asked. 'Wasn't it brilliant?'

Three attendees held up hands. Helen raised hers too and kept it there. She refused to miss out on the morning get together, even though she'd overheard the words 'butting in'.

She could contribute so much more than they had delegated. Which was why she pushed herself forward at every opportunity.

'Do any of my nurses have anything they wish to add?' There was silence all round. 'I know it's a harrowing time, but nursing is what we love to do, isn't it?' The sister with a giant ego droned on as if she was addressing a gathering at Speakers' Corner in Hyde Park.

'So thanks for what you're all doing.'

'No problem,' one said.

'Together we can beat this virus, can't we?'

There was a murmur of solidarity.

'I almost forgot. A special thank you to our volunteer.'

Volunteer. A patronising edge there. Seeing as Helen was working for free, they should at least give a decent job title. But she chose to ignore the slight dig. Accept the vague acknowledgement with grace. Pettiness degraded you.

The sister went on, 'Hasn't she got a wonderful beamy smile?'

Was she taking the piss?

It didn't matter because everyone in the group focussed on Helen and she seized the moment. 'It's important, don't you think? Patients need us to make them feel loved.'

At least they were listening. 'And while I have your attention, can we all please remember to stand two metres apart?'

The sister's face flushed red. She didn't appreciate being upstaged.

'Yes, this virus spares no one.' She cleared her throat. 'How do we get that message across?'

Several more clinical team members walked in and stood at the back.

'Those idiots who light barbecues on the beach do not understand the consequences. What it means for us.'

'No.'

34

'How important it is to stay at home. To wash hands.' She rubbed them together vigorously to make the point. 'And, as we've just heard from Helen, to social distance.'

Helen. Her heart flipped at the sound of her name. 'But you're all doing a fantastic job. I'm very proud of you.'

Positivity, togetherness, high spirits and a can-do attitude are infectious, she told herself as she fitted a surgical visor, gloves, and apron.

She entered the ward, which, first thing in the morning, heaved with activity. Busy? Rammed solid.

She noticed a nurse go from one section to another. Still wearing the same face covering.

Am I the only person who doesn't need reminding constantly? About the rules on shielding.

'Excuse me. You must change your mask for every bed bay,' she pointed out.

Staff in previous jobs had described Helen Rogers as 'boss lady', which she took as a massive compliment. She was once the top banana at Honey Estates. Everyone knew it.

Telling people exactly what she wanted them to do made things run smoother, didn't it?

She wasn't shy of dressing down the upper echelon either.

So who cares if it annoys them?

'Keep further from one another,' she told a couple of dithering doctors who were not observing the two metre rule.

35

Don't stare at me like that, morons. It's all part of my job.

Her surgical mask slipped down her face from all the telling-off sweat. It was time to swop it.

She disrobed in the narrow airless chamber and pulled on a fresh overall. Another slacker of a nurse reluctantly secured her ties with an audible sigh. A happy commotion erupted at the delivery of three portable ventilators. She overheard someone say, 'That would be brilliant if you could speak to her.'

Who were they talking about?

As Helen was about to leave, a ward sister she'd not seen before blocked her passage.

'You're the volunteer. Right? '

A lot more than that! But yes, technically.

'I'm Chris. I've come in to help.' The staff member was a few pounds overweight but nice looking, about fifty.

'Call me Helen.'

'It's hard to see you beneath that mask, dear. We need you for something.'

*There you go. S*he was indispensable. 'Anything at all.'

'That load of waste needs packing and moving. There's so much of it. We won't be able to move in the room at all shortly.'

'That's a job for the porter, isn't it?'

'We've got nobody free at the moment.'

'I'm sure I can find one for you.'

'No, we don't want you to get somebody else. We would like you to do it, seeing as you're all kitted up.'

'But there's a mountain of it.'

'Six times the usual because of the virus.'

'I can't do it all on my own.'

'It's not heavy, for God's sake. A child could lift it.'

'There are other volunteers.'

'We've had two drop out because they tested positive for Covid. After all, that's what they signed you to do, I'm told.'

She could hear it all before it was even uttered. The same old lines. *While they appreciated the help, bla, bla, bla.*

The rest spewed out of the fat sister's mouth. How they didn't want her inspecting the beds. Nor telling people what to do, ticking off the surgeons. Exceeding her remit as a volunteer.

'If you move those boxes, there'll be far more space. The doctors can change their gowns quicker then. Give them a chance to get on with the job they're trained for.' The sister crossed her arms firmly.

So shifting sacks is all they wanted from her! Clear the blue rubbish bags and dump the empty supply packs.

The nurses sniggered when they saw her bent double with her hands buried in shit. Helen Rogers didn't care. Surely they knew deep down she was way smarter than all of them.

She packed the first sack. Masks, dirty face wipes, and paper towels filled it right to the top and gathered together the opposite sides, tying them in a simple loose knot.

'That's no good, is it? You'll have to make it tighter than that.' The Sister from Hell hovered over her, eyeballing every move.

Seething, she refastened the bundle.

'Surely you know contaminated waste is highly infectious,' the Sister continued, rubbing it in.

There followed a lively debate between several members of staff about the used flannels and towels. What happened to them when they left the ward. How were they deep cleaned?

Some thought the hospital steamed them. But as infected material, they should burn them. Right? Not just disinfect and reuse.

She could hear the rude bunch enjoying themselves. All the banter in the background. Great for them. She had to grovel on the dirty floor. How she hated being watched over too.

The self-loathing, which started in childhood, rushed into her brain and with it the same old patterns of always having to play second-fiddle to others.

Ten minutes later Helen Rogers, human mule, tagged her first sack of toxic trash and shuffled it down the corridor to the bulk waste compound. Altogether, she tripped back and forth six times.

However, as she left the hospital through the rear entrance, she giggled. It had been ages since she'd laughed. They'd made her look a fool. But the royal ticking-off had provided the perfect excuse to leave for good. The gloss had well and truly worn off the job, anyway. Her only regret was she'd parked her set of wheels so far away.

When she got there, the leather interior of the Mercedes smelt delicious. Helen hit the audio button for the media system. The throbbing beat filled the car with sound. She turned it up, up, up. Played it full pelt. Using Bluetooth, she called Paul Honey's home number just to be sure there was no one at the house. It rang off the hook.

Perfect.

But she'd have to move fast if she wanted to put her newly inspired plan into action.

Chapter Seven

Helen Rogers decided against using the driveway and instead parked the Mercedes outside on the Chiswick street. That way she could make a quick getaway if needed.

She sat in the car undecided. Paul Honey always referred to the house as The Orchard, because of its location. One of the smartest in Bedford Park. She waited for signs of movement through the window. Nothing.

Should she go back in at all? She stared at her hand on the silver door handle as if it belonged to someone else, saw how the fingers trembled.

Her mind flip-flopped with indecision. Venture into the Palace of Promises or leave it all behind forever? Yes, no. Yes, no.

Do it.

She staggered through the front gate, weak at the knees, took out her key and let herself into the hallway.

Make it fast.

The visit should take minutes. Something to do at lightning speed. As soon as possible. But once inside she stopped, transfixed by the memories it held.

At that moment, Helen felt like she owned The Orchard. She'd visited at least ten times, but never earlier than eleven at night. And then only for quick sex in the study and to suffer the indignity of having Paul Honey kick her out before the clock struck midnight, Cinderella style.

At long last she had the house to herself alone. Mad now if she didn't enjoy the opportunity while she could.

The passageway was silent as a tomb. She remained there, back stiff against the green and gold wallpaper, wondering which part to visit first.

Perhaps start at the rear of the property and work forward.

The kitchen was virtually untouched from when she'd last been in it less than twenty-four hours before. Heart thumping, she crossed the broad galley and opened the fridge. The half-consumed bottle of champagne tucked into the side of the door begged her to finish it. She poured two glasses and watched the faint skim of sparkling foam settle.

Why two? Force of habit.

She imagined he'd soon come and join her. When he didn't appear down the stairs, she played a pretend game in which she was showing the five bedroomed residence to a buyer.

What terms would she use?

Adorable, awesome kitchen, gorgeous garden.

She wouldn't allow any more images of the ghastly night before to spoil her fun.

'Shall I show you around?' she asked the imaginary customer and got a real buzz as she flung open the cabinets and cupboards, looking for anything to take home with her.

He'd brought things on himself. It was all his fault. Autoerotic asphyxiation. Just like his other addictions. It should never have happened. As she unhooked a Victorian oil painting from the wall of the drawing room, Helen reminded herself how much money she'd made for him.

She considered herself a whiz at selling. It had not started out that way. Honey Estates took her on initially as a part-time telephone answering machine, not a negotiator. But the Bimbo receptionist, as they saw her, was a quick learner. She soon put herself in charge of all the advertising. The killer words. Classic. Stunning. Backyard paradise. Turnkey. Newly renovated. Redeemed to perfection.

Paul Honey wrote descriptive copy like a six-year-old. He was useless at English. So too were the rest of the half-wits he hired, whose selling skills were nothing short of pathetic. Despite everything else Helen had done, she'd not got as much out of it as a 'thank you'.

Why did he get rid of her? Lockdown wouldn't last forever. Wasn't he the one who predicted a massive house buying boom with a drop in sterling after the virus was over. Overseas investors were the way forward.

What did it matter? She could do real estate on her ear after what he'd taught her. All she needed was some rich Chinese punters looking to snap up flats for their kids at university.

She'd work for herself and rake it in.

Dodgy property deals elevated Paul Honey from Durham dropout to a millionaire several times over. Cash payments under the table. Just look at the bundles of fifty-pound notes hidden in the kitchen cupboards. Along with the plastic bags and needles.

She downed both glasses of champagne in quick succession, which by now had gone flat and tasted sour.

What about the lower level, which Paul crassly referred to as a basement? What was on that floor? There'd never been a proper inspection, and here was her chance. Plus, downstairs had a shower which he'd never used and she needed a freshening up.

She stripped off and stood under the tumbling water, letting it soak away the hospital crud, his crud, the bloody, cruddy past. She heard someone singing like a crazy woman and realised it was herself.

She stepped out and rubbed herself dry and then rolled up the damp towel to add to the rest of the things she'd stolen from the house. Twenty minutes or more had gone by so quickly. Helen started filling bin liners with her booty.

Time to vamoose. Get the hell out.

The master bedroom on the top floor. Do it next and leave the study area until last.

She raced up the stairs and opened the door to check out the hallowed sanctum to which he had denied her entry. A strong odour of pizza mixed with cheap perfume still hung in the air. And hot tears started down her cheeks.

Helen couldn't stop sobbing. Paul Honey was the real reason she was at The Orchard.

In her heart she'd been hoping somehow he'd appear from out of the timber-lined study with the springy divan, and they would start their affair all over again.

But it wasn't to be.

Chapter Eight

At seven o'clock that evening, Karen Andersen put on her motorcycle helmet. The lining smelt fresh from its run through the washing machine and the road beckoned.

She needed desperately to take the bike out. Get some air in her lungs. Delivering food to Quacker currently in quarantine provided the perfect excuse to leave the claustrophobic flat.

She headed south on to the Sutton Court Road, turning right when she got to Clarence Lane and on to the A306. Why was she doing this? Was it to escape the loneliness and drudgery of lockdown? The sadness over the death of Tomio Nakamura? To deal with Haruto being trapped in Liverpool for weeks? Or from concern that her time-to-time boss Quacker, cantankerous though he was, might actually have coronavirus and die.

At eight thirty she arrived at the caravan park in which he had hunkered down. A hand-written sign stated it was closed, and it certainly looked that way. Decimated. The combination of Covid lockdown restrictions and a rule change that owners of older vans were up for eviction was obvious by the sea of vacant lots.

Karen identified Quacker's plot easily because of the ageing Ford Fiesta with the 'I love hockey' bumper sticker, which was parked alongside a sky-blue mobile home.

Through a crack in the curtains, she caught the manic flickering of a TV screen. She was about to ring the small bell when she sensed movement in one of the neighbouring vans. It unnerved her. She placed the container of food on the step and hurried away.

Six or seven running strides, and Karen was back on the motorbike. The faint roar of its engine was enough to alert the management trailer which lit up. Definitely time to head off home.

She returned to London via the A22, joined the M25 at junction 6 and turned down through the western suburbs of the city on the M40. The route took her to Bedford Park, where there was a convenient petrol station.

She filled up and rode off. Traffic was light. Most sensible people had adhered to rules and stayed home. There was a sense of guilty pleasure in using the empty streets.

Karen Andersen had seen the local Deliveroo boy before. Several other times, in fact. Unmissable in his green cycling jersey, an oversized transportation box on his back, he flew about the place like a turtle on speed. The pavement was his racetrack. He took scant notice of red lights or the Highway code.

On those occasions, Karen had made a mental note to maintain a distance from someone she regarded as a complete clown. But driving through the deserted streets, she'd dropped her guard. So the risky one-wheel stunt just ahead didn't register, nor did the next chaotic move until it was too late, a swing-out directly on to the road in front of her.

By a combination swerve and brake manoeuvre she escaped a total rear-end collision but still clipped the bicycle which reared up and threw the rider and his load, causing a rattle and clatter which seemed to go on forever. The bike fell on top of him, the wheel sprocket spinning and clicking like it would never stop.

But Karen's skid did other damage. She'd thrown her machine over to avoid a wipe-out. But struck the back bumper of a parked car in the process.

She stopped dead and dismounted, leaving the Kawasaki in the road, and ran towards the rider who lay sprawled out on the street. But the six-foot-tall Deliveroo man was already up, shaking debris from his waterproof trousers and checking his phone, which by some miracle remained strapped on his arm.

'I'll call an ambulance for you.'

'No. Don't do that. And stay away from me too,' he yelled, waving a grazed hand in her direction.

'I'd better ring them,' she repeated, but keeping her distance.

'Do you want me to catch Covid as well? I said leave it and I mean leave it.'

'I'm sorry.'

'Fuck, you are. Didn't you see what I was trying to do?' The heavy jacket had saved him from serious injury.

'No, I did not. The pavement is not a cycle lane.'

He took off his gloves and slipped the backpack off his shoulder. As he unzipped it, a take-away carton slid out and deposited all its yellow contents on to the road.

'What's that? It smells good.'

'Indian food this time.'

The delivery boy grasped the bicycle chain clipped around his waist as if he was about to use it on her.

'How can I help you then?'

She crouched down to pick up the box. 'Don't touch it. You've done enough damage already.'

'Is your bike OK?'

'Yeah. No thanks to you.' He resealed the lid, locking in what was left of the curry. 'I've delivered to this street twice today without being mown down by an imbecile.'

'I didn't see you.'

'Well, that's bloody obvious. Which is why I use this.' He pointed to the camera on his helmet. He shoved the container down into the bowels of the backpack. He shook his one good wrist, which had a key band on it.

'What's that for?'

'My chain. For locking my bike.' He made a face. 'Ouch!'

'Have you sprained it, do you think?'

'It's aching, but it'll be all OK.' He pulled the cycle upright, then tapped the ground with his foot. 'Shit.'

'Have you hurt it?'

Without another word, he clambered back on the bicycle.

'Maybe you should get it looked at,' she called out as he pedalled around her in large wobbly circles to try out his ankle.

Karen checked out the Kawasaki, which stood in the middle of the deserted street, relatively undamaged from the prang.

'Look what you've done to the car!' The cyclist pointed at the tail end of a Merc. He completed a third circle in the road. 'It'll need more than a scrub with toothpaste to remove that dent.'

She hadn't seen someone sitting in the driving seat all along. A potential witness.

The Deliveroo driver pedalled off like the wind. Eager to avoid trouble. If he fell too far behind on the delivery schedule, his boss would want to know why.

Karen knocked on the window of the Mercedes. She noticed the rear seats were full of furniture and plastic sacks.

The owner, a woman around her own age with damp blonde hair, asked if she was leaving.

'Sorry. I've just hit your car.'

'I don't care about that. Can you move your bike? I can't get out.'

'I didn't notice you in there.'

'I'm in a hurry.' She pressed the starter button, and the engine purred into life.

'Okay. I'll shift it now and give you my insurance details later.' Karen paddled the Kawasaki forward. Before she could park it, the car pulled out and shot off at high speed.

Having travelled an eighty-mile round trip and broken lockdown rules, it was time to get out while the getting was good. If the police arrived, there might be awkward questions.

Quit while you're ahead.

Back home, she opened her front door off Devonshire Road to the familiar smell of new carpet. Karen steadied herself and mounted the stairs as a touch of post-traumatic shock set in. But there was shame attached too. Her out-of-control impulsive behaviour had often got her into trouble. This was just another example.

She vowed never to use the motorbike again on non-essential business. And also to keep the whole matter of Quacker's supper and the prang to herself.

And when Haruto called to discuss his uncle's situation, this made double sense. He'd apparently been trying to get hold of her.

She pretended she'd been working from bed on a counterfeit case, fallen asleep, and hadn't seen the notifications.

It was not just a white lie to cover the guilt she felt over her behaviour. It was also politic.

Chapter Nine

Haruto Fraser couldn't understand why Karen had slept away the previous day. And not returned his calls. Come to think of it, he didn't feel in top form himself, so he could hardly point the finger.

'Have you ever drunk whiskey?' he slurred before cracking up. 'This is an insane situation. Really crazy - ee.'

'It's sad,' she said.

'What's sad?'

'That Tomio had no friends. Is there a bed for you?'

'Oh, my God. No. You want to see it. His is bad. Sheets are all bruddy.'

'Bruddy?'

'Brud, brud. You know, brud from stabbing.' He realised he was making little sense, but Karen got the drift. 'Yeah. I think I should turn in. Or turn over. Or have another whiskey.'

The ceiling started to spin, so he ended the call and switched off the overhead light. Heading for a plastic chair, he missed the target and landed heavily on the living room floor. He was drunk as a skunk, wasted. It was all much too hard, and he lapsed into oblivion where he lay.

Haruto slept fitfully for some hours before coming around. Still pissed out of his brain and sweating, he had to get a grip. His head throbbed badly. Maybe he could sober himself up enough to leave. Risk the drive. Dodge the police. Everything was a bloody mess. Perhaps he could come back after lockdown and clear out the junk.

He stretched for his iPhone, which lit up too brightly in his beleaguered state. The alcohol induced blackout overtook him again before he could go any further.

At six the following morning, life returned. Haruto crawled across the floor covering which had served him as a makeshift bed for the previous few hours. The rug skidded sideways as he got himself upright. Sober but still hungover, Haruto's natural sense of order came back. When he picked it up to straighten it, he noticed a large access panel set in the flooring.

A surge of adrenalin widened his pupils. Why'd he not realised there was another level?

He staggered to the bathroom, took a leak and splashed his face. Life was full of surprises. So what has he got down there? A stash of child porn, or perhaps something even worse?

The trap door had an extension ladder attached to give easy access to the sub-basement. A single overhead light bulb lit up the room. Tomio must have forgotten to switch off on his last visit there.

His uncle had divided the space into a laboratory and office. Shelves, which looked like they'd come from Ikea, lined the lower part of the walls. Each overflowed with files and paperwork including yellowed newspaper clippings and pictures of Professor Nakamura at conferences, socialising with politicians or receiving awards, all blue tacked to the brick wall.

A dusty microscope from the 1950s stood on the top shelf. Envelopes, notebooks, pencils, and pens cluttered the office section. Maps, more photos and several books on biochemistry made an untidy stack in the corner. Centre shelves sat a closed MacBook Pro.

Whatever he used the underground area for, Professor Nakamura wanted to keep it well hidden.

What had driven him to such lengths? Something highly sensitive or even secret? Had that forced him to isolate so completely? One thing was for sure. He had a clandestine life. Like it or lump it, Haruto Fraser was now an unwilling part of it.

Chapter Ten

Karen had barely surfaced from a deep sleep on the Saturday morning when she got the FaceTime from Haruto Fraser. It made the hang up tone and crashed twice. Wherever he was calling from lacked decent internet coverage.

'I was in the bunker,' he said, when they finally connected. 'I'm back upstairs now.'

'What bunker?'

He gave her the news of the underground complex. 'He must have been half crazy. Sure of it. Some kind of reclusive paranoia, poor guy.'

'You don't look like you're all there yourself,' she replied.

'A rough night.'

'Did you, by any chance, crash on the floor?'

'I could have done.' His face was ashen from a combination of slow wave sleep deprivation and alcohol.

'I'm not looking my best either,' she said, keeping alive the fib of having slept most of the previous afternoon.

'I need something to wake me up.'

'Have you got milk?'

55

'Nope,' came his gruff response. 'Instant coffee, which tastes like mud. The rest of it is inedible. Seaweed. I don't eat that stuff anymore.'

'I'll try to get a home delivery to you.'

'That's not necessary.' He ran his hands through dishevelled hair.

'OK.'

'I can do it myself. Karen, if Tomio got involved in something criminal, I need to know about it.'

'Why do you think that?'

'Because of the attitude of the police. The state of the place. The neighbours not liking him. And why else would he dig a cellar?' He gave a noisy yawn.

'What's down there exactly?'

'Lots. But I've not had the pleasure of exploring fully as yet.'

'How long has it been there? Can you tell?'

'Right back to the nineteen eighties, would you believe?'

'Been doing a bit of digging myself, if you're interested.' She'd not wanted to raise the subject before.

To take her mind off the bike prang, a search of Google had netted a fair chunk about Professor Nakamura's career. Born in 1947 in Tokyo, he grew up as an only child in post-war Japan, studied at Kyoto University, before going to the United States.

'Then he moved to the UK in 1984. So that fits.'

Tomio Nakamura, owner of a secret hideout, had co-authored oodles of papers and six textbooks on biochemistry and immunology. None had been bestsellers, even in academia land. He shunned all publicity. Considered brilliant, but also more than a tad unconventional, he kept himself well below the radar of journalists out for a story. Only in recent times had he hit the headlines when his bizarre behaviour sparked a flurry of scandalous rumours. Several articles came out, one with allegations of sexual abuse of a student and another more recently related to anti-Chinese racism over the coronavirus outbreak.

'Is there anything covering the cyber attack on the net?'

She'd dug into the internet using a VPN and brought up a hacking allegation. 'There's a fair bit on it, I'm sorry to say.'

'I can't understand why he did that.'

'My bet is he didn't. And perhaps someone set him up.' Ferreting into the dark undergrowth of the worldwide web had also thrown up a most unconvincing Human Image Synthesis, computer-generated, which she was pleased to tell him about. 'There's a link to a dodgy clip on YouTube from a student forum. Shows your great uncle holding up an abusive sign. A total fake. Contrived, for sure.'

'Can you send me it?'

'Yes. Check it out for yourself. A young shoulders and torso with Professor Nakamura's head stuck on top. With the apps around today, it's a five second job for anyone to clone a photo as crudely as that.'

'I'll let you get back to sleep now.'

'I won't be able to.'

'I'm sorry I woke you,' he said.

'No, that's fine. Ring me at anytime. You know that.'

'OK.'

'I really wanted to hear from you.'

He gave a small grin. 'This place is getting weirder and weirder.'

'I can understand that.'

'I'd heard he lived on his own planet. But I always understood him to be as harmless as a fly.' He started rubbing his eyes.

'How can you be so certain he wasn't?' asked Karen.

'Why would he be so unpopular then?'

'Have you found anything else?'

'Not yet.'

'No pictures or stuff?'

'Like what?'

'You know what I mean.'

'No. But I've barely scratched the surface.'

'I think you've got this all wrong.'

58

'Let's hope so.'

'There's more. But I didn't delve too deeply. I was afraid you mightn't want me to.'

Haruto was silent for a moment, a sign she was treading on sensitive ground.

Haruto's FaceTime had been unsettling. Under the circumstances, finding a hand-dug cellar under the bungalow smacked of subterfuge and dodgy dealings. Particularly set against a background of the negative comments turning up on the internet.

But perhaps not. It depended on what else he discovered in the basement, rather than judge his uncle by what his critics bucketed on him.

Karen got up and pulled the curtains to allow in the light. Then fired up the kettle.

Instinctively she was on Tomio Nakamura's side because of her natural loyalty to Haruto. And also for the fact he was no longer alive to explain himself.

She recalled an old Danish proverb. 'If you want a lie to be believed, wrap it up in truths.'

Maybe that was the nub. Someone wanted the public to believe Nakamura was a closet sex offender and an anti-Chinese racist. So smother the lies with a veneer of respect for his significant contribution to science.

Karen needed to dig a bit more on her own. To root out evidence which would neutralise the attacks on the dead professor, without Haruto knowing.

Fake news is a dangerous and expanding practise. And digital image manipulation is only one of many tools hackers have in their arsenal. A clumsily cloned photo can kick off rumours. Turn opinion against a target.

In at least a dozen countries across the world, Karen knew that twenty-something law school drop-outs would be tapping out bogus stories on tablets. The sole motivation? To generate cash.

A thriving but murky business based one hundred per cent on the power of dummying up sensational headlines. *Read this. Click here.* Do so and add to the profits flooding in from sites like Google Adsense. They pay the content producer each time a visitor follows through on their ads. Though in itself a minuscule amount, the volume is enormous. So much so, top entrepreneurs employ fifty staff or more. The fake stories rake in a fortune for the operators.

But the so-called scoops are mostly show-bizzy, or focussed on celebrities or the royals. But why would clickbait bloggers bother with a little-known retired university lecturer?

This led Karen to conclude that it might well be political. Created by a hacker working for one of the nation-state cyber espionage units which crawled the web.

She grabbed a quick coffee and settled down in front of the laptop at the dining table before googling 'Japanese plus

Professor plus Kyoto University'. No mention of Nakamura. Instead, there was a long article on the seventy-eight-year-old Nobel prize winning immunologist Tasuku Honjo stating China had created the coronavirus deliberately.

Karen leant closer to the screen to read the words. 'If that theory is correct, it wouldn't have adversely affected the entire world. Because, as per nature, temperature varies in different countries.' She pulled up Crowdtangle. The quote had run riot on Facebook groups and forums alike.

But on Tasuku Honjo's Wikipedia page, he'd refuted it. 'In the wake of the pain, economic loss, and unprecedented global suffering caused by the Covid-19 pandemic, I am greatly saddened that my name and that of Kyoto University have been used to spread false accusations and misinformation.'

The misstatement had still circulated and spawned a tsunami of hate mail.

In February someone commented on a Chan4 chat board: 'I have known Tasuku Honjo for forty years. I worked with him in the US. He's telling the truth. I have also done much scientific research on the topic, but in biochemistry. The virus is completely artificial. It did not originate from bats.'

He'd gone on, 'I knew all the staff of the Wuhan laboratory whose phones are now as dead as they are. I will reveal the facts in a short while.' They signed it 'Anonymous and Concerned.'

But on a student forum, amid speculation about the identity of the poster, one of three names put forward was Tomio Nakamura. His background fitted, didn't it? Hadn't he gone to the same school as Honjo? Attended Kyoto? People swallowed the story hook, line, and sinker.

Pro-China activists were hot on the heels of anyone spreading myths about the origins of Covid-19. They needed a scapegoat to take the blame for the Zoom-bombing in Liverpool. The eccentric professor's profile fitted nicely.

But had Professor Nakamura ever written on the chat board at all? Or had someone been impersonating him all along?

Chapter Eleven

Karen Andersen was on a mission to clear Tomio's name. Who had tried to discredit him, and for what reason?

As she delved deeper, she became more excited as stories highlighting Professor Nakamura's weirdness cropped up rather than anything implying a sinister side.

She called Haruto to give him the good news. Perhaps the student body had misconstrued the professor's unorthodox behaviour. He'd once worn Dr Martens boots under a pink kimono for a #MeToo Uni debate. Sometimes disappeared for weeks on end without explanation. Small stuff. Nothing too outlandish.

'He just reads as a bit different. And he's lived here for ages. We Brits are all half barmy.'

'There's that to it.' Haruto, not exactly ecstatic at her input, sighed.

'Listen to this. "The weirdo carries his personal possessions around in a bucket," it says here. What's wrong with that?'

He told her he'd found five of them empty, stacked and labelled in the kitchen. 'He used one colour for each day of the working week.'

'Nothing criminal about being a loner,' said Karen, continuing with her judgement. 'He was "prone to angry fits" and "an odd bird who flew his perch ages ago". So what?'

'I guess.' Haruto still sounded sceptical.

'Most people don't spend two years studying for a Master's Degree in Microbiology and Molecular Genetics and another four getting a PhD in some esoteric subfield like protein and DNA interaction without ending up a tad loopy, do they?'

'But it doesn't explain the racist allegations, does it?'

'There weren't many of those.' Karen minimised it away.

'You know there were.'

'You've been looking?'

'True. In between clearing up.'

'But if you check the posts he appears in, they are mostly about people who studied under him. Have you heard of the Professor Watch list?'

'No.'

'It's put together by right wingers and is all about outing lefty professors. In retaliation, the left-wing sites are doing the same. They call out who they think are fascist lecturers. And so it goes. Doesn't always mean there's any substance to their claims.'

'But there are numerous allegations about him.'

'You're talking about the forum on the SOAS website?' They'd also got into the act.

'What's this about a shoe?'

'Yes, I read that. Someone wrote they caught him hurling footwear at the Chinese Arch in Liverpool. That's plain mad.'

'He was pretty damn strange by the time I met him.'

'Haruto, that bit of craziness happened not before but during lockdown. How did the informant figure out it was Tomio? Who saw him? Any CCTV? He was living as a complete recluse by then. You said he rarely ventured out at all by that stage.'

'Maybe he just ducked out, desperate to hurl the odd shoe at a Chinese symbol.'

'You know how rumours build. So then he gets accused of racism when someone hacked into a language lesson online.'

'You don't think he did that?'

'No. Not one bit of it. Doubtless some other nutter carried it out. But not him. Look at the picture, will you?'

Haruto read out the post which accompanied the fake photo. 'His shocking racist outburst reduced young students to quivering wrecks. You're probably right. Thanks.'

Karen, already tingling with excitement, moved across to the kitchen area and made herself coffee, which was the last thing she needed. 'Not probably. I'm certain. Just because someone is eccentric doesn't mean they are a bad person.'

'I appreciate your loyalty,' Haruto murmured softly.

'Why would a well-travelled Japanese professor turn against the Chinese overnight? And further, would he have lowered himself to carry out a cyber attack on a bunch of teenagers?'

'Yeah, unlikely. And the placards or posters must be somewhere in the house, I guess. He never threw much out.'

'And you've not found them in the basement.' More a statement than a question.

'Well, not yet. You should see the mountain I have to sort through.'

Karen felt Haruto needed more convincing.

'I'd better get on,' he grumbled. 'I've lots of forms to complete.' The funeral director wanted to hurry through Tomio's send-off because of Covid.

'I'm not giving up on this.'

'Don't drive yourself crazy with it. You've got other stuff to do.'

'I'll call you later. And by the way, I miss you.'

'Me too. The lockdown makes things hard on us.'

'I know. The sooner it's over, the better.'

Joining an online forum is a perfect way to embed yourself in a community devoted to a particular topic. You can join a debate with Nintendo fanatics on retro games or mums-to-be on water births. Mingling in with nationalists looking for news of those whom they consider traitors to China, *hanjan*, such as Professor Nakamura, is just as easy if discreetly done.

At ten o'clock Karen called up Chinese-chat1.com, the English-speaking assembly, which had been a source of much of the anti-Tomio problem. She clicked the place marked Register on the home page. Then the Agree button to abide by the terms of the site. Ironically, the rules included not posting slanderous content.

She filled in the name Betty Zhou, the new Gmail address she'd created and pressed Submit. Seconds later, she received a verification link.

The increase in the number of incidents since Covid-19 got plenty of coverage. She found the entries by Chinese students calling out anti-racist attacks in Liverpool quickly enough. Verbal abuse, robberies, and wanton criminal damage to Szechuan restaurants. A Sheffield Hallam student had had rotten tomatoes thrown at him, another his mask ripped off and then punched in the face.

So far they mentioned no names. A photo dating back twenty years, which showed a British-Chinese protest against allegations that foot and mouth originated in China in 2001, had sparked hundreds of responses such as, 'They are at it again. Why do they always point the finger at us?'

It didn't take long to find the original Liverpool Zoom entry. The initiator of the post had the username *China Girl*.

China Girl claimed to have identified the tutor who gave the disrupted lesson. She'd posted a screenshot of one of the offensive banners.

It read: 'With the disgusting barbaric animal cruelty you people do, you all deserve to get the virus.'

China Girl: I know the teacher who sent me this

Twincookies: This is horrible

China Girl: Also who did it

Twincookies: Why do this?

Snakeeater2020: Racism in Britain

CaptainSparrow: Tell me about it

GunsnBeerBoy: Far right freak

China Girl: Worse than that

Snakeeater2020: Some students sick and dumb

China Girl: Not a student

Captain Sparrow: Who was it?

China Girl: Bloody professor.
Twincookies: No way.

China Girl: Check what else

GunsnBeerBoy: Nationality?

China Girl: Japanese.

VanillaFiend: Where? In UK?

China Girl: Liverpool

Captain Sparrow: Old guy?

China Girl: Yeah

Twincookies: Subject?

China Girl: Biochemistry

VanilaFiend: Just googled. Got a name. TN?

China Girl: Pervert

Karen drilled into China Girl's earlier posts. The feed content, random and often rambling, covered the trivial to the political. Everything from which tone of red eyeshadow matched best with a white face covering to the 'black terror' the Hong Kong residents were suffering because of the West. Her hatred of Trump and the Far Right was deep-rooted. But consistent with the readership approach.

Who was China Girl? Thousands followed her Facebook and Twitter accounts. Many of them used blurry avatars created with bots from sites like Flickr.

When Karen rang Haruto later, she was buzzing. Her research confirmed one thousand per cent, Tomio's innocence. Since the start of the global pandemic, the internet community had singled out and scapegoated Professor Nakamura for many hate crimes in Liverpool.

'I've found nothing in the house to connect him with the class attack either.'

'I thought as much.'

'Only the blood stains. What about them?'

'Don't blame him fighting back.'

Set up or not, Haruto was certain about one thing. The cremation should remain a quiet affair with restricted numbers.

Karen agreed. 'Notify as few as you need to?'

'I think so. He preferred his own company and just loved working on his pet project.'

'Whatever that was,' she murmured.

'Well, I'd have to hack his Mac to find out. I'm not ready for that. Maybe after the funeral.'

Chapter Twelve

She'd been on the net all Saturday. Bulletins of interest to Helen Rogers ran up on her computer constantly. Stranded Brits Abroad Pay a Fortune to Come Back to the UK. And Midwife Shortage as NHS Scoops Up Staff. Furlough Explained.

Reading on. 'This means you send an employee home. They do not work for you at all, and you reimburse them under the Coronavirus Job Retention Scheme.'

He could have kept her on. He didn't have to get rid of her.

Tall Paul. The man with the moolah. The guy with the lie. 'I am a hundred per cent going to leave my wife. Silly Jilly.' Ha ha, oh yes.

Helen embezzled as a one-off, initially. But she so enjoyed the flowers and the flirtation which followed. So she suggested they repeat the exercise. And he'd been up for it.

From then on, each time he approached her desk, it gave her a tingling sensation. There'd been nothing else on her mind but Paul Honey. She had waited her entire adult career for this life change. At thirty two, it had been the closest she'd come to a proper love affair.

A golden future lay ahead. Dreams that tantalise. Like a house of her own, a personal trainer, the well-cut clothes and spa weekends. His wife Jill plastered all across her Facebook account the spoils of the rubbish marriage.

Helen Rogers could have had them for herself. She could have been Mrs Honey. She'd almost made it.

She flicked on the television news. 'The government puts brakes on the housing market until coronavirus restrictions end. People should delay moving house if possible. All viewings to be put on hold.'

She resolved for the hundredth time to move flat the second she could.

The coffee maker, stolen from 'The Orchard', delivered a piping hot espresso into the plain white china mug which she'd nicked from Harrods. Not what she would've bought in normal circumstances, but it beat the ugly chipped cups which came with the bedsit.

Life would be bearable when the gut-wrenching pain went. Helen had to get away with the crime she committed. Just this once. Put it behind her. In the same way, Paul deserved exoneration for concealing his hard-earned gains from his grasping coke-sniffing wife.

She had to. Somehow.

She wouldn't allow herself to feel any guilt about their love affair, even if she was bursting at the seams with regret at how it'd all ended and still longed for the time of the Bollinger bonks, as he'd described them. But right now it was vital to hear the latest about him.

And the person who would know was his dear partner.

Making the actual call was much harder than she imagined.

'Did he owe you money too?' Jill asked when she answered the landline at the Surrey house.

'Why do you ask that?'

'Everyone's calling me. One after another.' There was a momentary silence. 'Oh, I am sure you've heard that Paul died over the weekend?'

Her heart thumped so loudly she was certain Paul's wife could hear it over the phone. It sped up to ten thousand beats a minute.

'He's dead? What a shock.'

'Yes. Completely unexpected. A stroke, they think.'

'No.'

'And it looks like he also had Covid as well.'

'Oh, I'm so sorry.'

'It's been so awful. I don't want is to play the messenger. Horrible, to break the news to the rest of the staff.'

'I can do that for you,' she stammered.

'Incredible as it sounds, there's not a penny in the accounts. Forgive me. Nothing to do with you, of course.' Jill sniffed. 'I wasn't sure if you were still working there. Belle said you were leaving.' She put heavy emphasis on the name.

The senior negotiator's wife?

73

'I left it to her to email out the news yesterday. All I got back from six members of staff is a gripe. We have not paid them for three months. Can't meet their mortgages.' There was a momentary silence. 'My husband has just died. And all they think of is themselves.'

'I am so sorry. I never received that.'

He fired me.

'This is the first you've heard? The news about Paul's death?'

'Yes.' Helen kept her pitch even. *So the nightmare was real.* 'He was such a mentor to me.' She coughed lightly.

'That's nice of you to say. Shit, this is a horrible experience. Odd you didn't know and should ring, anyway.' A trace of bitterness.

'Is there anything I can do?'

'There's a funeral to organise. I don't have the vaguest idea where to start. They've sent through a load of instructions on how to hold a streaming event.'

'Do you need any help?' Helen clicked to a page on her computer.

One internet story reported how British coronavirus victims could have funerals either postponed or the deceased buried quickly with no mourners over virus fears. Funeral chiefs revealed they could stream their services online if the government bans mass gatherings to stem the pandemic.

'Would you, Helen? I hate organising and stuff.'

74

'Horrible for you.'

'No one knows this, but we separated years ago.'

Then Paul hadn't been lying about his marriage after all.

'I'm still his wife, technically. So I inherit everything. Which now amounts to nothing more than a mountain of bloody debts.'

'How awful for you.'

'So you can see why it's pissed me off, can't you?'

'Yes, I understand completely.'

'Do you really?'

'Of course.'

'It sounds bad when someone you love has just passed away. But he was such a bastard. I'm sure you wouldn't think that though, would you?'

'No, definitely not.'

'I'll lose my house too. Because he re-mortgaged it to buy a property in London for his mistress, who then has the cheek to call me as if I know bugger all about them.'

Helen opened her mouth to speak, but nothing came out. The phone felt clammy in her hand.

'If you can support me in a few ways, great. That is why you rang, isn't it?'

Does she suspect me? Is she playing games?

'You are a guru at selling houses, aren't you?' Jill continued.

'I'm an expert at it.' She countered the implied sarcasm.

'Well, I need to sell the love pad as soon as possible. But you can't do viewings now. How does that work?'

Was she for real? Did the Honey woman expect Helen to answer? But she managed to get out, 'You're permitted virtual ones.'

'How can you organise a sales presentation of the Orchard without going inside?' Jill challenged. 'Impossible.'

'I use the video from the purchase.'

'That's clever. Didn't think of that.'

'Not that long ago, after all.'

'Do you still have it?'

'It'll be on the Honey Estates system.'

'But I don't want the company to sell it, which is the whole point of me asking you.'

'Right.'

'No way. Can you take the slide show thing off the site?'

'I could, easily.'

'It would make it quicker, wouldn't it?'

'Yes.' Helen would have to hurry before they changed the password.

'Obviously the commission is yours if you sell the place. And I know that bitch Belle won't get her hands on it.

76

Incredible. How she was having an affair with him all along, don't you think?'

He was seeing Belle?

'I really can't believe that.' she said.

'Nor could I when I found out. I'm almost pleased he's dead.'

After the call, Helen stomped angrily around her flat.

She'd had a fantasy about killing Paul's self-centred wife, of getting rid of her because she stood in the way between them. Imagined the piece in *True Crime Newsletter. Love Triangle Affairs, which end in tragedy... And now a real life honey trap joins the list.* But it had been the wrong person all along.

What a turnaround. Paul was dead, but it was Helen Rogers who felt as if she was choking to death, barely able to breathe in her fury.

The clothes she'd torn off the rails had not belonged to his wife, but Belle Adams. How could that have been? He must have been a real dickhead. Imagine cheating on me with that slut.

Perhaps Jill had got her facts wrong. Had she mixed them up? But somehow Helen knew it was true and felt an overwhelming sense of worthlessness.

At least she'd amassed a stack of money, a ticket across the Atlantic and a car, albeit with a bloody great dent in the bumper.

Chapter Thirteen

Karen Andersen had plenty of fresh cases land on her desk that day. She certainly wasn't short of work. During lockdown, pirated goods were flying off online shelves. With the police and Border Force not working on Intellectual Property crime, or IP as it is known, because of Covid demands, it was down to private investigators like her to cover the counterfeit sector.

She made a toasted sandwich, and the flat filled with the tangy aroma of hot cheese. With the TV droning on in background, she brought up the product image of a red handbag. A client support chat sprang up, which she ignored. She pressed the 'buy now' button. Ten minutes later, the knock-off Gucci was on its way to her, she'd even progressed the car on to the evidence package stage.

The bike episode was history, or at least the extraordinary news about Haruto's adventure up north had almost wiped it clean from her mind. But Quacker's call brought it back. Had he spotted her when she dropped off the stuff at his caravan? Was that why he was calling?

'Have you made progress on the counterfeits?' He gave a quick cough.

'Working on it as we speak.'

'Now's the time to gather intelligence. It'll be mayhem with fake goods everywhere when they finally lift restrictions.'

'The sweatshops don't stop for Covid, do they?'

'Gearing up for the inevitable spike in demand when the dodgy outlets reopen.'

A plasticky noise in the background sounded like a bottle popping back into shape.

'Did you hear that? The caravan makes all these strange noises. Any word from Haruto,' he asked?

'Yes. I'm afraid his uncle died of the virus. So he's staying up there to organise the funeral and also work off his quarantine.'

'Sorry about that. Rather quick, wasn't it?'

'How are you feeling, anyway?' Karen was keen to change the subject. They had yet to settle on a strategy regarding Tomio's secret bunker.

'I'm still under the weather to tell you the truth. And my temperature is above normal.'

'You should be in a proper house and not a freezing caravan.'

'No, it's not that bad,' he coughed. 'Yesterday it felt like I had a tight band going right across my diaphragm. Makes it rather hard to breathe sometimes. But I feel better today. Keep up the good work.'

Around two in the afternoon, Karen received a further tip off. A private investigator in Manchester called. A couple of clothes outlets in the Shepherd's Bush area were doing a roaring trade in counterfeit trainers.

Checking up on them in person would give her the excuse to rediscover the essential link between the mind and the body which had been missing since lockdown. Remote sleuthing had its limitations.

The afternoon felt cool under the limp sun. What better than a quick run to Shepherd's Bush for work purposes?

She called Quacker with the update.

'Karen, where are you phoning from?'

'Approaching Ravenscourt Park. The moment my legs begin to move, my thoughts begin to flow. I intend to see it for myself.' She panted. 'The mask and gloves are the perfect cover. They'll never pick me.'

'Don't even think about it.'

'What?'

'It's a job for the police.'

'But I can get the proof first hand.'

'Yes, and we'd lose our online status. It'll undermine all the work we've done so far.'

He had a point, she thought. Only companies with robust identities like Partridge Security could stand up to evidential scrutiny. Too big a risk.

'OK.'

'You can't leave the house for that. It's breaking government rules, never mind about the hefty fine involved.'

Karen didn't enjoy being reprimanded. But she knew Quacker was right and returned home with her tail between her legs.

The investigation was a trivial matter, anyway. Small fry compared to the pandemic, which was killing thousands, ruthlessly tearing families apart, with loved ones separated forever by indiscriminate death.

She kicked away a paper bag in frustration but, seized with guilt, picked it up with the tips of her latex glove and deposited it in a handy litter bin. Covid-19. You could catch it anywhere. Even by opening the door to someone you've not invited, as happened with Haruto's uncle.

Life seemed so unfair.

Who'd set him up? And, more to the point, why?

Chapter Fourteen

Haruto Fraser caught a waft of the bean-based canned food, which took him back to his years at junior school.

He unlocked the door of the bungalow to let in the fresh Merseyside air. It was four in the afternoon and the rain had stopped. Just three days into the lockdown. Time for a spell in the garden.

Haruto crouched down in the dense overgrowth, still wet from an earlier spring shower. Intent on videoing a stray cat stalking a mouse, he slipped and fell into the bushes and both creatures fled at high speed.

The clip was too ridiculous to waste, so he WhatsApped it on to Karen.

'Where are you?' She messaged back. 'And why are you chasing that poor animal?'

He pressed the call icon, and she answered straightaway. 'Forget about that. You're right. Tomio was a good guy. Why didn't I see it before?'

'Too close to the subject, perhaps.'

'He was more than a little unhinged.' He laughed.

'This Covid is driving everyone crazy.'

'I think it might be catching. I feel a bit mad myself. Maybe just living here is making me act odd.'

'There could be a family common factor.'

'Now that's an idea. Quite a good one. Erm, can you hear voices?'

'No.'

'You're sure?'

'Other than a bumblebee buzzing away. Yes.'

'It's as if I'm being watched.'

'Perhaps the cat has returned and is keeping a wary eye on you.'

'Very funny. Oh, and by the way, thank you.'

'For what?'

'Because I respect Tomio better now than I did.' Karen's constant defence of his uncle's bizarre behaviour had made a total difference. 'I'll call you later.'

A couple of days of combing through his possessions had put Haruto in a maudlin mood. Conflicting emotions swept over him as he stood in the brambles, and he found a fondness for his uncle grow within.

However dismissive he may have been at first, he now tolerated the idiosyncrasies, even admired them. The two-hour bleach baths, sleeping on the streets at Christmas, fasting, keeping binoculars by each window for his ornithological interests, all seemed normal and just an example of the complex individuality of the human spirit.

After ten minutes, the imagined voices faded away, and he went back inside.

As an act of respect, he'd rearranged nothing too much in the bungalow and instead invested the time in organising a simple funeral. But a big cleanup lay ahead. So he reckoned he may as well start.

Haruto cleared the surface of the antique Japanese hardwood desk and polished it until it shone. Was Tomio's spirit still here and the reason he felt watched? Could anyone see in from the street?

He drew the curtains together. Crossing to the front door, he slid the chain into position. At the kitchen one, he turned the deadlock twice for good measure.

Perhaps the reason why Tomio kept the doors barred and locked was rational? All at once Haruto understood the cellar. Solitude. Away from prying eyes. Logical.

Fifteen minute headstands, mismatched shoes, or walking naked around the house would appear very weird to anyone looking in.

So far he hadn't come across any hard-porn magazines, manacles, or questionable video cassettes. Just the usual paraphernalia associated with someone leading a long and solitary life. And one that was now over.

For the rest of the afternoon, he didn't bother with much. Haruto's interest had refocussed closer to home. He wanted to learn more about his uncle. Filled with a sense of regret that he'd not known him better, he set about sorting, exploring, assessing, identifying.

As if they were joined at the hip genetically. Were like two peas in a pod.

Chapter Fifteen

It was a little past six in the evening. The early spring sun had gone down and a cool breeze freshened the flat through the open window. Karen breathed in, enjoying the smell of a recent rain shower. Haruto's gratitude for her loyalty to his uncle had left her sky-high. She couldn't stop smiling. His approval meant the world to her.

Thank you. I respect Tomio so much more now. All thanks to what you've told me.

It exhilarated her. Defending the ones you loved was part of a deeper relationship. And that extended to their eccentric relatives, however remote the connection. The urge to sleep with him again was all-consuming. She'd never been as close to anyone before in her entire life and liked the way she fitted so naturally into his arms in bed, the electricity between them.

She would do everything in her power to clear Professor Nakamura's name. Haruto and his uncle had become inextricably linked in her mind. So she had the bit between her teeth as she fired up the computer. Curious and impatient, Karen threw herself into it.

Having found one dodgy clip on YouTube, surely she could turn up another.

For example, who was this China Girl? How was she connected to the truth about Professor Tomio Nakamura?

She logged into the online forums from the night before using a Virtual Private Network. Ignoring what she'd covered from her previous research, she drilled through open source networks looking for posts on blacklisted professors.

Bingo.

A new entry she'd not seen before caught her eye. A discussion board on the student website *The Liver Bird* discussing a major review into sex abuse across the country by university staff.

It was China Girl all over again.

This time she'd posted a link to the text from a published newspaper article in 2018 on lecturers who'd broken sacred #MeToo rules. The piece covered the investigation into 136 staff-on-student and 109 staff-on-staff reports of alleged assaults. The findings cost 86 teachers their jobs across the country. Those listed under Liverpool University included the name of Professor Tomio Nakamura.

Clicking on the top of the discussion list instantly brought up well over fifty replies and shares.

What! No! She dropped her head in despair and cursed to herself.

So it was true after all. It had to be. Here it was in black and white.

China Girl claimed to have suffered from traumatic stress since her attack by a professor in Liverpool and even posted class photos.

Karen pulled herself back from her desk before slumping down heavily in the chair. It was a heavy blow. The sex allegations were a severe disappointment. Why hadn't she read this before? How would Haruto take it? She'd built his hopes up prematurely based on what she wanted to believe. Now how could she tell him? Would she even have to? She couldn't bear the thought of it.

Outside, it was as black as pitch and pelting down with rain. Then the laptop ran out of battery.

I won't ring tonight. I'll leave it until tomorrow.

Time for bed.

Chapter Sixteen

That evening Haruto Fraser pondered for five full minutes why Karen hadn't called back before going to bed. It was a quarter past eleven. But he felt pretty relaxed about the situation. So without giving it another thought, he headed for a good night's sleep.

The dusty single divan in the second bedroom was a more comfortable option than the saggy couch, and he didn't stay awake for long. Although exhausted, he tossed and turned.

In his dreams, he replayed several scenarios. He saw Tomio Nakamura in every strange sequence, always beckoning for Haruto to follow him. In one dream, turning a street corner led into endless fields of rain-ravaged wheat where farm workers, armed with pitchforks, hunted him down. In another, his uncle clung desperately to the bow of an ancient ship. Shouting for help before slipping off and into the dark waters.

He woke with a jerk to the dawn chorus of birdsong. Still dressed, he lay half on and half off the bed. Next to him was a copy of Gordon Hoople's book on the interaction of technology and society *Drones for Good*, which Karen had given him to read. A reminder of his latest enterprise, pre-Tomio Nakamura.

As he clambered back on top of the faded green quilt, he saw the problem. The clutter pile he'd not bothered to move earlier had collapsed on him while he slept.

Haruto went to bed on nothing more than a bowl of miso soup in his stomach. Now he was ravenous for anything in the food department. Breakfast beckoned.

The compact kitchen, previously piled high with dirty dishes, was at least in some state of working order. A home delivery to replenish stocks with freshly baked bread and newly laid eggs wasn't due until later. So instead he feasted on beef jerky and a can of evil-smelling black beans, eating them straight from the tin with a buckled fork.

Haruto was pragmatic about what he could do about his uncle's unfair treatment. It'd all been a storm in a teacup, hadn't it? But there remained the laptop to analyse. A necessity he'd put off out of respect.

He descended into the chilly basement and retrieved the MacBook. Returning to the relative warmth of the kitchen, he placed it on a flimsy table and opened the lid.

It was time to sortie into unknown pastures and perform some ethical hacking. He figured as Tomio's next of kin, this was a necessary part of his self-imposed responsibility. One last test, he told himself.

To start it up without having access to let him in, he held down the power button and Command-R together. The apple sign and the progress bar popped up.

He took a mouthful of tasteless black coffee as the machine entered the recovery mode. Utilities. Terminal. User. TN.

When he got the message to enter a new password, he typed 'HarutoWozHere' then clicked Save before restarting the laptop.

It powered back to life, half battery remaining, and he logged in with no problem.

An initial scan through the folders and files brought little of concern. No obvious evidence of anything related to the Zoombombing. Karen had been right. A total fabrication. That was a relief. And so was the rest of it. No kid porn. Snuff videos. Or films of students having sex.

But buried deep inside a folder marked 'Sea Voyage', there was another folder Tomio had named 'Miasma Report'.

He clicked on it. Ignoring the odd text, he focussed on several research papers, which appeared to cover transcripts of phone conversations and screenshots of Facebook and WhatsApp chats. The content was all about bioweapons.

A separate folder marked 'Japan' contained hundreds of documents. He opened one at random. Inside it held observations on testing being carried out at the Japanese National Institute of Infectious Diseases in the western suburbs of Tokyo. What about the rest?

Several pages, clearly typed on a portable typewriter before being recorded on a scanner, lay in front of him, alongside others hand-drafted on yellow lined paper.

On one, Tomio had scribbled, 'Why now?'

Underneath, in red highlighter, he'd scrawled 'Marburg. Lassa. South American. Crimean-Congo.' Also, heavily underscored, the words '2020 Olympic Games' stood out. The comment, 'Will they postpone?'

Haruto scrolled to a folder labelled 'jpgs' and opened it. Amongst the hundreds of images were a series of photos of men bulked up in astronaut-style protective suits. Within this was yet another folder marked 'Lab Upgrade'. It contained pdfs of scanned plans with attention lines and various comments, 'Proposed chemical showers' and 'Heavy duty air filters'.

His uncle had added 'built 1981 - hazardous viruses. Infectious BSL-4 pathogens 2015. Why so late? China Sea (controlled by Imperial Japanese Navy during World War 11 and handed back in Treaty of San Francisco, 1951).'

In a collection of papers on Covid, he found something of interest. '2019-n CoV could be American-made aimed at sabotage of economy. A superpower struggle. Centred around 5G. But this is according to the Russians!'

Amongst the documents Haruto came across one which included a list of student names under the heading 'likely to be for hire'.

There was nothing about the Zoombombing, sexual impropriety, or anti-Chinese prejudice.

That was a deliberate misrepresentation.

However, from what he gathered, Tomio Nakamura had been working for an intelligence organisation. He'd been collecting and analysing material on qualified people in the north of England who might be suitable for foreign agencies to recruit.

Haruto's uncle had been passing on state secrets. But not to the British, Japanese, or American secret services.

Professor Nakamura must have been working as an agent for China all along.

Chapter Seventeen

At seven o'clock the same morning, Karen Andersen got up, ready to face the music.

On the previous evening she found incriminating evidence on Haruto's uncle, Professor Nakamura. She hadn't wanted to pass it on, but had to do it, eventually.

Time to explain to Haruto she had everything wrong on Tomio after all.

The aroma of the bitter coffee made her feel nauseous as she powered up her laptop. She threw open a window before emptying her mug into the sink.

The page had disappeared. It required a Google to bring up the article again. The piece had come from *The Guardian*. She pulled up the online site and ran her eyes over what read as the original story. But there was no mention of Liverpool. How could that be? Had Karen dreamt it all?

She'd definitely seen that in the editorial.

They had called Tomio Nakamura out as a sex abuser.

Named him as one of the disgraced professors.

She was doubly sure of its existence. Clear as crystal. But where had it gone?

She went back to the online student paper to check it out on their site. They had the same feature as in the Guardian newspaper.

Headline: *Universities Investigated.*

Multiple examples of staff sexual assault cases and 86 of those accused had either left or were being pushed out. Both the University of Edinburgh and the London School of Economics clocked up five, the highest number forced to leave their posts.

No mention of Tomio Nakamura.

Why couldn't she find it now?

Karen ran along the top of the website and found the hyperlink to the student discussion board. After scrolling through ten pages, she arrived at the post. *China Girl* had created it, using a link to the supposed original article. She clicked on it. The piece lay right in front of her eyes. The one which included a reference to Nakamura.

She hadn't imagined it all.

Not completely crazy, at least not yet!

She'd struck gold.

An amateur hacker had lifted a section of the *Liver Bird* editorial. And used a PDF editor to change the copy. They then reloaded it, adding an underscore to the address. It meant on clicking the link you would go to another site altogether.

Karen stretched her arms out above her and closed her eyes. *Thank God I didn't ring.*

What a find. Brilliant stuff.

Don't get too excited, she told herself. But it was hard not to resist. What'd been going on? She bounced around the room impatiently, desperate to call Haruto.

Keep looking. There's more to it. Just persevere.

She returned to the forum with fresh vigour, knowing the rest of the fake copy would be easier to analyse.

The photos of Nakamura at the front of class were additional evidence of hacking. Created from Getty Images stock shots circa ten years back and then dummied.

A hacker normally deletes an edited webpage straight after they kick start a conversation online. But this one had survived.

Her hands tingled as she took a screenshot and saved it to a file marked 'TN'.

She scrolled on. China Girl hadn't stopped there. She'd developed the theme. Shady images of a man groping a woman's breast. The caption. 'I got this with my phone. Nakamura has to go.'

Another showed someone fondling a young girl's thighs, her lacy knickers full exposed. A blackboard was clearly visible in the background. China Girl had downloaded both from the adult section of a photo sharing website.

'Can't you lot do better than that pathetic attempt?' Karen shouted to the laptop, feeling her excitement growing, becoming almost manic with happiness at the breakthrough.

Knowing she had to complete her search and keep checking to be certain, she went on to another site. There was nothing else detrimental to the Professor. No mention of inappropriate behaviour of any sort, nor his being dismissed for sexual misconduct. Even the Zoom allegation had begun on the forum.

As a self-proclaimed activist for the Communist Party, China Girl, with matching profiles on Facebook, Instagram, and Twitter, had whipped up a hurricane.

Karen wanted to help Haruto at all costs. He'd just been trying to defend his uncle from the many accusations against him. With all she needed now to prove her case, she was on cloud nine and couldn't wait a minute more to call and share the news.

When she did, he took an age to answer. He listened without interruption as she blurted everything out. But when she ran out of steam, his reaction floored her.

'Karen, I don't want you probing into this anymore. Do you understand? Can you just leave it alone?'

He was furious.

Part Two
BEIJING

Chapter Eighteen

I n Beijing Professor Wang, or Wig Wang to his hard drinking comrades because of his Hingling Hairpieces Emporium, stared with satisfaction at the April 2020 copy of Scientific Life. His mug shot took pride of place on the front cover.

The journalist had quoted him. 'For success today, business people must have a full and luscious head of hair?' The same glossy photo appeared on page three with the entire interview. His cars, fitness regime, philosophy. Whatever it was down too, he prided himself on maintaining a youthful appearance for his forty-six years so he could appear in his own adverts.

'Baldness can affect your image and self-confidence. Take action now!'

The business had brought wealth and prestige to Ned Wang. As a celebrity, it added a social cachet to his list of life achievements!

Recently China had trialled a unique credit system which took into account citizens' good behaviour. It docked points for jaywalking or missing a court bill and was growing in popularity even amongst the public. The penalties, such as losing the rights to book flights and train tickets, were seen as a clever idea. The professor was sure he'd score highly in that, too. Working undercover for the CPC puts a citizen way ahead in those stakes.

No one would pick it. Just the phone gave things away. Known as the red machine, it was a sign that the research and testing outfit was not quite what it appeared on the surface.

The company received faxes from Zongnanhai, the leadership compound within the government operation. Although no longer in general use, the Chinese establishment still used them because they were a highly secure way of sending messages. Comrade Wang was an esteemed, approved, committed-to-the-CPC, loyal servant of the party. With fingers in many pies, he also ran Hinling Pharmaceuticals as a cover for an arm of a bioweapons production facility.

Prestige was essential, wasn't it, no matter how you got there? It sometimes surprised him no one ever asked if he used his own remedies. He had no need. His jet black mop was a legacy of his gene codes for ectodysplasin and was nothing to do with miracle treatments.

He thought forward to the International Conference in New York at the end of the year. If indeed it went ahead. He had already submitted a paper on biochemical mechanisms regulating human hair growth and a copy of the article to add to his biography.

There'd been a lengthy silence from Professor Tomio Nakamura. But they kept conversations to a minimum in case cybersecurity had discovered the rapport between them. Misinterpreted it.

He wondered if that might already have happened. It was possible the Ministry for State Security had picked the contact while they were busy hacking Liverpool University computers. The MSS was one of the most secretive intelligence organisations in existence. Sometimes this worked against them. Some departments didn't know what the others were doing. Each of its sections operated in complete isolation.

He chuckled to himself. Most of them regarded all Japanese as arrogant and long term enemies. They would never imagine someone like Tomio Nakamura cooperating with a senior member of the Chinese Communist Party.

However, it was highly possible the recent stories he'd read online, that the professor was a troublemaker and storyteller, were of their own planting. Fake news was something the nation understood and didn't underrate its importance. China prized secrecy and spin because it was an effective tool against the decadent liberal societies whose dangerous ideas about individual freedoms threatened the stability of the entire state. The more civilised Chinese should have colonised the West. Not the other way round.

Yes, Professor Wang, successful magnate, and newfound celebrity! Someone happy to do whatever the Party asked of him. He was ready to serve when required. A beacon of reliability for the top echelons of power. Nothing was more important to him. Why wouldn't he? It had taken years to work up to his present position. Having got there, it meant a committal for life. What higher priority than belonging to the chosen group? The powerful few responsible for a fifth of all humanity. None.

He readily agreed with what the party drummed into the Chinese consciousness, that the Americans planted the coronavirus strand while on a scientific exchange trip to Wuhan. If it was the official line, then it was Wang's position. The United States were big players in the propaganda offensive. China must be too. It was essential to have a defensive biological programme of their own. Japan had used germ warfare against them in World War II, hadn't they? Just another reason the CPC felt compelled to join the game.

With Professor Wang's reputation as a highly qualified academic, they welcomed him into the DX21 initiative, in developing the deadliest bioweapon of them all.

Chapter Nineteen

Tarbock Green, April 13, and the air was fresh with the tangy salinity from off the Mersey. It had been a warm Easter bank holiday. Having sneaked a stroll or quick jog, residents headed back indoors to watch Netflix. A lone police car raced flat out along the quiet lane leading to the village, its two-tone siren clearing the way.

Inside the Hyundai, Kylie Brown, and Raj Patel discussed the job in hand. The last time the pair visited this particular property was on March 28. That was over a fortnight ago. They'd gone to warn the elderly occupant Professor Tomio Nakamura that someone he'd been in a fight with had contracted coronavirus. Tonight the reason was much more mundane. The report from Emergency Services had just arrived to advise that they had extinguished the runaway bonfire.

It hadn't raised concern straight off because Merseyside Fire and Rescue were out day and night dealing with similar situations, up to eighty or more during the Covid lockdown. With the municipal tips closed and residents using the quarantine period to empty their attics, they'd turned to burning their junk to get rid of everything from broken bed posts to kids' high chairs, all stored away just in case, even though the children themselves had left home ten years before.

It wasn't against the law. And it was also perfect weather for the main cause of intentional arson, the Great British BBQ.

The driveway was free, so Inspector Brown parked where the car belonging to the professor's nephew had been during their last call. Where was he now?

She turned off the blue strobing light. The firefighters' boots had made indent marks where they'd tramped down the tall grass by the gate.

'He must have left,' she said. Jumping out, she fitted a mask quickly to avoid the smoke.

They tried the front door, which was still double locked, and noticed somebody had repaired the broken window since their previous visit. They ambled through to the rear of the bungalow. The garden was a blackened mess.

'The flames stopped short by inches.' Inspector Brown pointed to the scorch marks left by a petrol trail leading up to the house. 'Another ten minutes and the whole lot would have gone up.'

Her counterpart nodded in agreement.

Having prised it open to check for occupants, the fire crew had hastily secured the back door. Tearing away the gaffer tape, Raj and his boss went into the kitchen. They found it neat and tidy. Fridge cleared, defrosted and propped ajar with a beer bottle.

'Odd. He did a good job cleaning up. Just wish he wasn't so careless with his bonfires. Shall we take a peek?'

The bungalow stank less of smoke and more of disinfectant. Kylie Brown led the way, while Raj followed on reluctantly. Women loved to get on the inside of other people's houses for whatever reason, he'd observed in life.

In the front room, with the limp drapes pulled tight, the darkness and a strong smell of bleach gave it an eerie atmosphere. The female officer flicked all the switches, but nothing happened.

'Terrific,' she said.

The diminutive Bangladeshi turned on his torch to allow her to open the curtains. The feeble light failed to reveal too much. Somebody had arranged the contents in a meticulous manner. Cartons of books made a neat stack piled away to one side.

'Smells like someone's been at it with a mop.'

Raj swung his flashlight around the room before pointing it at the wrinkled rug.

'Perfect for me to trip and break my neck,' she said, lifting the corner to smooth it out. The trapdoor lay exposed in front of them. 'Hello, hello, hello. What have we got here then?'

'Maybe check with the station first, boss? We might need backup.' He took out his phone, and the screen lit up.

'What! Let them take all the credit? You willing to have a go?'

Raj shrugged. He saw Kylie had gone into hyper mode.

'Things getting interesting here. He lights a fire. The pours a trail of petrol up to the premises. Knows no one will notice because it's barbie Monday. Locks up and leaves. Hopes house burns to cinders for whatever reason.'

'And there's a secret cellar.' He had to agree and raised his eyebrows.

'I think our man was trying to get rid of something, don't you? I should have got his mobile off him when I had the chance.'

She lifted the trap door carefully.

'Hello!' she shouted. 'Anyone down there?'

Nothing.

The walkie talkies crackled. 'Let's go down, shall we?'

The ladder was stable and slid down sweet as a nut.

Before his colleague could take a step, Raj interrupted her. 'Let me, boss.'

'Thanks, mate.'

Half way down he hesitated, uncertain of what horrors might lie ahead.

'Have we looked at the circuit breaker?'

'Good idea. I should have figured that out myself.' Inspector Brown returned to the hall and found the switch. 'Electricity's off. Obviously he expected to be gone for a while!' She pushed up the mains switch on the Electrical Consumer Unit and all the lights came on.

Raj let out a satisfied grunt and vanished down the steps into the cellar.

'Anything?' Kylie asked as she gingerly descended after him.

In the middle of the underground room stood a full size office shredder. Several thousands of shredded documents filled the large black bags stacked against the wall. Otherwise the chamber was empty and smelt of damp paper and old blankets.

The odd part was that someone had gone to enormous trouble to clear through the deceased estate. And then put a match to it.

Chapter Twenty

Karen hadn't spoken to Haruto Fraser for ages. When she first got the rebuff, she pulled back. His reluctance to have her help him any more with his uncle's affairs including the online funeral stung like salt on a wound.

She called again on the eleventh of April. He'd been in London for days and not even bothered to tell her.

He never mentioned the plan to move in together and used Covid as an excuse to avoid the subject. Or so it appeared.

'I thought it was just a cold. But perhaps not. I ache all over. My head is thumping, my eyes burning, and it's as if I've been half strangled.' He coughed lightly. 'I don't want you to catch this.'

Same again a week later. 'Still sweating, hot as hell, dizzy and shivering,' he grumbled. 'The TV's on for company. Here I sit in a complete daze and feel like a steamroller has run over me. This is a bloody nightmare, Karen.'

Then there'd been a FaceTime. She hadn't set eyes on him for weeks. His shock of black hair reached down to his shoulders, and he'd grown a full beard. He was sitting alongside an elegant Japanese cabinet, which she assumed had come from Tomio Nakamura's house.

'My sinuses are agony, and my eardrums ready to pop. I know I shouldn't but I've been massaging my inner ear with cotton buds, trying to take the fucking pain away.'

But not on a single occasion did he initiate a call or a WhatsApp. Something had changed, but what?

Around noon on the same day, her bell rang. Karen looked out of the window and saw a police car parked opposite. She fitted her mask and freed the latch on the door. The two officers from the Met acted quickly to reassure her. Nothing serious. No one had died or anything. The call was simply a response to routine enquiries on behalf of another unit.

'I wonder if we could have a few words about Haruto Fraser? I believe you're quite close.'

'Yes. He's not living here though.' She heard her voice crack. 'Because of the coronavirus. I understand he is self isolating at a flat in Islington. How can I help?'

'Won't take too long. We're following up on a suspicious fire in Tarbock Green. It started in the back garden. Got out of control. April the thirteenth was the date. Do you know anything about that?'

'No.' Her heart thumped.

'The police in Liverpool tracked Mr Fraser down by his vehicle registration. Been up there seeing to a relative's affairs, I believe?'

'Yes. His uncle died.'

'We called at his address in Islington. He said he was in London then. It was the first he'd heard about the incident.'

She explained it was against lockdown regulations for them to be together. Which was why he couldn't answer in person. Surely they understood!

'He's not saying you were with him personally. But he informed us you'd spoken on the phone. So could you verify where he was, please?'

Karen opened her mobile. Over twenty calls to Haruto's number. She showed them to the officer.

'They'll have to analyse satellite records to see exactly where he was when he received them. It's easy enough to do. That's if they want to pursue the matter. Our colleagues in Liverpool asked us to pay a visit. We appreciate your time.'

'Well, I know he burnt off brambles or something. The garden needed weeks of work, apparently.'

The officer in charge turned to her sidekick. 'Perhaps a weed blowtorch or a flame gun?'

'But he'd left by the date you gave me.'

'Easter Monday?'

'Yes.'

'Great. That's all the information we need at this stage.'

'When did you speak to Haruto about this?'

'Oh, we've come from seeing him just now. Probably three quarters of an hour ago.'

Three quarters of an hour? Plenty of time for him to warn her.

'Was much damage done to the property?' Karen asked, as the officer swivelled round to leave.

'Fortunately, very little. And garden bonfires aren't illegal. But the Fire and Rescue Service reported finding evidence of petrol having been used to start it. Multiple points of origin. Also, they arrived just in time before the entire house burnt down.'

Her face grew hot under the mask. She blinked away the shock, aware of the growing frown and the hairs lifting on the back of her neck. Why hadn't he told her about all this before they'd paid their visit?

'But I expect they're curious about why he would take that approach. He doesn't own the residence, does he?'

'No.'

'If Mr Fraser wasn't there and didn't start the fire, there's no issue. Arson has been on the rise since the lockdown.'

'Haruto would never light a bonfire with petrol. He is very security conscious. Very.'

'Ok. Well, thank you very much. That's it for the present. We'll get straight back to Merseyside so they can continue their investigation. Mr Fraser suggested it might have been a gang of kids from a local estate. They've apparently pulled this type of stunt before, to quote him.'

Karen climbed the stairs and removed her mask. There had to be a simple explanation. *Had to be.* But when he didn't call her after a quarter of an hour, she sent through a brief message.

'I've just had the Police here. I told them you were in London when this fire business happened.'

Five minutes passed. With no response, she opened the settings app on her phone, went to Sounds and then Text Tone to check it wasn't on silent. Finally, the familiar alert chimed as his reply arrived.

It read 'thanks.' Nothing more.

The disappointment at his lack of elaboration brought tears to her eyes. Her insides sank into numbness. She swallowed hard before tapping out her response. 'I think maybe we should cool things between us for a bit.'

Her stomach churned as she watched the screen, willing it to return an apology for him acting so distant. He'd been ill after all, hadn't he? The news of the fire at Tomio's house must have been a shock. Perhaps the virus had affected his memory. Could Covid-19 leave you with amnesia? Anything he concocted would have let him off the hook with Karen. Anything at all.

No reply came for several hours. When it did, it was just a simple four letter word.

'Sure.'

Chapter Twenty One

Haruto Fraser unlocked the windows back and front to draw a cross breeze into the Islington flat. His temperature had recorded normal on the Monday and he didn't want it shooting up again.

He sank into the leather couch, still sticky from cleaning fluid. His breathing was less laboured and his sense of taste and smell had returned. He planned, as soon as he felt fit enough, to throw himself into his drone work. Put Tarbock Green and Tomio Nakamura on the back burner of his life. News of the fire had well and truly buggered that idea.

It looked as if someone had tried to burn the house down after he'd left it vacant. Perhaps just an accident? The rough element from the local estate, aware the property was empty, sneaking in for a quick barbecue? *Whatever*.

All around his bare feet sat boxes of artefacts taken from the bungalow. The outside air cleared the dusky odour given off by the old notebooks and diaries. But it didn't sweep away the reek of regret and shame which remained. Sometimes life handed you a bummer, but you couldn't just up and distance from it, particularly if your uncle was a spy.

In the interests of state security, privacy was under siege. Nothing was sacred. A good example was the US Navy's PALS programme, where they trained dolphins for underwater espionage activities. The DARPA initiative, trialled, with the idea of using plants to gather intelligence, kids' watches with listening devices embedded. Astute abusers had hacked into children's net-enabled dolls. And now there was Tomio's underground cellar.

Haruto sat cross-legged on the carpet Japanese style and thought about it all. On top of everything, Karen had finished with him by text. That had hurt like hell, beyond just painful. But he understood why she'd sent it. They became so fixated on Tomio, he'd lost his sense of priority, of how to maintain close human relationships with people who really mattered. But splitting up with his girlfriend would simplify things. Perhaps he should return to Japan for a bit to atone for his relative's sins and shameful behaviour.

He made three piles. Items to keep, others to discard, and another for undecided. A folder containing coupons for a transatlantic crossing from Southampton to New York in November went into the first one. Despite his reclusive instincts, Tomio Nakamura was a cruise-liner affectionado. All his life his uncle always preferred going by sea when practical rather than hop on a plane.

When Haruto found the vouchers, he'd planned to use them to take Karen on a trip. And maybe ask her to marry him on the voyage. But proposing had been a crazy thought, a ludicrous idea born out of the madness surrounding his discovery of the secrets Tarbock Green held.

Decision reversed, he took the tickets out of 'keep' and placed them amongst the pile of items for disposal. Chris

Partridge had told him she was raising funds for the NHS. The donation of an Atlantic crossing on a luxury liner would raise money in the auction.

He opened up Tomio's laptop. It was the hundredth time he'd been through the computer, examining records picked at random. A link on the desktop led to a video on You Tube. He had yet to check it out properly.

The film was obviously a promotional one for Buddhism and done somewhere in Liverpool. Lit by six red lanterns, the room emulated a small Buddhist temple. Intricate wooden carvings of men, dragons, gods, and animals covered the elaborate ceiling. Inside a sparkling glass case sat three gold-leafed Buddha statuettes. Below them the altar lay decked out with flowers, fresh fruit, and tiny icons, gifts from the devotees. Along the walls hung several scrolls of calligraphy.

How things had changed since Covid! Nowadays every church, monastery, and temple was closed to halt the spread of the disease. But in this clip pre-pandemic, at least forty people crammed elbow to elbow, the majority white Liverpudlians with a few Chinese faces amongst them.

The young girls had shaven heads, wore brightly coloured dresses and danced together. The men watched, fingering beads which they all had around their necks. Monks in flowing orange robes wandered at random in the background. One of them, seated akimbo, struck a large brass bowl which sent forth deep toned vibrations.

A sense of calm came over Haruto as he sat mesmerised by the clip. What was it doing there?

Summoned by tinkling bells and the patter of tiny drums, the congregation assembled at the altar. Men lined up together on the right. The women formed a separate line on the left. It was a ceremony for repentance of sins, vows for forgiveness for wrongdoings, with promises to reform.

An ancient monk bowed low in front of the statues. Who was he? Haruto lent closer to the screen. The elder's silken robe trailed across the floor as he carried three slender joss sticks up to the shallow black caldron simmering away from the flames beneath. He carefully placed the offering along the cast iron edge of the great cauldron. The congregation chanted in rhythm to the steady beat of the drums as they shuffled around in a loose circle, reciting the sacred mantra.

The senior monk seated himself, legs akimbo, on an ornately woven pecan chair. Everyone bowed. One very young girl approached the altar, lit a stick of incense, held it over her head like a wand and circled the room several times. She placed it in the cauldron, gave three and a half bows and went down on her knees to make a formal request to Dharma, goddess of enlightenment.

The elder who they referred to as Shifu or teacher nodded assent. He spoke in mandarin, reading from the Buddhist text. His followers either closed their eyes or gazed at him in adoration. During the lecture, someone who clearly understood the language and what was being said let out one burst of laughter at some secret humour within the elder's words. The camera swung round abruptly to focus on the devotee, guilty of the inappropriate transgression.

There was no mistaking the identity, Tomio Nakamura.

Chapter Twenty Two

By definition, a spy is someone who is paid to betray his or her own country.

Haruto Fraser was no stranger to the world of espionage. His Scottish born father had been privy to inside information on the Directorate for Signals Intelligence, Japan's version of the NSA, while serving as a diplomat in Tokyo.

In addition, a childhood friend now worked on an underground floor in C1, the office building within the high-security compound which houses the country's Ministry of Defence. Using a mass surveillance system called XKEYSCORE, his classmate, who'd always wanted to be a comedian on Nippon TV, instead had ended up sifting through people's emails, online chats, internet browsing histories, and data on their social media activity for them.

There was a difference between defensive monitoring and what Nakamura had embroiled himself in. Who was the contact in Beijing Tomio referred to as Ned? A handler, friend, or a colleague? They appeared to have several years of history between them. There was much reference to the Chinese Communist Party. Had he become a secret recruiter?

Espionage activities since Covid-19 were real enough. The press reported almost daily on examples. Issues included whether the UK should limit students from China enrolling in classes involving sensitive work. Maybe Tomio had found potential assets in the form of PhD graduates with first-hand access to Britain's advanced technology?

No one knew better than the professor how research departments worked at Liverpool University. And who would suspect a Japanese scientist colluding with their old foes? Perhaps recent accounts of his public China-scepticism had been trumped up as a front for something far more sinister? It was the fake-news smokescreen the Chinese secret service was so adept at creating.

The suspicious activities of Haruto's uncle placed a heavy burden on his shoulders. And who could he confide in?

Professor Tomio Nakamura had once made Britain his home. The country had welcomed him with open arms and tolerated his eccentricity. Yet it appeared he had repaid UK's warm welcome by working with Beijing on the latest biological weapons aimed at the West.

And how would Karen Andersen, who prized her country's safety above her own, feel about Haruto if she ever found out?

Chapter Twenty Three

It was only the second time Professor Wang had been out in his car since lockdown. Forced to fill up at the garage in case of shortages, he drove straight back home through the weird and deserted streets.

On this occasion, with the restrictions easing, he headed to the markets. The long period of compulsory containment had raised within him a longing for the sights and smells of old Beijing. The familiar aromas of exotic vegetables, pungent spices, and even the freshly cut carcasses were a comfort he had deeply missed over the last few months. And he so preferred the lively atmosphere to the sterility of the modernistic cosmopolitan city.

Shops and offices had reopened on every street. The country's long fought and disciplined battle with the coronavirus had paid off. *On the surface.* Employees swarmed back to the factories, carefully observing the one metre social distancing rule. Some companies even allowed their staff to work without face coverings.

As the pandemic faded, everyone took up again the serious business of making money. Time to pull your fingers out!

A CEO's speech, quoted on the government's website as an example of the right approach, told them to 'Remove your masks and let your dreams soar!'

Professor Wang's dream at that moment was freedom from his lonely isolation in a luxury apartment. In the newly built districts, as everywhere else, normal life had been on hold. With the complete standstill lifted, cars and trucks filled the streets like nothing had changed.

How he'd missed it all! A traffic jam one minute, erratic random driving the next. The chaos was all part of Beijing's charm. Speculation on what the crazy driver had in mind kept the professor wide awake. Who could tell? Did he even have a licence for his spanking new Hyundai? On each trip, you took a risk.

Despite being barely recognisable from the place he'd grown up in, every corner of the capital held a special meaning for him. He loved Beijing and China more than his own life.

Which was why his vital mission must remain his secret and his alone. It was a public service. His sacred duty to the state.

At Tiananmen Square he swung left and entered Nanchizi Street, which led to the East Gate of the Forbidden City. The spectacular sight never disappointed.

Just getting out lifted Wang's mood. Ever since the sudden death of his loyal wife Xixi six months ago, he could not shake off the depression which had enveloped him, blackening every thought he had.

The professor drove back home, his thoughts going over their life together. After a quick shower, he chose clothes which she said always suited him. A well-cut dark suit and polished black shoes. Perfect for the initial meeting with

Colonel Li, reputed to be the most colourful member of the ultra right faction within the Party. Ideal for a dinner sprung on him over WeChat, rather than via the usual red phone, the normal channel of communication between the higher rankers within the CCP.

When Professor Wang arrived at the St Regis Hotel, the Maitre d'Hotel guided him to an executive dining room. The style of the upmarket venue matched his expectations for the meeting with someone of Li's standing. Two armed guards flanked the entrance. Inside, racks filled with expensive French wine stretched the full length of one wall.

No wonder the young graduates all wanted to join the CCP! Way to go!

Plenty of freebies at the top of the second largest political party in the entire world.

The PA, a thin, athletic type wearing an ill-fitting jacket, bowed low when Wang entered. His boss, Colonel Li, thumbed through a copy of *The Chinese Film Market and* nodded in greeting but remained seated in a plum red brocaded chair.

'Ah, Professor Wang. Or should I refer to you as Wig Wang?' The colonel smiled and extended his hand.

Wang had done his homework too. Li, one of China's wealthiest men, conformed to what he expected, the class image of a son of the Maoist regime. To a man they never missed an opportunity to espouse the ideals of socialism and the socialist state, but acted as capitalist in every way serving on

123

the boards of banks, industrial groups, commodity trading firms, or indeed any foreign company which needed a Chinese partnership. It was a good lurk, whatever the industry. And Li's was showbiz.

The movie business bought a lot from Hinling's Hair Pieces Emporium. So he tolerated his nickname in the interest of profit.

Wang believed the party leaders had lost the plot on leadership. Prosperity, which was supposed to take a backseat to doctrinal behaviour, dominated every aspect of their decision making.

Colonel Li was typical. He used his wealth to have his kids in socially with the other princelings of the top set by sending them to the best schools. And also to keep his girlfriends sweet and deter them from going public with embarrassing details of his sex life.

'I bought three Apple computers today. Not all for me, of course.'

Professor Wang told Li he rarely shopped online, preferring to do it in person.

'In the past month I have had so many gadgets delivered I have lost count of them,' said his host.

He cast a dismissive glance at Professors Wang's locally manufactured Oppo smartphone.

They had little in common other than Party involvement. Exactly what did Colonel Li want?

Li whipped out a photograph of his rather plain niece who had aspirations of being a model. Wang got the drift. Some indication of what was in prospect.

It was how the Party system worked. Senior members wanted well placed jobs for their relatives. And the professor obliged when he could. Say, by creating a vacancy in the sales department. But he knew from experience that hair pieces sell better when advertised using pretty young girls, and therefore he waited with a certain concern to hear what Li had in mind.

'We should start with cocktails.'

The colonel ordered three 'hurricanes' as he lambasted the Americans, his second favourite topic of conversation next to after the latest mistress in his life.

'Wuhan has reopened its shopping malls. Let's see how the Yanks like that!' he gloated, sitting back and straightening his red silk tie.

'The National Health Commission reported that we have discharged all Covid patients now.'

'They're not too proud to buy our masks and gowns. And when we provide them, they say we are doing it to make China look good.'

The assistant downed his rum cocktail in record time, hoping for another.

'How does the US pursue its moral crusade against extortion in other countries when their own system is so corrupt? Money taaawks!!' His fake Southern American drawl raised a polite smile from the professor.

On cue, the Maitre d'Hotel turned up during a pause in the Colonel's tirade about double standards. The three men ordered quickly before the colonel went back to his favourite subject.

Wang concluded that the political opinions were a barely disguised tactic to see how loyal he was to the Party.

'As you know, when Comrade Xiaoping was still with us, he urged China to leave the development of the aircraft carrier as a major offensive asset entirely to the Americans, saying they end up as rust-buckets, expensive and redundant before launched, and that the real reason the USA keep building them is as cover for their bioweapons industry. They are not beyond using them to wipe out the population of our nation. And now the West has the temerity to accuse *our country* of deliberately spreading the coronavirus to weaken them and cause internal racial divisions?'

The ravioli risotto provided a break in the conversation, with Wang cautiously holding back careful not to take part in the loose talk.

'The Party has a high opinion of you, Professor. What is your personal view on this?'

'It is that we should all keep our hair on.'

But Li didn't laugh. 'Your pioneering research in that area will put China as the leading nation in the field.'

'I hope my work contributes helpfully towards the advancement of our great country.'

In this way, the professor remained tightlipped about his involvement with the deadly DX21 biological weapons programme.

You never knew exactly who you were talking to in Beijing. Many layers populated the factions within the party.

There was a growing group of ultra nationalists who believed the country should expand its borders and conquer the world by whatever means necessary. They resented being used just as cheap labour and detested Western values. The comrades favoured terms such as 'hostile nations', 'lab leaks' and 'foreign barbarians'. Most of the super-wealthy covered their true beliefs but paid lip service to the Party platform for good reason. That way they could maintain influence within China and continue to accumulate wealth overseas, acquiring businesses particularly in New York, London, and Toronto. But a recent spate of high-profile disappearances and abductions had generated an atmosphere of tension and fear. These days it was smart to keep your views to yourself.

So when Colonel Li waxed lyrical about the newly created social credit system of justice and how it was superior in every manner to the American lock 'em up and throw away the key' attitude, Wang nodded and smiled in agreement.

'Make punishment proportionate. Then you have an intelligent way of penalising the public for their misdemeanours. And a more effective deterrent.'

127

Colonel Li illustrated it by quoting from his own experience. A former beauty queen and celebrity who'd often been on his arm at various events, had refused to apologise to a love rival in a defamation lawsuit. As a result, the party had banned her from travelling out of the country.

'I told her so myself. You deserve it. The punishment fits the crime,' said Li. 'She did not disagree.' He paused before continuing. 'You are no doubt wondering why I asked you here for dinner tonight. Firstly, may I say how sorry I am to hear about the death of your wife. But I have a favour to ask of you.'

The light chat involving one of the colonel's beautiful girlfriends was purely a preamble leading up to the main event.

The colonel tapped the table thrice. At the signal his assistant leapt to his feet, bowed and left the room at a brisk pace.

'You are going to a conference in New York in September? I read about it in *Scientific Life*.'

'I'm delivering a paper at the meeting.'

'How do you propose to travel there?'

'I'll cross the Atlantic by ship.'

'Alone?'

'Yes.'

'Then there is indeed a favour I need to ask.'

The request floored Wang. Something completely out of the blue. So unexpected.

Chapter Twenty Four

On Saturday Karen woke early to the aroma of vanilla and almond wafting through the window from the cherry tree across the street. She decided it needed to be a day of reckoning.

Two weeks had passed since the police visit about the fire at Tarbock Green and the text she'd sent to Haruto putting their relationship on hold,

She checked out the world news. Ninety per cent of it was pandemic-related. Karen dug out some old shorts and a T-shirt. She ran hard around the blocks, trying to leave behind her emotional pain. The last time they'd FaceTimed, he appeared unkempt and exhausted. It made her feel sick to the stomach that she couldn't be with him, even more so after what she'd learnt about his uncle.

Karen jogged home and prepared a cup of coffee she barely kept down, tense with anxiety about Haruto. The daily sprint behind her, she filled the rest of the morning with mundane household tasks. Then made seven calls on the fraudulent goods case, including two to Quacker who'd signed off her report.

However, Tomio Nakamura was never far from her thoughts. His cremation had come and gone with little fanfare. The death announcement and the internet page which accompanied the funeral notice was no longer there. It was as if he'd never existed. Karen Andersen seemed to be the only one sufficiently interested. Who'd worked out there was more to his story. Not just gossip on social media? What if he was innocent?

But Haruto the hermit, had made it crystal clear. He did not want to talk about his uncle. Perhaps he'd discovered something more incriminating when hacking into Tomio's laptop. Because from that moment forward, he'd cut off with Karen on the subject. But their love affair unravelled with it. She couldn't discuss either with him anymore.

Keep yourself busy!

Using public transport was a no-no. Essential workers used the underground, but no one else. Nothing was open. Quacker's nagging haunted her as well. To go out was irresponsible.

Blocked in all directions, Karen felt her life was on hold. But for what? Private investigators sometimes strike up conversations with strangers on buses just to learn what's happening around the place. But with the pandemic restrictions, passengers had to sit two metres apart, making that impossible. Even close neighbours avoided social contact on their fitness walks. Barricaded coffee shops lined the High Street.

With the potential to pick up and pass on Covid ever present, the streets lay deserted, but the risks remained. Chris Partridge, front line as a senior nurse working in intensive care for the NHS, told harrowing tales of life in the unit.

131

When Karen couldn't get her head round things, she took to the road. A bike ride to vent her frustrations via the throttle. The clean country air blasted away the cobwebs. But ever since the accident, she'd not straddled the Kawasaki once.

She checked on the date out of interest. It had been four weeks exactly. Still no formal follow up on an insurance claim. But what if the problem resurfaced?

Take the bull by the horns, clarify the position. Move forward.

She left the flat and headed up on foot to the main road, turning on to Turnham Green Terrace to walk back to the exact spot on The Orchard where she clipped the bumper of the Mercedes.

Karen often went that way on her fitness runs and several times imagined she saw the black Merc, but on each occasion got it wrong.

She navigated a short-cut across the grassy expanse of the park and jogged on to Acton Lane. Her thoughts ran in tandem. Wondered why the driver hadn't wanted to take details for insurance purposes.

Karen paused for a breather at the site of the accident. But no sign of the car. After five minutes of indecision, Karen crossed the block-paved driveway and rang the doorbell long and hard. She stood back, alert for activity from inside. Nobody answered. A quick glance around confirmed the place was vacant. Not uncommon for a property on the market.

She retraced her steps along the perimeter of the park where several local residents occupied open spaces to do their social-distance exercises. A lonely old woman in a soiled orange puffa jacket and filthy trainers sat on the ground and watched them enviously. The scene was surreal. It could have been out of a Nordic Noir movie.

By the time Karen had reached the corner of Devonshire Road, she had convinced herself that the house was a rental, and the Mercedes she'd battered a hire car. It made total sense. It'd been full to the gunnels with furnishings and clothes and the owner unphased by the expensive dent in the paintwork.

By genius luck, she was off the hook. A best-case scenario which explained everything, anyway.

There was nothing more to worry about. Karen's conscience was clear.

With the catharsis, she felt somewhat easier. Nevertheless, the accident had put her off the bike big time. It'd take massive mental effort and a lot of psychiatric help to get her back in the saddle.

With all that had happened in her personal life during the past four weeks, Karen had lost her nerve completely.

Chapter Twenty Five

Helen Rogers arrived, all masked up, at The Orchard in a black Uber just past five in the afternoon. She noticed straightaway the offensive odour of dog urine on the front porch. Still, it was good luck and a change in her fortunes.

Psychologists say you should not make serious decisions within a year following the loss of a loved one. That's when you're at your most vulnerable. But Jill Honey had let Helen know she had to sell either the Chiswick house or her farmhouse and stables. And so she got the transaction for the London property.

The Government had eased restrictions on viewings to help the housing market and she'd organised an appointment with a potential buyer in just fifteen minutes. The social distancing rules were clear. Keep two metres spaced apart or well behind.

'Have you received much interest?' The client wore dark glasses and a bright red and blue polka dot face covering which muffled her voice.

'Heaps,' said Helen. The posting of the old virtual viewing had attracted enquires. But even more flooded in from the Honey Estates database she'd hacked into only minutes before they changed the password.

'How did you get my email address?' The viewer asked suspiciously.

'I have a huge mailing list. Not sure how you got on it.' Helen felt lightheaded from a flutter of fear. The company would be dead against a former employee accessing the system. Had they rumbled her?

'Perhaps you could start at the top and work down?' she suggested.

'Yeah,' said the customer, backing away. 'You wait down here.' She turned and shot up the stairs.

Helen followed the client's progress as she opened and closed the cupboard doors in the floors above. The oak framed wardrobes gave a solid sound as her buyer slammed them shut one after the other.

The woman is an arrogant fool. But clatter and bang all you like. It's OK if there's an offer in prospect at the end.

Helen Rogers slipped off into her favourite fantasy. She saw herself on the deck of a luxury liner, sailing to the USA on the cruise of her dreams. Escapism always lifted her mood and made the humdrum reality of her life more bearable. As vivid as watching a film. She filled her mind with images like these whenever she visited The Orchard. Sometimes she held intricate conversations in her head. The trip on the ship was a scenario she ran repeatedly and also stopped her thinking about the death of Paul.

Fifteen minutes passed. When the lady reappeared, she'd removed her dark glasses and mask. Her face triggered a vague sense of familiarity in Helen. Had she seen her before?

'Can you wear your face covering, please?'

'Why?' The woman crossed her arms.

'We're supposed to keep them on. Government regulations,' she chivvied. 'It's important to stick to distancing rules, otherwise they will put the sector back into lockdown.'

'Never mind about that. Where is my stuff?' She demanded through narrowed eyes.

When Helen finally realised that it was Belle Adams, the wife of a partner in Honey Estates, she thought immediately of the Crime Watch programme on Suzy Lamplugh, the attractive, smiling, dark-haired estate agent reported missing, presumed dead after showing a property in West London. An unsolved case.

'What stuff is that?'

'Someone has stripped the place. Where is everything?'

'They have cleared it for sale.'

'Where's the art?'

'What art?'

'My old painting. I bought that for him at auction. Clothes in the wardrobes.'

'I have no idea what you're talking about.'

'I'll get it back somehow. You tell her that.'

'Who?'

'You know who.'

'Can you leave here now? I thought you were interested in buying the house?'

Helen Rogers felt a trickle of sweat running down inside the mask as she edged her way out the front door.

'While we're on the subject, explain this to me.' Belle shuffled up to her and stared straight into her eyes. 'Where's his car? Paul's Mercedes? It was a company asset. You've not heard the end of this, I can assure you,' she yelled, stomping off and muttering about calling the police.

When Helen got back to her flat, she played her former lover's Zoom funeral for the tenth time. After learning about his two-timing, she'd become obsessed, running the clip with Belle Adams in it. Why hadn't she picked her out straight away?

Often she thought about getting rid of Jill, poisoning her. Then she would have Paul to herself. Perhaps she had to poison this one too.

She pulled Belle's full-length evening gown carefully down over her head and checked herself in the mirror.

Brightening the walls of her dingy room, Helen had stuck a collage of glamorous holiday destinations. Prints of the QE2. Bermuda. St. Moritz. Also cutouts of expensive things, bottles of champagne, Cartier watches, a photo of a private jet.

She stood on a chair and ripped them from the wall as the tears streamed down her face. She'd been rumbled, blown. It was fast forward to reality. Acceptance of being just another thirty-two-year-old singles failure.

Her inbox dinged. She expected it to be 'the knock on the door'. But it was anything but.

A Chinese businessman, whose sister lived in the UK, wanted to buy the property and could organise a cash sale. Later on, a calmer and focussed Helen Rogers came to an agreement on a Skype call. At around eleven in the evening on June the first, they settled the price. Although the market value was three million pounds, he'd offered a little over two and a half. Still, it would be a quick transaction, and she reduced her commission to seal the deal.

Maybe Paul's wife was super simple or mega amenable. Or needed the cash for her next cocaine binge. Helen Rogers couldn't believe she agreed so readily to the amount. When she called her up to put the offer forward, Jill Honey jumped at it.

Almost money in the bank.

No one had figured out what Helen had in her account from the previous commissions. It all added up.

When Helen applied for the job with Honey Estates, she'd falsified her address and conjured up fake references.

But she had to dispose of the black Mercedes as soon as possible. Parked outside the flat collecting parking tickets was a way they could trace her. Plus, it had a ruddy great dent in the back.

Chapter Twenty Six

On the fourth of July, Boris Johnson announced to a thirsty public that pubs in England could reopen. Quacker sat up straight at his makeshift desk in the dining room. Pondering the situation, he hoped the casinos and clubs would follow shortly and his life could return to normal.

He joined his wife in the kitchen, eager to convey the news.

'Did you see that according to the Office for National Statistics, the highest rate of deaths from coronavirus has been among male security guards?'

'I would've thought healthcare workers myself.' She was in the middle of arranging some cut flowers. Chris Partridge had discharged herself from frontline duties at the Northwick Park Hospital, but thank you gifts, cards, and bouquets still arrived by the truckload.

'Construction labourers and bus drivers are amongst the worst affected as well.'

To please his wife was one thing Quacker wanted today. More than anything else. He'd talked her into giving the wards a rest, assuming she'd be happier not having to decide herself to leave hospital work. She'd done more than her fair share. To come out of retirement as a nursing sister at her age. All to ease pressure on the NHS in its moment of crisis.

The gesture, however, wasn't entirely altruistic. He'd persuaded her to bring her organisational talents to bear on Partridge Security.

So they spoke for ten minutes about invoicing matters before she went quiet. This was a habit which had become more frequent recently.

Quacker sensed his wife was withholding from him. He doubted it was a surprise gift, like an extra set of fishing gear or a year's subscription to the Drive Through Car Wash. From long and bitter experience, it was likely to be bottled-up resentment. All over some thoughtless comment he'd made.

'Anything wrong, love?' He hated asking. When the genie was out of the proverbial bottle, ouch. No putting it back.

'Nothing,' she replied rather icily. 'Just having a mooch out the window.'

'So, if nothing's amiss, perhaps you're up to something which as your husband I should know about.'

'And I suppose whatever you got up to at the caravan park is not something your wife should know about, is it?' She narrowed her eyes. 'Well, if you really want me to tell you, I'm planning a holiday.'

'And does this involve me at all?'

'That's up to you.'

Quacker thought a quick break not a bad idea as he had barely recovered from the coronavirus attack. And a weekend away might fix her mood. 'Fine by me. Depending on what you have in mind.'

'Oh, I see.'

'And how we get there.'

'Great.'

'And where we go.'

She raised her chin and eyebrows at the same time. 'Anything else?'

But the destination was indeed a problem. Chris enjoyed places like Goa, which he didn't. So he hoped she intended it to be a trip within England, Wales, or Scotland. Even though they were about to allow flights for the summer, the prospect of getting stuck abroad left him uncomfortable.

'And then there's when?'

'If you can spare the time, you mean.' Conference organisers had postponed all Quacker's speaking assignments on his usual topics, such as stalking and rape cases. Or they'd moved them online. So no easy excuses remained to get out of it.

'Would you like to come for a walk?' Quacker attempted to break the stalemate.

'Only if we can talk about it sensibly.'

'I think it's an excellent idea,' he said as they made their regular circuit of the local streets. 'We both need a brief spell away from London. Cooped up under lockdown gets so tedious.'

Chris brightened up. 'I hoped you would see it my way.'

'But you still haven't mentioned when, dear.'

'November.'

'Oh.' He fell back a step. 'I wasn't expecting it to be that far in the future.'

'It's important to plan ahead. This virus won't stay around forever. Then everyone will book.'

'I suppose you're right. But if we're leaving town for a couple of days, why wait?'

'Because by then you'll be well and truly convalesced. I want you to enjoy it. So that's settled then. Good.'

Back home, Quacker had an uneasy feeling about exactly what he had agreed to.

Chris broke the ice as they walked through the door. 'You might just use the sanitiser.'

Dutifully, he ran the tap and splashed water over his chunky hands. His wife got to work on a Partridge Security survey, her cheeks glowing from the brisk walk and the satisfying victory.

'Thanks for doing that for me,' he said.

'Nearly done with it at last.' The long overdue study on the rate of deterioration of modern fibres and textiles had been one of the latest breakthroughs in forensic science.

'This break?'

'What about it?'

'So you're not considering the caravan?'

'Definitely not,' she flared up.

'I'm uncomfortable about taking a flight, Chris.'

'What I have in mind doesn't involve any air travel. Look at the sky. How many planes do you see?'

'Oh, that's all right then,' Quacker smiled as his spirits scored. 'So it's not somewhere abroad.'

'For your information, I will be off whether or not you join me.'

'Do you intend to reveal a few of the details to your husband?'

'Well, since you want to spoil it all. Especially when I've been trying so hard to keep it a surprise. We are going on a cruise, Quacker dear.'

'Oh.' Her husband gave a bark of joy as he visualised a leisurely tour down the canals. 'Quite fancy a barge trip.'

'Not that.'

'A nice romantic ride down the River Thames, perhaps?'

'No.'

'Around York?'

'No.'

'Well, down the Rhine Valley then? Is that what you had in mind?'

'Better than that. A luxury cruise.'

'That's when you climb onboard and sail for an entire day. You arrive at a wonderful destination. Then they dump you off to explore the place. But before you can, they want you back on board.'

'How d'you know any of that? We've never been on one.'

'Plenty of people I've met have done them.'

'And loved them.'

'What about your lady friend who missed the boat chasing some old boyfriend in a transit port? Cost her a fortune to catch up with the ship by air.'

'Well, how typical! Now you've got the details out of me, you're straight away trying to put me off. Pour cold water on the idea. Empty the ice-box. If you insist on knowing, the tickets were gifted. Some people, unlike my husband, appreciate what I do for them.' She crossed her arms and sucked in her mouth, eyes filling with disappointment at his lack of enthusiasm.

'You never mentioned that before, dear. That you were given a holiday for free.'

'I shouldn't have had to. You don't need to bloody come. I'll find someone else to go with me if you won't.'

144

'Of course I will, if you still want me to.' Quacker knew he was in trouble. 'You can't blame me for being curious, though. Where are we headed exactly?'

'A seven-day crossing from Southampton to New York.'

Chapter Twenty Seven

B y July, the impact of the lockdown on the aviation industry had been dramatic. Flights out of Heathrow decreased by over ninety per cent. As the approach path to runway 27R ran right over Karen's flat in Chiswick, the change was extraordinary. Apart from the reduction in noise pollution, the air itself regained the freshness reminiscent of thirty years ago. The sky gained a deeper blue without the burnt fuel emissions, and the stars at night reappeared in all their original beauty. All of which had a positive psychological effect on her mood. Nevertheless, it was short-lived.

Stuck indoors working on a fraud case for which the evidence had collapsed, she often lapsed into twenty-four-hour black moods.

Sunday the tenth was set to be exactly that type of day. She woke missing Haruto and feeling sorry for herself, and kept reminiscing on their weekend routines when they were together.

Sometimes when he'd stayed over on Saturday, they'd played about in bed until noon, then ambled up to Bill's on the High Road for brunch. If the sun was shining, they wandered along one of the many paths alongside the Thames.

Haruto pulled her back to an emotional equilibrium when she became too manic or felt too fragile. Just being together made them happy. Where had it gone wrong?

Karen relived these moments as she left the flat to do her regular excursion to the grounds around Chiswick House. She bought a take-away coffee at the Garden Cafe and headed for her favourite table on the terrace next to the windows.

She was halfway there before realising someone else had bagged it already. Her world stopped for a beat as she realised who it was.

'Am I that predictable?' she asked for want of an opening gambit.

'Some habits never change,' Haruto said with a grin, 'I knew I'd find you here.'

She turned as if to go, but her knees weakened. He scraped back the iron chair and stood up. Karen noticed how well his white sports shirt went against the jungle green shorts. A paper mask dangled loosely under his chin.

'Come on. You always like to sit here. Look, I need to talk to you.'

'All right.' Reluctantly she sat down facing Haruto. 'Are you feeling better now?'

'Yeah. A little. There's something we must discuss as we're together. Is that OK?'

'Sure.'

Don't hurt me again.

'I've been stalking you.'

She smiled. 'That shouldn't have been necessary. Ninety per cent of people's daily actions are routine. Predictable with only a few mathematical equations. Simple ones too.'

'Well, yes, but you are completely random, so unpredictable. In a good way.' He gave her a warm glance.

'Maybe I am.' Her hand shook the paper cup. 'The MIT is doing a study on it with electronic black boxes.'

'We are all just robots.' Haruto grinned. *His old self.*

'Probably true to some extent. That's what we are. We think we have free will. But we're still programmed by our genes. And the environment, for that matter. It's why we tend to act in a repetitive way every single day. All of us.' Karen's self protective barrier remained intact for the moment.

'How've you been anyway?' he asked. There was genuine affection behind his words.

'Ok,' she lied, taking a sip, well aware that lifting the cup might spell disaster with her hands shaking so badly.

'Sorry to spring this on you. To turn up like this. I should have called.'

'What is it?' She had a sinking sensation. 'You're leaving?' Her eyes filled with tears, but she blinked them away.

'You want me to?' He was playing with her a bit. 'I thought about moving to Japan. But I'm not so sure now. The virus is just so bad everywhere. You didn't get it, obviously?'

148

'No.'

'That's good. I've been very worried about you.'

'Thanks.'

'Have you picked up the latest? Quacker and Chris are off together on a cruise across the Atlantic?' He looked over at the lake. Two dogs had jumped in after one of the ducks.

'No.'

'They've not mentioned it to you?'

'He doesn't tell me much these days, other than what's wrong with my reports. Anyway, so what? Lucky things.'

'You reckon?'

'Well, nice for them to get away.' She managed a sip of her coffee.

'It's not your sort of thing, you told me.'

'There were a hundred cruises still sailing in March, which was bloody madness.'

'Helped to spread the virus without a doubt.'

'No fun locked in a cabin with just dry sandwiches for dinner, is it?'

'So that's the reason you aren't keen on them?'

'I said I'd hate quarantine on a cruise during the pandemic. Yes. Hell on earth.' She cleared her throat. 'So where are they off to?'

'The Princess Hyacinth from Southampton to New York. It's a seven-day trip.'

'Haruto, how come you know all this stuff and I don't?'

He cupped his hands over his mouth, as if ready to confess something. 'The tickets belonged to Tomio. I came across them at his house. In fact, I gave them to Chris Partridge a few weeks ago.'

'Oh.'

'She rang this morning to say Quacker is going too. She also asked not to mention the vouchers were mine. Otherwise he'd pull out.'

'Why would he do that?' It was a hypothetical question, for Karen already knew the answer. Haruto and Quacker shared one of those older to younger male competitive relationships. Both as bad as each other.

He shrugged and smiled.

'Well, I wasn't aware of it, anyway. And I won't let on. So that's the sole reason you wanted to see me?'

He sat in silence for a moment.

'Why did you give them to Chris?' There was a burning sensation in her chest.

'I didn't give them to her,' he said, emphasising the *give*. 'I intended it as a donation for the NHS fundraiser.'

'And she's not passed them on.' Karen rolled her eyes. 'Awkward. You should have kept them for yourself. You're too generous.'

'Why?'

'Well, then you could have gone.'

'But not unless it was with you. Otherwise I'd be bored stiff.'

'You never asked me. I've never been on a cruise.'

There was a brief silence.

'You said you didn't like them.'

'I never did.'

'Would you really have wanted me along?'

'I would have loved to.'

'Oh shit. I'm sorry.'

'It's OK.' She blinked the thought away.

'Maybe you still can.'

'No, I can't. You've given them the tickets now, haven't you? And anyway, why'd I want to cross the Atlantic on my own?'

'With Chris.'

'Don't be ridiculous. Let Quacker have it. That's fine.'

Haruto put his hands behind his neck.

151

'I am so sorry, Karen. It's all my fault. I've buggered things up once again.'

'I was only trying to help with your uncle, after all.' Haruto having engineered the meeting, it at least had given Karen an opportunity to find out what had gone so wrong between them.

'I know that.'

'I didn't mean to pry.' She breathed in the pleasant aroma of cut grass wafting across the grounds.

'I never took it like that. You found out things, that's all.'

'Why did you just freeze me out?'

'I wanted to hide his weirdness from you. The way he lived his life. I was so ashamed.'

'Is that honestly why?'

'Yes.'

'But I'd picked up on it, anyway. Soon worked out that he had some secrets.'

'That he was a spy?' He looked straight into her eyes. 'For China?'

She had to be careful and resolve amicably the subject which had torn them apart. At the same time, she needed to reassure him. That he could trust her and she was on his side.

He rested his chin on his hand. 'I should have told you.'

Karen waited in silence, knowing things were heading in the right direction.

'It seems he was helping the Chinese with a biowarfare program. Something pretty sick.'

'Are you sure about all this?'

'Certain enough. I wanted to block it from my mind. Pretend it never happened in the hope it would all go away. You kept asking me questions. Wouldn't leave it alone.'

'I understand now.'

'I needed to put it all behind me. Destroy the evidence.'

'So that's why you decided to burn it all in the backyard?'

He gazed steadily into her eyes. She sensed he was searching for some sign that she believed everything he was telling her. 'I didn't light the fire.'

'Phew. I thought as much. Who do you reckon did then?'

'To be honest, I haven't got a clue at this stage.'

'Tomio's life was always a mystery, and the entire story is full of loose ends. Not that it's any of my business, really.'

'I figured once he'd been dead for a few months, everything would resolve itself for the better. I didn't want to get involved in all his shit, and I certainly didn't want you drawn into it either.'

'But taking down his digital obituary? Should you have done that so soon after his death?'

For Karen, this was a risky moment. It would show she had continued to check into Tomio's background. Hadn't he specifically asked her not to? She feared he might go back into defensive mood and close off.

He flinched. 'But I didn't.' A look of intense worry swept across his face.

She needed to proceed with caution. 'Haruto, the death notice is not online any longer.'

'Are you sure?' He took out his phone to check.

'I assumed you removed it.'

He raised his eyebrows. 'Me?' he replied, testily. 'Why would I do that?'

'Well, it made little sense, really. It was so impressive how much you did for him. Truly.'

He scrolled through several pages. 'But you're right. What's going on?'

She pushed the point further. 'There were Wiki page references. Remember them? They've gone too.'

He shook his head. 'Wow.'

'Haruto, there's virtually nothing on the net to confirm Tomio has even died.'

He looked confused, baffled by what he'd just heard. 'Which explains why his contact in Beijing sent a message this morning.' He took Nakamura's iPhone 4 out of his pocket.

'Saying?'

'It's encrypted. So I can't read it.'

'Do you want me to unscramble it for you?'

'Yes, please. If you can.' He passed the phone over.

'You trust me enough for this?'

'Yeah.'

'Are you sure?' she teased, while she forwarded it on to her own.

'I am. You know I love you, don't you, in my own fashion.' Haruto reached across and touched her hand.

Suddenly everything that had caused so much pain faded away. She rose quickly from the table.

'Speak to you when I'm at the flat. I'll need my software for this.'

The coffee was stone cold, so she poured it out on the grass and binned the cup.

Karen went back to Devonshire Road at double speed. Using Encros chat, she opened the brief message.

It read: 'Tommy. The time has come for Miasma. I will be on the Princess Hyacinth from London to New York. See you in the Atlantic. And I won't be travelling alone. Ned.'

She called Haruto to let him know. He said, 'Oh, by the way, I meant to tell you. I've bought a cabin for two on the same crossing. I hope you've got your sea legs on when we travel. And while we're about it, there's something else you had better read.'

Chapter Twenty Eight

Professor Nakamura worked in the development programme of a deadly bioweapon in the Chinese Republic. Haruto felt it in his bones.

He'd tracked down a speech allegedly made by a senior officer of China's Military Commission, which was used in an address to his fellow officers in 2016. Tomio had saved it to his research file and added his own note: 'Possible fake news by right-wing activists in the US.'

'We, the proud descendants of China, demand land for our survival as a race! It is a historical destiny that our country and the United States must come into unavoidable confrontation on a narrow path and fight to the death.

'Only by using special means to clean up America can we lead the Chinese people there. Non-destructive weapons, which kill millions at a time, will enable us to reserve the USA for ourselves. There is no point in destroying cities and buildings. We need them for the future.

'Biological techniques are unprecedented in their ruthlessness. If Americans do not suffer death, then the Chinese must. If we, the people, remain strapped to our present borders, a total, societal collapse is inevitable. We have to move our population on.

'When we face war with the West, half of our nation might perish. That means 800 million. Just after the liberation, our farms supported 500, while today the official figure is over 1.3 billion. Our land has reached the limit of its capacity. We have tried a single child policy? It was not enough.

'In the future, who knows how soon, the great collapse will occur. Half the population of the USA must be swept away. It is indeed brutal to kill one or two hundred million Americans. That is the only path to secure a Chinese century. A century in which the Communist Party of China dominates the world.'

The same Sunday evening, six hours after they met in the park, Haruto FaceTimed an excited Karen who suggested they should be careful of what they said on the net about Tomio Nakamura in case of hacking.

So when they hooked up, instead of discussing the next global conflict, they chatted about slightly less important matters such as the atrocious state of Karen's flat, the unsuitability of the piano for the size of the room and the prospective trip together across the Atlantic.

Modern forms of espionage lie hidden in all aspects of our daily lives. Apparently each one of us unwittingly commits an intelligence offence every three minutes of the day. Google, Facebook, and even Netflix know more about our online activities than ever before.

Covert operations. Specific conversations on the subject had popped up in Karen's brain the moment she heard Haruto's uncle had passed on unauthorised state information.

She recalled one with Quacker way back when he first assigned her work for Partridge Securities. As some cases were for the Home Office, he'd asked her to sign the Official Secrets Act.

'Not necessary, is it? Under Section 5, everyone's bound regardless, whether they've signed it or not.'

'The legislation is intended more to remind the individual they are under such obligations. How do you feel about doing some intelligence work, anyway?' Quacker enquired, putting on a blank expression in a poor imitation of the character Smiley in *Tinker, Tailor, Soldier, Spy*.

She remembered her response at the time perfectly well. 'Not madly enthusiastic about it.'

'Gone are the days when spies loitered in some Middle Eastern Kasbah, hoping to pass themselves off as a native trader but sticking out like dogs' balls to everyone. Today it's all drones and computer stuff. The sort of thing Haruto is into.'

'The Big Brother element of modern life.'

'No point being sentimental about it, Karen. All Governments spy to protect their people.'

'I'm aware of that, believe it or not.'

'They often use security companies to carry out their work as they are in a prime position to pick up inside knowledge.

158

Obviously they are working on the ground in a legitimate role in these various countries. The agents have plenty of opportunity to enlist willing amateurs. Easy to find someone with an axe to grind. And tempted by a few hundred dollars.'

'Isn't that treason?'

'It's referred to as intelligence, Karen. And, for your information, is one of the important functions of all overseas embassies. They don't just issue passports and visas, you know. Prison visits that the Second Secretaries make to drug addicts and so on are cover for parallel roles they perform.' Quacker had an unfortunate habit of becoming pompous quite quickly.

'A spy is someone who passes on classified material for financial gain, surely?'

'Not always *sells*. Some give it without renumeration. The police, for example, often use a family member to get evidence in a rape or murder. And we all know employees are unintentionally giving away national secrets from their living room via Alexa almost every day!'

'You make it sound like everyone's at risk.'

'Think about it. They say you can never trust a spy. Nor a journalist, for that matter, if there's a story in the offing. Or a politician, if his position is under threat.' He had a unique knack of getting to the nub of a subject. 'It's easy as pie to break the law under the Official Secrets Act without even knowing it.'

When Karen told Haruto about the conversation with Quacker, he protested. 'We're talking bioweapons research here.' And it wasn't the undercover agent aspect as much as where his uncle had been sending his information. As a qualified biochemist in the nineteen eighties, Tomio had worked with the Japanese Secret Service. So the recent Chinese development was reprehensible to him. With their long history of conflict, China and Japan weren't natural bedfellows.

So why? Haruto surmised it was Tomio's stubborn ideological bent. Perhaps Japan's refusal to acknowledge its belligerent past might have tipped him towards taking the dangerous steps to state treachery.

'In most cases, people get trapped or blackmailed into giving away classified information,' Quacker had claimed. 'It is surprising the number of employees who don't appreciate how the report they are writing, on say medical research, or the air conditioning unit they are designing for a nuclear plant, in the wrong hands could put another nation ahead militarily.'

Karen saw Quacker's name when her iPhone lit up on Sunday night and she had a surge of guilt. With everything going on, she'd completely forgotten to forward the file on the second fraud case.

'A heads up to make you advance Partridge Security matters. Time we wrapped up that report.'

'No problem. I'm so sorry. I'll get onto it in the morning.'

'A few other bits and bobs while I've got you on the line. We're taking a trip across the Atlantic from Southampton to New York.'

'Right.'

'Aboard the Princess Hyacinth,' he added with a touch of pride. 'One of the first sailings after lockdown in November. I believe it's a rather dressy affair. Out with the black tie and cummerbund. Someone Chris looked after during Covid gifted her these tickets. So we're going the whole hog as VIPs. Splendid how some people reward the NHS staff, isn't it? So generous.'

'Yes. I heard something about it from Haruto,' Karen felt her body temperature rise a notch.

'Well, I can't see how he would know anything about it,' Quacker scoffed. 'I haven't long learnt about the trip myself.'

Not the best moment to break the news all four would be sailing together. Nor that a Chinese bioterrorist might join them on board.

Part Three
THE CROSSING

P rofessor Wang let out a slow sigh of relief. He had successfully packed up his lethal cargo from the northwards freight department at Hamburg's Hauptbahnhof. The vial of DX21 lay carefully concealed away in his briefcase.

The long 9,400 kilometres journey from Beijing, dubbed the New Silk Road, runs across the largest land mass on the planet. Crossing the borders of Kazakhstan, Russia, Belarus, Lithuania, and the Russian exclave of Kaliningrad Oblast to the north of Poland, the ten-day train ride finally ends in Hamburg. All frontiers had passed without issue. The lethal vial contained hidden away in the presentation case of Wang's hair products.

It was midday, Wednesday, 11 November. The very date the Germans signed a ceasefire agreement with the Allies over a hundred years back. Wang had no interest in the World War One Memorial Day. Nor any historical wars in Europe. His concerns were for China and its future role and its own contribution to her destiny. The Chinese professor's part was simply to deliver the deadly virus to agents earmarked in America.

So far everything had gone to plan. Registration for the Biochemical Engineering and Molecular Biology Conference due to take place in Greenwich Street, New York was a

Chapter Twenty Nine

Professor Wang let out a slow sigh of relief. He had successfully picked up his lethal cargo from the inwards freight department at Hamburg's Hauptbanhoff. The vial of DX21 lay carefully concealed away in his briefcase.

The long 9,400 kilometres journey from Beijing, dubbed the New Silk Road, runs across the largest land mass on the planet. Crossing the borders of Kazakhstan, Russia, Belarus, Lithuania, and the Russian exclave of Kaliningrad Oblast to the north of Poland, the ten-day train ride finally ends in Hamburg. All frontiers had passed without issue. The lethal vial remained hidden away in the presentation case of Wang's hair products.

It was midday Wednesday, 11 November. The very date the Germans signed a ceasefire agreement with the Allies over a hundred years back. Wang had no interest in the World War One Memorial Day. Nor any historical wars in Europe. His concerns were for China and its future role and his own contribution to its destiny. The Chinese professor's part was simply to deliver the deadly viruses to agents embedded in America.

So far everything had gone to plan. Registration for the Biochemical Engineering and Molecular Biology Conference, due to take place in Greenwich Street, New York was a textbook cover. The forum of leading scientists and researchers from all over the world would exchange notes and ideas on their latest findings in disease control. With his technical background, the professor would merge with the other academics, raising no undue suspicion.

Where next? Wang had one day left before the departure of the Princess Hyacinth to New York via Southampton. He wondered what to do with himself to fill in the afternoon.

Just ten minutes before the rendezvous, Yoyo Chen had texted him to say she was running several hours late. The flight from Beijing had been delayed.

Hamburg! What a city! The air carried the full freshness of the surrounding farm areas, blended with a tangy breeze coming off the North Sea.

The cosmopolitan metropolis inspired mixed emotions in other ways. He'd planned to revisit the museums but still strolled over to St Pauli, where his grandfather had set up home in the nineteen twenties before the SS had sent him to his death in a labour camp.

With his lunch arrangements cancelled, Wang took a taxi to a shop which he knew sold jigsaw puzzles. With the box under his arm, he headed to the Institute for the History and Ethics of Medicine. He'd visited the display twice before with its array of old microscopes. Reading about the role doctors and nurses had played in the state-sponsored eugenics programs made him feel better about his work for the Chinese Communist Party.

He tested himself out on the box-shaped device which the Nazis used to measure intelligence. How would he score? As the analogue digits clicked into place, Ned, as his friends knew him, adjusted his glasses, ready for the result. Ninety six. Not bad out of a possible hundred. His confidence high, he reread the text message he'd sent Tomio Nakamura.

The professor's mind addressed a more immediate challenge. How was he going to handle Yoyo Chen? Having a young woman thirty years his junior accompany him on the sea voyage was madness. Already she was being a pain.

Initially, the idea of taking her along was straightforward. He thought he'd programmed it to perfection. Surely, the fashion-obsessed girl would occupy herself with shopping, the beauty saloon, the live entertainment. If he kept her on a tight leash and monitored her every movement, she'd be as easy to manage as ABC.

But it was just Day One, and the proverbial wheels had fallen off. She was messing him around even before they'd stepped aboard the boat.

Professor Wang moved on to a laboratory where medical students had once honed their dissection skills on the cadavers laid out stiffly on the cold stone benches. Today the visitor to the hall reflected more on his own immediate concern. Miss Yoyo Chen.

Her delay was irritating. Failing to appear distracted him from a much more pressing worry. The security scanners on board the ship. He checked and rechecked his watch. He left the museum and returned to his hotel. At four, when she hadn't appeared, he texted her, but she failed to reply.

By seven o'clock, with still no word, Wang's mood had turned from annoyance to anger.

Primed for the next update, he sat in the hotel's foyer and listened to the streaming music and ordered a large glass of sweet German Riesling to pass the time. How had Li manoeuvred him into his ridiculous plan?

Mistress dispelling was growing fast in China and a lucrative money maker. To avoid a divorce, wealthy wives paid thousands of Yuan to see off an overly ambitious girlfriend. Business executives, keen to replace a favoured one with someone younger, were also ready clients. And the colonel had asked Wang to be his personal dispeller! Could be worse. Nine days with a former concubine to himself on a luxury crossing of the Atlantic.

Li set the twenty-five-year-old model up in an apartment. Even provided a shiny blue BMW3 coupe. In addition, she received a generous allowance.

'And she's a great lay if you're interested,' he'd added as an afterthought. 'If you want to keep her on once I stop paying for her car lease in December, she'd most likely settle for a two door Audi sports model.'

It was an odd request. Wang felt compelled to go along with it at the lunch, out of pragmatism. Or the intimidation implied. Li was well connected with the heavy set in the CPC. So he initially agreed, hoping to wriggle out of the pact closer to November. However, once Yoyo contacted him, Wang changed his mind.

Not only beautiful, Li's unwanted mistress possessed a politics degree from Tsinghua and had spent a period in the UK. To top of it all, she had a great body. Slim, almost perfect to his taste. Colonel Li needed his head read.

Although they'd yet to meet in person, the professor had seen plenty of photos of her both dressed and undressed. He had tried to link up with her in Beijing in May, but she'd been dead against it, flirting but keeping a distance. And what a flirt! Taunting and teasing on FaceTime. Her giggling made him feel alive, and youthful desire consumed him whenever they hooked up online.

The remote relationship helped him cope with the grief associated with the sudden death of his beloved wife.

When he caught sight of her slender figure entering the vast foyer, he forgave her on the spot for messing up his entire afternoon.

Yoyo Chen was undoubtedly the prettiest girl Wang had ever laid eyes on.

The professor couldn't wait to be alone with her.

When they ate dinner together in the restaurant, he took her lack of conversation for shyness at meeting in person. Another attractive attribute. They'd soon strike up a rapport, which would make a difference.

But from the moment they entered Wang's hotel room, all her reserve disappeared. Without bothering to even unpack her wash bag, Yoyo stripped off her clothes and slipped naked between the sheets in silence.

Wang undressed slowly and got in beside her. Trying to recover from the excitement of their online romance, he clambered on top of her straightaway. But it wasn't there. A nagging doubt crept into his mind. Was this the same person? Why was she so different?

He favoured the missionary position for their first time because he knew that way he could reach orgasm. She remained rigid and let him take complete control. Wang loved the expression a woman wore during sex. But what he saw in Yoyo's eyes wasn't ecstasy or embarrassment. He read a coldness bordering on disgust.

Maybe he'd made a move too soon?

'No, I need you in me,' she said as he pulled out prematurely. He rolled over on to his side of the massive mattress in silence, unconvinced. It was like having sex with a robot Chinese Barbie.

Worse, Wang suddenly didn't want to even sleep in the same bed. However, in the hotel no other option existed. So he balanced on the edge, keeping his space while she sprawled out in the middle, legs wide apart. For hours, her sleepy mumblings kept him awake. He lay wondering if he'd gone crazy being talked into all this.

The following morning when she woke, he rolled over on top of her. Once again, she neither resisted nor responded. But when he finally entered her, he struggled to stay hard, as if on a long journey to nowhere. He was devoid of sensation and couldn't climax, try as he might. The sex had been a total letdown. A fat zero on the scale, especially after all the anticipation.

But he'd committed to Colonel Li. And he had to fulfil his promise to take her to the Big Apple with him, at the very least. He must not break the contract under any circumstances.

To add insult to injury, Yoyo got up and used the toilet just when he needed it desperately. But while waiting for her to finish, the answer came to him.

The suite he'd booked on the Princess Hyacinth had another bathroom. It also had two bedrooms spaced well apart.

Besides, there was the full run of the ship. No requirement to spend too much time together once aboard. He must find Yoyo a new lover. Someone closer to her own age. She'd make her own fun, for certain. And there'd be no digging into his personal and business affairs.

He'd be free to operate on his own, unencumbered.

Chapter Thirty

'There you go.' The driver brought the taxi to a stop at the Southampton Terminal drop-off. 'The Princess Hyacinth in all her glory. Very nice too.'

Having had her face out the window half the ride, Karen Andersen flopped back in the seat with relief. The strong chemical smell from the tree-shaped trinket swinging from the rear-view mirror had made her retch repeatedly on the way down. Haruto leapt out to grab the suitcases, but not quickly enough. Before he could stop them, two crew members whisked their baggage away and out of sight.

The twenty-three-kilo weight allowance was barely adequate, but the cameras, microphones and recording devices they carried were small and sufficiently portable to conceal in their carry-on luggage. They also had brought along Tomio's computer and uncle's ancient mobile phone, so that they could go through his files during the trip.

The Partridges were already aboard. Having distanced themselves because of lockdown in the lead up to the holiday, Quacker was hassling to meet up socially. As self-appointed party organiser, he'd lined up happy hours together and a range of shared events the young couple would far rather have avoided.

171

All autumn Chris Partridge had steered well clear of the contentious subject of the tickets. Therefore, the young couple kept the original reason for Tomio Nakamura's dubious mission aboard the Hyacinth carefully under wraps. Haruto decided it was political common sense for it to remain that way as long as possible.

So when they walked into the check-in hall ninety minutes after the Partridges, it'd been intentional. They intended to keep themselves to themselves when they could for several good reasons.

But as they were showing their e-ticket, passports, and credit cards, Quacker called on Karen's phone to suggest being fashionably late was not the best way to do things before a major sea voyage.

'We've arrived. And just going through security.' She stepped forward to have her photo taken on a webcam.

'Well, you've still got ahead of you a body temperature check and a health form to fill in. You'll find us having something to eat in the Queens Head on Deck 7.'

Tomio Nakamura's contact should be somewhere on the ship, if he was sailing. And the message said he'd not be travelling alone. So Karen and Haruto hoped to pick them out from the other joining passengers, in particular from amongst the several groups of Chinese tourists. But how would they recognise Ned, anyway? They had very little to go on.

At the registration deck, each were given a cabin key, a plastic embarkation card and another for buying drinks and souvenirs on board.

'It's a lot easier than all that stuff you have to do to get aboard a plane these days,' she remarked, taking in the airline-style X-ray. A metal detector completed the security check, and then it was straight on to the gangway and into the Grand Lobby on Deck 3.

'Let's do it,' said Haruto. With hesitant steps, they made their way to the restaurant.

Karen wondered if Chris Partridge intended telling her husband about Haruto's generous gesture. Perhaps things had progressed too far. Hard to tell him at this stage without incurring serious embarrassment. That her boyfriend had been the one to gift them their tickets.

As predicted, Quacker was already halfway through a late lunch when they spotted him. It was precisely what they'd tried to avoid, a closeup in depth chat about the ship in general and the accommodation in particular.

'It's not the more expensive full-balcony affair,' he said, oblivious to his wife's attempt to change the subject. 'but it is still not too bad. We're number 4101 on 4 Deck.'

'So how was the journey down to Southampton?' Chris directed her question to Karen.

'And, dear, according to the steward, it's one of the best for a transatlantic crossing because it's so protected,' Quacker

173

continued his train of thought to Haruto getting into stride on the topic.

He crossed his arms. 'Even at twenty knots in mid-Atlantic our sheltered balcony remains wind-free, just as the word suggests. I don't suppose you've checked yours out yet, have you? You got here so very late.'

'What are you having?' Chris asked, handing the menu to Karen.

'Some say you don't get to use your open-air terrace in November.' Quacker wittered on, 'so it was an excellent choice, dear. Not that I hadn't expected to be able to stroll outside and stand at the rail, watching the ocean drift past.' He eased back in his chair. 'I hope the two of you haven't got an inside cabin. They would be very sloppy. If so, perhaps upgrade it if you can.'

'I think we'd better check it out,' Haruto said. They excused themselves and went off to settle in. According to the crew, prior to the five o'clock departure they had to give all passengers a full twenty-minute emergency drill.

Their own quarters, although spacious and comfortable, were located a little closer to the Partridges than Karen had counted on.

'Do we know for sure Tomio would have taken cabin 4101?' She swept the room with her phone for any hidden cameras.

Haruto threw himself on the bed. 'Yeah.' He gave an amused shrug. 'So save your efforts. It means that if Ned and his friends make contact, they will tap on the Partridge door, not ours.'

'If.'

The ship's alarm sounded, summoning them to the muster station for the drill and welcome speech delivered by the Captain over the Tannoy.

After returning their safety jackets, they went up on deck to watch the departure in full.

With no sign of Quacker and Chris, they stood close together, their bodies touching as the band played them off. They copied other excited couples who snapped selfies and toasted 'to the holiday'. What would the week bring? The whole thing had a slightly surreal side to it. The luxury and romantic setting overshadowed by potentially life-threatening danger.

Moored in the relatively narrow channel, three harbour tugs guided the massive cruise ship out towards the Solent. They eased along past the old Titanic dock, where thousands of shiny vehicles gleamed in long rows, ready for export.

A light breeze added to the perfection of the moment. Laden with the unmistakable tang of the sea, it gave a promise of what lay ahead. As they reached open waters, the pilot boats peeled off, and the powerful twin screws began to churn up the wake.

Haruto pointed out Cowes and then Ryde to starboard and Portsmouth to port.

It wasn't until they'd rounded the Isle of Wight and the Princess Hyacinth steamed into the choppy Channel that they saw the Partridges ploughing their way through the merry throng towards them.

'Oh, you're over here, are you?' said Quacker. He didn't seem overly bothered at having missed them during the departure. 'We heard you knock earlier, but I was in the shower and Chris wasn't in a fit state to answer. Our fault. But at least we've found you now.'

The couple exchanged quick glances. There was no point in admitting they hadn't knocked on the Partridge's cabin door.

'No problem,' said Karen, 'we should have waited longer. Maybe we could catch you in your grand stateroom later?'

Chapter Thirty One

Why do I feel so bad?

Standing at the rail of Deck 8 of the Princess Hyacinth as Southampton docks fell away to stern should have been a dream come true for Helen Rogers. It was anything but. A mood of black despair had replaced early elation about the trip.

Her eyes stung with tears at the depth of Paul Honey's betrayal. At the time she arranged the ticket nine months ago she remembered her excitement, believing it was for the two of them and all along he'd planned to take Belle Adams, the partner's wife.

The dark sea sliding past the ship filled her with a sense of dread. Why was she so afraid?

Her finances? The dodgy sale of Paul's house had fallen through unexpectedly and she had already spent the expected commission. She shivered and tried not to think about the growing overdraft.

Helen wore a flamboyant dress stolen from the cupboard at The Orchard, expecting to be in a celebratory mood. But she wasn't in the slightest. A keen wind cut through the thin material and she started shaking with cold.

Back in her cabin she'd change and toss it overboard. Dump it for good, just as she did with the Honey Estates company credit card some bastard had blocked. Out at sea, it now all seemed irrelevant and silly.

With a strong and chilling wind in her face, she struggled towards the nearest companionway to escape.

After the huge build up to the trip, the reality had been an anti-climax. She'd waited all those months for what? A bunch of movies cooped up alone in a steel box on the sea. Suffocate. Drown. Hang herself, most likely.

Out of the biting cold, but in depression, Helen wandered around aimlessly before climbing the broad red-carpet staircase leading up to the next deck. Not watching where she was going, she walked straight into an elderly American couple, who'd sat beside her when she first arrived with her carry-on baggage.

'Well, hello there,' the man said. 'You were at the swimming pool earlier, weren't you?'

Yes, they'd glared at her then as if she was a piece of meat in a butcher's window. And they were doing it all again. 'That's correct.'

'We are so pleased to bump into you,' he went on. 'We've been keeping an eye out for you.'

The American fumbled for an age in his trouser pocket. He showed Helen the credit card she had dumped at the pool bin, certain that would be the last she would see of it.

'Noticed it in the trash. Just as well. We were on our way next to the Purser's office. Then my wife saw you. So that won't be necessary.' He held it up, read out the name. 'Honey Estates?'

'Yes, that's mine. Thank you.' It would have been unwise to deny it. He handed it over, and she stuffed it straight in her bag, barely suppressing a sudden urge to throw up, nauseous with fear. 'Silly me. I mistook it for my other, which is out of date.'

'No, it's valid. And if someone unscrupulous picked it up, who knows? I'm Marty Wyatt. And this here is my wonderful wife. All we know is you are Mrs Honey?'

'Helen.'

'I so adore your English accent. My name's Sal, by the way. Have you made this crossing before?'

'No. First time for me. So exciting.'

'Well, this is our fifth.' She tapped her walking cane five times on the deck in emphasis.

'We're trying to get our weight down,' Marty confided. 'So we really should have stopped at our fourth!'

'But *you* don't have that problem,' Sal looked her straight in the eyes. 'Now, there's nothing we haven't learnt about this ship. So if you have any questions, ask us. We will probably know.'

'Well, thank you so much.' Helen began backing away to escape.

'Are you travelling alone?' asked the elderly American.

Mrs Wyatt wasn't going to let her leave before finding out everything she bloody could. Everything. Unable to hold back the female instinct. 'Yes, I am.'

'We thought so. But we understand why you're on your own?' She tilted her body closer. 'Your husband?'

Helen pretended not to hear the question. She didn't have one, did she? But Sal was in her space, practically on top of her. So close, she wanted to shove the meddling old bitch away. Topple her down the staircase, stick and all. Thump, clatter, clatter.

'You've just lost him, haven't you?' She whispered sympathetically.

'Yes,' Helen replied without a thought. 'How did you work that out?'

'Oh my God, I guessed as much.' She puffed out her chest. 'I said to Marty, she looks like a young widow to me. I can always tell.'

'How?'

'There's a sad look about you. I don't mean you're not very attractive.'

'Those exact words.' He clapped a heavy hand on his wife's shoulder. 'And she picks up on people quicker than anyone I know.'

'It must have been recent, your loss?'

Helen delved for a tissue and dabbed at an imaginary tear.

Sal's eyes sparkled with pride at having guessed correctly. 'My first husband died only six months into our marriage.'

'Moved to the Lord. And Sally came to me.' Marty closed one eye in a lurid wink. 'We got married forty years ago come next week.'

'So Honey Estates was your business?'

'Yes, it was.' An immediate auto response. 'I run it by myself now.'

'Oh, how brave.' Sal leaned on her stick. 'And I bet you booked this cruise expecting to be together too, didn't you?'

'We did.'

'I figured that right, too. Any hour of the day you want to talk about it, please feel free to join us. We're always here.'

As they left, she caught sight of her reflection in a mirror. The new 'Helen Honey' smiled back at her. The widow! And a business woman. She felt empowered and would play the part as if someone had written it specially for her. It was perfect.

She didn't need a randy waiter or poverty-stricken aristocrat to make her trip. On board there would be all types. Wealthy individuals to impress with her knowledge of the market and about how the global shutdown in response to the coronavirus pandemic had effected real estate worldwide. Who knows? Eventually, there might be an opportunity to set up her own realty empire. After all, she actually knew heaps about the residential side of property.

Helen recalled a conversation with Paul more than a year ago. He told her it wasn't the same as in the 2008 bubble when prices in Spain, Ireland, and Costa Rica dropped off a cliff through over leveraging and reckless lending by the banks.

'This time it's different. The market will bounce back quickly in places like Paris and Lisbon, for example.' Paul said repeatedly.

The old Helen Rogers had picked up everything, and the new one stood ready to use the knowledge to her advantage. Now she had a viable business plan with potential far beyond the returns from nicking the odd handbag or necklace.

She couldn't wait to glam up and explore the dining room and meet as many future clients as soon as possible. All it would take was a break. Just one, and she'd be on her way to the American dream. Helen Honey, the socialite of 2021 and toast of the Hyacinth. She had to keep sharp and alert. The reinvention process was already working big time.

She imagined herself soaking in a whirlpool tub before hosting an in-cabin soiree for her well-heeled clients. Lengthy visits to the hairdressers' salon. Then off to indulge in a range of beauty treatments available in the Gold Spa area. In her imagination, the future was all so clear. A personalised trainer? Essential, as befits someone who can look over Central Park from their own huge penthouse.

From that moment on, the fulfilment of Helen's ambition beckoned. She had just one goal in mind. A determination to gain access to the upper echelons of society denied to the hoi-poloi.

What better plan? And deep down, the original idea. The purpose of the crossing. Of course it had been.

She threw her shoulders back and walked to the lift, head held high. There was an endless supply of capital aboard the Hyacinth, and a lot had her name on it.

Chapter Thirty Two

Professor Wang was in a salty mood. He'd seen as much of Southampton Docks as he wanted. At least, for the time being. But he preferred to stand and freeze through to his bone marrow on the outside deck of the Princess Hyacinth. Anything to avoid the stateroom and Yoyo Chen. She was truly bugging him.

Not at all happy about the separate rooms deal, she took the division of their luxury quarters personally. All the way from Hamburg to Southampton she played the wounded victim. Things looked set to carry on for another three thousand nautical miles.

Now on the New York leg, she seemed hell bent on devising a multitude of trivial ways to irritate him, like plucking at the sleeve of his jacket to get him to leave.

'You've seen enough,' she nagged. 'Let's go in.'

'You make your own way. I'll join you later.'

Why had he not left her behind? It had become a nightmare already.

'No. You come back with me. Where were you before?'

What business of hers was it, what Wang did? He'd given her the slip and knocked on the door of the cabin 4101 in case Tomio Nakamura was aboard, but there'd been no answer.

This presented the problem of organising another visit there. How would he do it with her always tagging along?

The couple went back to their cabin without a word between them. Wang cursed the agreement he'd made with Colonel Li. What had possessed him to give in to it? Was it only to keep sweet with the influential Party official? Or because he was notoriously ruthless. Not the slightest compunction in eliminating the girl if it suited him.

But whether out of decency or fear, Wang had caught himself in a trap of his own making. And the cost? *Yoyo* gave one-word answers, moped around or played on the entertainment system, driving him crazy.

Sure, he fancied her chatty and flirtatious personality, but she'd changed completely since they met. The girl now spent twenty-four hours a day behaving more like a paranoid teenager.

His own fault.

Wang showered in his private bathroom before putting on a smart grey suit. He found Yoyo ready and sitting on the sofa. She had dolled up for dinner in a stretchy dress which clung to every curve of her perfect body. Ned had to admit it. Even the ridiculously high heels added something as well.

'You look like an old man. You should wear younger clothes. See?' She opened her phone to show pictures of Colonel Li in an outfit of tight jeans and leopard skin boots, which might have suited him with thirty years off his age.

'I don't need you to tell me how to dress,' he growled back. Even before the words left his mouth, he knew he'd made a mistake. With seven long days ahead, this was the last thing he needed. A full-blown flare-up.

'But maybe you're right,' Wang added to soften the outburst.

Encouraged, Yoyo looked up from her phone. 'You should wear something more casual. It is not a formal night.'

'So what do you suggest?' Ned asked, in a further effort to appease her.

'The grey roll neck.'

'I will buy one in the shop tomorrow.'

'You have already.'

How did she know that? 'Have you been in my cabin poking around in my stuff?' he fumed.

'No. You were wearing it in the magazine.'

That surprised him. Her interest in his publicity shots didn't fit with the self-obsessed cold fish image he had of her to date. It was clear, from her expression, Yoyo had read all about him and wasn't faking it. This pleased him. He decided to change into something which would impress her. Perhaps it might ease the tension between them too.

Back in his own room, he pulled out the roll neck jumper. Matched by his less formal trousers, it would still strike the right note at dinner.

186

Having warmed to her for the first time since they'd met in Hamburg, he splashed on a bit of cologne. Maybe a misjudgement of her character on his part. After all, she was more than twenty years his junior. He'd try again to get some rapport going.

Perhaps explain about his private meeting onboard and take her into his confidence a little more. Not tell her everything. Compromise sufficiently so things worked better between them.

He went out into the living area. Yoyo sat with her back to him, processing a text. Her hair was silky and smooth, tumbling down exquisitely over her bare shoulders.

She turned to look up at him and her eyes glowed bright with approval.

She smiled in a way that showed the appealing side of her personality. Exciting.

'Why don't we go to dinner?' suggested Wang, moving close to her.

As she pressed 'send' on her phone, he just caught sight of the message.

So, she was still in touch with Colonel Li.

187

Chapter Thirty Three

Miasma theory is an obsolete medical concept which held that diseases such as cholera and the Black Death were caused by a noxious form of 'bad air' emanating from rotting organic matter.

It spawned the use of the word in everyday conversation as a way of describing an unhealthy atmosphere. It also served as a title for the classified report on secret bioweapons compiled by Professor Tomio Nakamura.

On the evening of 14 November, as Karen watched the Southampton docks fade away behind the ship and darkness close in around her, she herself was in a state ranging between mild alarm and confusion.

Quacker had just imparted the news there'd been a visitor to cabin 4101 before the departure fanfare. Was it somehow connected with The Miasma Report?

Because of the unexplained removal of the online death notice, combined with the text received on Tomio's phone, there was the strong possibility Ned, whoever he was, had tried to make contact. Could the seemingly far-fetched scenario be shaping up into a reality?

It was a quarter to six. Time to prepare for dinner. They went down from Deck 7 all together and then back to their separate cabins.

'If Tomio had survived Covid, he'd be aboard right now.' Haruto had already memorised the complex route through the companionways.

'Whoever tried to get into 401 is likely to make another attempt.' Karen did her best to keep up with him as he strode confidently down the passage. 'Unless we can find him first.'

But who was this Ned, anyway? How would they pick him out from the fifteen hundred passengers? What collusion had brought the two eminent scientists together on the ship now speeding its way towards New York?

Back at their stateroom, they pondered their next move. Karen shivered and turned up the thermostat.

'They must have arranged a meeting place. But where? That is the question.'

Haruto rechecked the message for the fiftieth time. 'In the text he wrote, "See you in the Atlantic".'

'He could mean "on" the Atlantic. It's a typo. Perhaps the cabin itself? 4101? We should have taken that one ourselves, maybe.'

'So we have just seven more days to find him.'

He had read most of the documents he found on his uncle's computer. Tomio's ethical position was unequivocal. He blamed the allies for failing to bring to justice certain Japanese military personnel for their crimes over six decades ago, and for the effect that had on medical and social ethics.

But along with the various tirades about Japan's bioweapon activities, Haruto had noticed an article on a new Category A agent referred to simply as DX21.

'Which could be a code name?' Karen wondered.

'DX21 was a synthesiser made in the mid nineteen eighties to create sound effects.'

'Of course it could be that. Still it doesn't add up, mixed in with the rest of the articles.'

'Exactly,' said Haruto. 'He refers a lot to "the exchange". As if they're swopping something.'

'When you looked around the basement, you didn't find musical equipment or anything.'

'No evidence Tomio was into electronic music and all that stuff. Plenty that he was full bottle on China's development of advanced biological compounds, though.'

'Your uncle wrote to this Ned. He said the Miasma report was an essential part of the project. What did he mean? Was he talking about a bioweapon sample or what?'

'Or just two elderly musicians looking for a New York record deal.'

She grinned. There was always that hope. 'That means if his contact thinks Tomio is on the Hyacinth, he'll expect him to have this stuff with him?'

'Possibly.'

'Then he's likely to go to cabin 4101 to retrieve it.'

They'd offered to drop by and see the Partridges on the pretence of comparing decors. It'd been Karen's brainwave. An opportunity to quietly check out the cabin. So once Haruto zipped her up in a shimmering blue dress, they headed over for pre-dinner drinks.

'This time you've caught us ready and waiting,' said Quacker as he opened the door.

'Come to see our little balcony? Let me show you.' Chris was wearing shocking pink. 'Lovely the way they've done it.'

The three of them crammed into the limited area, the fresh breeze tainted with a trace of diesel.

'The entire outside space is within the hull. Then the side facing the sea is open to the bracing salt air.' Quacker stated the obvious. 'Clever design, isn't it?' Moving out to join them made for a tight squeeze. 'The sheltered balcony is slightly deeper than a standard one with the glass railing, which is what you've got, I think. That also means, of course, when you're sitting down, you only see sky and not water, which is quite a disadvantage.'

'Want to swap?' Haruto thought it worth a try.

'Oh, no you don't.' Chris Partridge put in quickly.

'We have a larger stateroom too,' Karen added, seeking confirmation from him. Perhaps the more substantial size would swing the deal for them.

'I knew you'd be after this one if you saw it.' Already rosy-cheeked from the earlier champagne on deck, she flushed to the colour of her dress. 'Was that the only reason you came? To compare?'

Karen motioned for Chris to relax and backed out of the enclosure. 'We weren't in the least trying to upset the arrangements. Perfectly happy exactly where we are. Haruto's offer to switch was just him being polite.'

'How about that drink? Let's not get fractious,' said the former inspector. 'A chance to celebrate all being together.'

'Yes, please, if everyone's having one.' Haruto wandered over to read the titles of a row of books lined up neatly on the oak shelves.

'And on a Transatlantic, you've nothing much to see but a broad expanse of grey water, haven't you?' Quacker opened the fridge.

'Try slaving away on endless shifts for the NHS. This is a dream. A flat patch of ocean stretching out before you. Bliss.'

'Can I use your bathroom?' Karen asked.

The boss of Partridge Securities took a determined grip on the bottle of Prosecco. 'You know where it is,' he said, launching the cork. 'Shame we don't have any cheese.'

After fifteen minutes of small talk, they made their move to leave.

'We'll catch up in the dining room, shall we?' Quacker showed them the way out.

The couple had looked forward to an intimate dinner together. Under the circumstances, a compromise was necessary. It would relieve the minor hostility which had built up between the two women. Besides, they were in a super relaxed mood, having used the visit to plan four miniature recording devices around cabin 4101.

Chapter Thirty Four

Helen Rogers was as high as the sky. Excited, she made her way to the dining room on the Princess Hyacinth, bang on eight o'clock.

How spectacularly the sea rolled by under the canopy of bright stars. She thought she'd bust a gut with so much pent up energy. What did the trip hold in store? She noticed so many interesting individuals while exploring the boat. The days ahead were full of promise. So what if they had to sail through the odd winter storm? *Bring it on. Let's rage, baby.*

The ship's entertainment meant plenty to do on board. A casino, shops, the pool, lectures, shows. With classes covering photography to bridge, there'd be masses of opportunity to meet new people. Even ballroom dancing was worth a whirl.

The daily briefing sheet advised the dress first night was casual as not all passengers had received their luggage. But Helen dressed up to the nines. No way would she miss this chance to be the centre of attention.

The cruise liner was everything the brochures said. And she'd fantasised about it long enough! She had completely forgotten the slump in mood on departure. In the magnificent dining room, the polished oak panelling, the shapely columns, and high ceilings gave an old-world grandeur. What a ship!

Perhaps Paul Honey's reservation was a part of her destiny after all. If things had gone differently, he would have been Hyacinth-ing with her, wouldn't he? But stop! She didn't have to mooch now she was bobbing along on the ocean. On board, no one would know anything about her past.

Remember the Wi-Fi.

She double checked her phone to make sure the settings were on airplane mode. It would be too awful to get a ridiculous bill. Before departure, she logged into the ship's system to go online, using a travel router to connect her three devices. Helen had kept the surfing short to less than thirty seconds. That's when the counter registered the use. However, at sea you couldn't do that. High charges lay ahead.

She worked out her daily spending allowance to the penny. There was a spa booked and a small amount set aside for the casino. But she must resist a natural urge to indulge her expensive tastes.

'Helen Honey.' She used her new name several times on the way to the dining room. What a lovely feeling it gave. Great acting. Tonight she would shine.

The ship's crew were more than geared up for Covid. The cruise company was desperate not to have any cases breakout on board. They'd planted Purell dispensers everywhere. Upturn palms! Despite having already used so much anti-bacterial gel, her skin was flaking, the waiter still insisted on giving another squirt of the ethanol based sanitiser for good measure.

Helen easily found her table from the seating plan at the door. The other names meant nothing. The room was a sea of white cloths and sparkling silverware. When she finally weaved her way up to it, one couple had already begun on their first course. She recognised the woman immediately. OMG. The bully from Brent. The Sister who'd bossed her around on the ward.

'You on our table?' Chris Partridge asked brightly.

What was she doing there? Wasn't she supposed to be back at the hospital saving lives?

The husband struck Helen straightaway as the windbag type. Bored out of his skull unless he was doing the talking. He rose politely before she could conjure up an excuse to find an alternative table.

There was no avoiding it, was there? She had to take the seat bang opposite them.

'We are expecting others to join us shortly. They should be here any minute.' He looked at his watch.

'Never expected to see you here!' Sister from hell wore a tight-fitting dress at least a couple of sizes too small.

Helen flashed one of her widest smiles. 'Northwick Park Hospital.'

'I didn't pick you straight off without your PPE. This is hubby Donald, though everyone calls him Quacker. I'm Chris, if you don't remember. Sorry, I can't recall your name for sure. Helen, wasn't it?'

196

'It is actually.'

'My wife always thinks she's met people before. Right this time, obviously. Bit grey out there. Is this your first cruise?'

'Yes. My late husband wanted to take me, but now...' She trailed off unconvincingly but still managed an excellent attempt at a sad sigh. No one dared to ask too much out of natural politeness.

Helen Rogers got her confidence back. She could make an entertaining dinner guest and babbled on to fill the awkwardness. The check-in went terrifically well, didn't it? She'd found her stateroom straightaway. What about them? Had they heard the weather was about to turn wild and stormy? How Paul would have loved it when it was rough. It added to the thrill, but she was not so sure herself.

Eventually the conversation drifted towards their shared experience at the hospital. Chris raised her chin and thrust her chest out. Well, that was how she was.

I'll huff and I'll puff and I'll blow your house down, Helen.

But what happened next definitely wasn't on the cards.

Sister Partridge sang her praises to the pear tree and back. How she was the best aide they had ever come across during the crisis. Coped magnificently with the workload. Quacker would've had to witness it himself to believe it. How exhausted they all were towards the end of a shift.

After having the arse charmed off her, the former volunteer decided she'd rather misjudged Chris Partridge.

No. She'd not been a problem. Nor the tall, attractive Japanese chap who joined the table. But his girlfriend. Without her black leather jacket and motorbike, Helen wasn't a hundred per cent certain, but she looked the spitting image of the idiot who'd bashed into Paul Honey's car. Surely not.

And that conjured up stressful memories from her recent past. It all threatened to ruin the evening.

So the new Mrs Honey decided she'd best avoid the lot of them for the rest of the voyage.

Chapter Thirty Five

Where have I seen her before? Is it possible? From the moment they arrived at the table and Chris Partridge introduced the blonde woman called Helen, Karen had been racking her brain for the answer.

Meanwhile, Quacker's wife was holding court. For the first time since they'd boarded the boat, she brightened up. The conversation turned to the pandemic. With practical experience on the front line, Chris had many stories to tell. She went on for a full twenty minutes straight and not taking a breath.

Having made excuses about needing an early night, and without further ado, Helen headed off.

'Anything we said?' Quacker shifted uneasily and fiddled with his napkin.'Funny bumping into people like that.'

'Disappointed she's left, are you?' his wife asked, lifting one eyebrow.

He coloured as she sat well back in her chair and turned her head.

'What pudding should we order then?'

But the group fell silent. Chris got up and sailed off in the general direction of the toilets. Or so they thought.

'Sorry about this.' Quacker looked awkward.

'Anything the matter? Can we help at all?'

'She gets jealous of me with other women.'

'Oh,' said Karen.

'Can't understand it. I am not exactly Brad Pitt, am I?' he quipped, trying to make light of what was an uncomfortable situation.

'She has seemed a bit irritable with us too though.'

'Has she?'

'Just a little sensitive, that's all.'

'She got this crazy idea. Ridiculous. Thinks some woman moved into the caravan with me back in March. And I don't seem to be able to convince her otherwise.'

'Why did she think that?'

'That night I first stayed down there. Someone left a lamb stew in a carrier bag on my doorstep. When Chris FaceTimed in the evening, she found me tucking into it. Typical. Jumped to the conclusion the lady in the van next door had cooked it for me. She's the type who walks around in the summer with everything hanging out, so my wife decided she was after me. Ridiculous, but there it is.'

'Quacker. I'm sorry. It was me. I left it there.'

The story tumbled out. How she had driven down to Sussex that March evening.

Chris Partridge marched back to the table with a stiffish expression.

'Dear, it was Karen here who did it.'

'What? What are you on about?'

'Brought the food down to the caravan the night you called.'

'So you reckon I don't cook for my husband, do you?' she said, turning on her. 'That I'd leave him to starve. Is that what you think? I had a full delivery of chicken and chips sent that evening. Cost me about twenty quid.'

'Really?'

'I thought you weren't supposed to drive,' she shot back.

'I wasn't.'

'What if you'd had an accident? Back then, that's all we needed with the NHS bursting at the seams. Patients arrived in Casualty for minor ailments and left worse off. Actually picked up the virus in the waiting area.'

Karen excused herself, glad to escape the conflict. Haruto followed on a few minutes later. The full story of the bike prang and its aftermath came out as she shook with cold on the open deck.

'Why does the NHS make people feel so bad, whatever they do? This affects everyone, and most are just doing their best. I guess it's because the staff are under tremendous pressure,' said Haruto.

The two huddled together for warmth as the building waves broke against the hull. They agreed the first evening had turned into a tedious melodrama about nothing.

'You OK, Karen?' Chris had followed them out, finally realising she had offended them. Gone too far. Quacker stood in the background, guiltily triumphant that they had verified his story at last.

'It's true. I did have an accident on my motorbike that night, everyone.'

'How bad?' He was straight into it, inspector's hat firmly in place.

'Nothing much really,' said Haruto, answering on Karen's behalf.

'Was anyone else involved?' He ignored the input.

'A young guy doing a Deliveroo delivery. He appeared out of nowhere.'

'Where was it?'

'The Orchard in Bedford Park.'

'Was he OK?'

'Yes. He was fine.' Karen shivered in the breeze.

'But you never reported the accident?'

'No. I should have done, perhaps.'

'Maybe not. If, as you say, he didn't want you to.' Haruto rose again to her defence.

'I don't think it was my fault, actually.'

'If he wanted to take it further, he would have mentioned it,' he continued and attempted to change the subject. 'Anyone know what star that is?'

'Well, he wouldn't have known who she was.' Quacker rocked from foot to foot.

They all needed to shout. Impossible to hear a word over the roar of the waves and the wind.

'He knew about me,' Karen pointed out.

'How come?'

'I rang the company the next day to check and gave them my number. Apparently he'd told them he came off his bike, but was OK.'

'Well, that's fine then.'

It seemed time to clear the air. She should have left it at that. Instead added, 'But I also smacked into a car.'

'Much damage done to that one?' asked Haruto.

Karen took out her phone and scrolled to the picture she'd taken. The photo showed the dent on the lower cowling.

'Two hundred quid max to pop that out,' he commented.

'And the rest.' Quacker moved in closer to peer at it too. 'A completely new Mercedes section. That will set you back a lot. Far more than that. You made a proper job of things, didn't you?' He shifted into pompous gear. 'That's put paid to putting you on the company insurance.'

'This is not making me feel any better,' Karen remarked.

'Did you pay for the damage?'

'I couldn't. The car went off. Never saw it again. So frankly, no.'

'But since you've got the number plate, it is easy to find out who it belongs to. Quacker can do it.' Chris butted in, determined to have her say on the matter.

'I have no intention of making any such request.'

'It'd only take you five minutes.'

'It's not as straightforward as you might think using the plates. The DVLA doesn't just hand that information out willy-nilly. Besides, there's a Data Protection issue.'

There was a heaviness in the air. Everyone knew Quacker had lots of contacts. If required, they would willingly carry out such an inquiry. 'I doubt if they'd want to pursue the matter.'

'I bet they would with a hit and run,' said Chris. 'The Metropolitan police are meticulous about that.'

'It wasn't, though. I didn't leave the scene, did I?'

'Then there's nothing further to worry about, is there? I think all this Atlantic air calls for a nightcap.' Everyone was as eager as him to escape back into the warmth.

As it was the first evening, the English-style pub was buoyant. Apart from Karen, the crowd was upbeat and very noisy.

'Come on!' Quacker yelled across the din. 'Where has your sense of humour gone?' He intended to enjoy every aspect of the cruise as much as possible.

'Let me buy this round. On us. After all, we're quids in. Not paying a thing for the crossing. And bloody marvellous it is too.'

He went to the bar, and Chris followed, a hand on his shoulder and bending his ear. When he returned with the drinks, he was alone.

'Just to give you a heads up. We might stay in our cabin tomorrow. So if you don't see us around, it's not we're trying to avoid you or be antisocial. As you suggested, Karen, my wife has not been herself lately. I think she's still exhausted from what happened during the pandemic.'

It was now clear he'd passed on Karen's private remarks earlier about her irritability and that there would be consequences.

Chapter Thirty Six

Day two of the Atlantic trip. Karen and Haruto hoped the crossing would be seven nights at sea with nothing on their minds but each other. There were no coastlines or islands to distract them, but there was plenty else.

They boarded the boat fully aware Haruto's uncle, a Japanese biochemical professor, had been working on a research project before his death in March and colluding with a Chinese scientist known only as Ned. So they both signed up for the uninspiring biomedical seminar in New York unaware of what lay ahead.

Haruto had noted, from the Partridges, that someone might have tried to access cabin 4101, the one originally booked for Professor Tomio. With suspicion aroused, they used their visit to plant surveillance cameras and monitor any unintentional activity. But, as Quacker and Chris remained isolated in it, the only images they picked up on the tape were of Chris's bitching about the couple, and her husband doing his best to smooth things over.

'We're set for a mid-Atlantic storm. I had a look at the synoptic on the Purser's notice board,' Haruto mentioned as they strolled along Deck 8 after breakfast. 'Better get our exercise before it hits.'

Karen fought the brisk breeze, fixing her eyes on the horizon to suppress a touch of nausea. 'Oh dear. There are those who love stormy seas on a cruise. I'm not too sure that includes me.'

A long blast from the Princess Hyacinth's whistle interrupted her words.

Haruto, a seasoned sailor and untroubled by the ship's heavy roll, glanced at the faces of each passenger they passed, on the lookout for the ethereal Ned.

'Sorry I dragged you into all this. I never wanted to, believe me.'

'You didn't drag me into anything.'

'Rather relieved Tomio is not around to deliver his shit,' Haruto leant against the safety rail of the Princess Hyacinth and looked out over a choppy ocean.

If Karen hadn't realised how deeply he resented Tomio's treasonable acts before, she did now.

'I'll wipe the laptop clean when we are back in the UK.'

'But you can't erase the data yet. There are so many unanswered questions. Like, what was the motivation? Why did he do it?'

'Because he could. In his position, he had access to so much material.'

'And, indeed, what did he expect to get from it?'

'Money?'

'Do you think the Chinese paid for the tickets?'

'Obviously.'

'And you really believe a free cruise and new car would be sufficient enticement? After all, he's risking everything. Career, reputation?'

'There could be millions in it. Biotechnology is a billion dollar industry. Agricultural products use the same pathogens as weapons. It would be easy for him to cover what he was doing. He was a consultant for several companies, which trusted in him implicitly.'

'But surely they would have caught him out somehow?'

'How can a company know whether someone is researching development of a super fertiliser? Something to enhance crop growth and feed people. And not a bioweapon to destroy them? Corporations don't allow outside scrutiny. Say it leaves them open to industrial espionage.'

The icy wind cut through Karen's flimsy top. 'Perhaps it's widespread in labs everywhere. There's nothing to prevent any country concealing weapons if they take that tack.'

Karen took his arm to steady herself against a powerful gust which threatened to blow her sideways.

'It depends a hundred per cent on national compliance. The moment countries cite any sort of risks to their citizens, whether it be nuclear or bio, they have the moral high ground and can justify developing their own.'

'So arms treaties mean nothing, then.' She caught sight of a cargo ship ploughing eastwards and wondered if they were having more fun than her right then.

'Nope. Tommy wrote, you won't find them until felled. Nice, eh?'

'But Tomio's not alive to defend himself.'

'Bioweapons, manufactured in complete secrecy, leave no trace. Obviously scientists involved are incredibly useful to an opposing state.'

'I'm still not convinced that Tomio sold on his research,' said Karen. 'Everything online seems to point to just the opposite.'

Haruto stopped. 'Why do you always defend him?'

'Who lit the fire? Who removed the Facebook notices? Why do the Chinese maintain he's alive?' she asked.

'Perhaps they don't.'

'So why is your uncle still listed on the program as a guest speaker?'

'Because I never contacted them to about it.'

'No, but I did.'

He gave her a sudden angry glance, then shook his head. 'You never mentioned that to me, did you?'

'Sorry. I was just trying to help. It seemed unimportant then.'

'But you should have said.'

'You could have asked.'

'And you never shared with me your motorbike accident too, come to that. How many other bits of information are you keeping to yourself?'

'You told me to fuck off. Remember?'

He rocked back and forth to control an outburst and turned from her, gripping the rail tightly.

'Well, you did. In a way.'

'I never did,' he said softly.

'Why did you push me away then?'

'I find it so humiliating that a relative of mine spies for China. Filled with shame when I learnt and still am today.'

'Don't be. It was nothing to do with you. And anyway, I'm not at all convinced he ever did, as said earlier.'

'But I am. There's no question about it.'

'Well, there is. And it's important to learn why. Besides, it's tearing us apart.'

'Stop being so dramatic.'

'Things aren't the same anymore. I hide stuff from you. You're doing the same with me. And it all began with Tomio.'

Her pulse raced as she waited what seemed like fifty years for his response.

'True.'

'And we should get the answer at that conference in New York. Or even here on the ship. It all depends on us finding Ned, whoever the fuck he is.' She shivered. 'Anyway, I need to go inside.'

He grabbed her hand and drew her close to shelter her with his body. 'I guess you're right.'

She snuggled up to him.

'OK. There are at least a hundred Chinese aboard, maybe more. I think we're wasting our time. But if you insist.'

'I promise if we turn up zero onboard or at the conference, we put it all behind us. Get on with our lives. Erase the data on the computer. Then. Not before.'

'I might hold you to that.'

The two ran back into the warm hotel-type smells of the interior. On the ship's plan they checked, in all categories, for any Atlantic Room listing. Quacker rushed up, puffing, blowing, and grey in the face.

'Where in Chiswick did you say you had your accident, Karen? If it's where I think, you might be able to help police with their enquiries into a suspicious death. A certain Mr Paul Honey.'

211

Chapter Thirty Seven

Yoyo Chen never stopped talking about Colonel Li. At every opportunity she managed to manoeuvre the subject around. Mention his name, or something or other he had said or done. The infatuation was obvious. Her all-encompassing obsession with texting him turned Wang's stomach more than the churning sea that Sunday morning.

What was the point of bringing her along at all? She still hankered after her married lover.

Plus, if he met up with Tomio Nakamura and she found out, the news was likely to pass straight back via Li to top leader Yu Huning, a current member of the party's Politburo Standing Committee, First Ranking Secretary, and Chairman of the Central Guidance Commission on Building Spiritual Civilisation.

Wang returned to the eight hundred piece jigsaw he'd bought in Hamburg. He was way beyond the three quarter mark. Yoyo hated the puzzle as much as he enjoyed it, so thankfully it'd driven her out of their stateroom and into her own room for a couple of hours.

He started sorting the remaining sections by colour and pattern, setting the edge pieces aside. But his overstressed brain focussed on the other major challenge. How to contact

Professor Nakamura without Yoyo getting to know about it? His best chance lay while she was at the hairdressers.

Satisfied with the plan, he turned another piece picture-side up on the board.

Resist the urge to finish this too quickly.

He divided the piles into the smaller subdivisions with scientific pedantry and arranged them roughly where he knew they would go in the puzzle. Professor Wang positioned each one slowly and deliberately, allowing only the slowest movement.

String it out. Spin it out forever if possible.

Preoccupied, he barely noticed Yoyo when she came back into the salon an hour later. Then he heard her say, 'Oh, you're almost finished.'

She sat and watched him.

'You want to help me lay the remaining pieces?'

'Maybe,' she replied.

He'd reached a stalemate with the last gaps. There were too many. But then a possibility dawned. Unless he was mistaken, some parts of the puzzle must be missing. He checked under the box lid. Then on the floor, before standing up to shake his trousers in sudden frustration. Where were they?

Yoyo pulled a coquettish face. Then she giggled.

'What's so funny?'

'You're funny and so cute,' she said. 'You are like a child.'

213

He failed to see the joke. But at least she was in high spirits.

Then, because of a mischievous look in her eyes, he realised she'd hidden them.

'Where are they?' He demanded.

She burst out laughing.

'Have you taken them?'

She laughed even harder.

Wang's heart pounded, his body rigid with tension. He must resist, somehow, the overwhelming urge to smack her across the face.

At the sight of Wang, perplexed and staring at the unfinished puzzle, she doubled up again. Yoyo went off in sniffs and snorts, squealing with laughter. To her, it was the most hilarious event ever. She re-emerged seconds later from her room with the missing pieces.

She filled in the remaining holes as quick as thinking about them.

'See? I am cleverer at this than you.'

Who was this mad creature? Why did she drive him up the wall? Was it just her sense of fun or did she have a darker streak?

Who knows? The eternal mystery that is woman.

In which case was he overreacting? Losing it for no good reason? Wang's thoughts shifted from Yoyo-hateful to recrimination.

214

Had she intended it as a childish joke, nothing malicious at all behind it?

From the moment they boarded ship she nagged him to let her try on the wigs he was taking to the Greenwich Street convention. And so, consumed with guilt over his short fuse, he ducked into his bedroom and selected two of the most luxurious.

She discarded the first. Wrinkled up her nose. 'I don't want an Uyghur,' referring to hair taken from the Muslims locked inside the re-education camps.

White blonde and waist length, the synthetic one took her fancy at once. 'I like this.' She put it straight on. 'What do you think?'

'It suits you. You look beautiful in it.'

'Yes?' She clapped her hands together.

'You can have it. It's all yours. A gift from me.'

Yoyo picked up her phone, opened the camera and turned it to selfie mode. She photographed herself from several angles and uploaded the shots to an English-speaking Facebook page, before texting them on to the Colonel.

'I know he will love me in this.' She attached a copy.

'Why are you sending that to him?'

'He likes to get many pictures of me.'

'Yoyo. Li is married. You are with me now.'

Even though he was counting the days.

'Then why do you want to leave me and walk the ship by yourself?'

He'd tried to slip out twice to track down Tomio. As usual, she was right there on his coattails. Listening in on his phone calls to China. Always too close all the time. He began to feel like a prisoner in his own home.

'I've grown used to being alone since my wife died.'

The very mention of Xixi transported Wang back. How she'd prepared ahead for her own burial, common in Chinese tradition. But what a shock when she dropped dead at a lunch. He was at the office. No chance to say goodbye. Nothing. He observed most of the rituals. Removed all mirrors and covered any statues with red paper. Outside, the widower mounted a gong to the right of the entrance. But instead of burning her clothing, he kept most of the special outfits in his closet. Just a few things to remember her by, along with the framed photos of their life together, which he placed neatly around their apartment.

He knew he shouldn't compare Yoyo to his beloved wife, but he couldn't help it. Xixi often addressed him as Dang JiaDe, which meant 'Master of his home'. She never answered him back or hid his jigsaw pieces or poked fun at his love of fine wines.

Nor criticised his style. If Wang elected to put on his satin Tang suit with the mandarin collar and frog buttons, she'd slip into a cheongsam with little stiletto heels. If she was in a full-length dress, he would wear a black tie and tux. Together they made the perfectly balanced Chinese couple.

While Yoyo was almost twenty five years younger, he loved his dead wife so much more.

He broke the completed puzzle into large segments and returned it to the box.

'There's a lot of entertainment for you on this cruise.'

'But the weather is too rough today.'

'And remember. You have your hairdressing appointment at four o'clock.'

'No need now. I have the wig.'

Yoyo Chen knew nothing about how much Wang detested her neurotic behaviour and pointless chatter. Nor that he was carrying a vial of a deadly bioweapon hidden away in his room. Something with the ability to kill within two hours. And right then, he would have happily used it on her.

Chapter Thirty Eight

B e sociable. Helen Rogers, or Helen Honey as she now styled herself, had to hook up with someone, anyone.

She didn't want to fall into the classic trap. Forced to sit with the same boring couples at table the entire cruise. And there were real risks as well. After all, Florence Nightingale's husband ran a security firm.

Eventually he might learn more about her background. Those types are all the same. Fishing, suspicious, snooping. And also that rather pretty girl, what was her name? Karen something. The one with the blue sequins

She might recognise me from the glimpse she had through the window of the Merc the night I nicked it.

However unlikely, there was no doubt she was a nosey type too, spending half her time staring at the faces of every single person anywhere near her. What was her problem?

Either way, it wasn't worth the risk.

So at six o'clock on Sunday evening she decided to keep her spa appointment, even though the seas were a rollercoaster.

Helen rifled through the Louis Vuitton carry-on case she'd swapped for her fake one during the first-day chaos. The bag switch had netted heaps. Cashmere jumpers, jewellery, and best of all, an exquisite Cartier watch.

Yes. She deserved a little pampering.

And aboard the Princess Hyacinth the opportunities were boundless. Dozens of high-status individuals wandered the decks, keen to show off their wealth, often in easy-to-steal items. This was only the beginning!

Helen sat in the waiting area of the health club, unimpressed by the lack of freebies on offer, a few cheap lotions and a pile of face masks. She hoped for much better than that. However, the staff had tucked away all the sample products. Early for her appointment, she had the time to reflect on matters she'd rather forget.

Then things started looking up.

After washing her feet with scented water, the attendant showed her into a security area which contained a safe for personal belongings. She opened it and slipped in her stolen watch. She felt something odd in the back. Peering in, Helen could see a solitaire diamond ring sitting on top of a pile of fifty-dollar bills.

When she left the changing room after the massage, she pocketed the jewellery and stuffed the money deep into her bag, leaving one note on the counter for the spa assistant.

She barely reached the door when an elderly lady, in great distress, rushed into the centre.

'Is this yours, by any chance?' Helen asked brightly. The five-carat diamond sparkled under the hundred watt LED down lights.

'Oh, my dear.' The woman brushed away her tears. 'I was beside myself with worry. It is so special to me. From my late husband. Thank you so much. And the dollars that were in there? Do you have them too?'

'I didn't see them, I'm afraid. Maybe someone else handed them in. I noticed the safe was already open when I put my own things there. Let's ask the technician. She'll probably know.'

The young woman, a picture of health, was flat out sanitising the front desk.

'I left some money in the locker?' The former client wriggled her ring on to her finger in its rightful place.

The assistant flushed an iridescent pink. 'There was this lying on the counter. I thought it was a tip.'

'Not from me, sorry.' Helen Rogers murmured,

The spa girl put back the note quicker than she'd taken it. 'We always advise our clients to charge everything to their accounts. You don't really need to use cash onboard at all.'

'But that wasn't mine. I didn't leave anything either.'

The attendant waved the fifty-dollar bill from one client to the other, confused and undecided.

'I drew out a thousand dollars for the casino just this morning. I have the withdrawal receipt right here.'

The woman fumbled in a clutch bag. 'Oh no. It wouldn't be here, because it was with the money, wasn't it?'

'If you find the slip, we can show security.'

'It is so awful when this sort of thing happens on your second day.' Helen Rogers stood her ground, ready to deflect any risk of involvement. 'Would you like me to buy you a cup of tea?'

'No thanks, my dear,' said the lady taking in the glittering Cartier watch on Helen's wrist. 'I'm sure the dispenser will have a record of my withdrawal.'

There was an awkward pause.

'You should be more careful, really. You never know who is onboard.' Helen turned to show off her yellow anti-theft tote bag. 'These have so many pockets. You can find them in the ship's shop.'

'Maybe I should pick up one myself,' she said.

'You should. I've had things stolen, and it was awful. Most times you don't get them back.'

Escape time. She slid off, leaving the spa assistant and the victim exchanging distrustful looks.

Helen went in search of a quiet area to regroup. Unthinkable for security to catch her with a thousand dollars. Anyway, barely enough for a few spins at the roulette table.

She joined the milling passengers, complaining about the state of the sea and the weather.

Safely tucked in one of the toilet compartments, Helen went through the tote bag she'd lifted off a snoozing passenger en route to the spa. It was completely empty except for a tube of sweets and two unwritten postcards. It had come in handy after all!

Having transferred the locker cash to three separate pockets, she dropped the receipt into the toilet bowl. She heard someone enter the room, so she pressed the lever.

The resultant noise was loud enough to raise the dead. A whoosh, followed by a wump, ended with an emphatic thunk. The ship's huge vacuum system sucked away all evidence of the theft. Macerated it into pulp and pumped it into the black water tank buried below the Plimsoll line under Deck 1.

The sound of the suction pumps doing their work was sweet music to Helen's ears.

Chapter Thirty Nine

'I've got some information on the guy you ran into on your motorbike. Let's find somewhere to sit, shall we?' Having waylaid them, Quacker was on the hunt for a spare table.

As the wind picked up, whistling around the ship's various fittings and projections at an ever-increasing velocity, the fresh air freaks abandoned the deck and any free cubby holes and cosy spaces became rarer by the second. But after a few minutes they came across a suitably private area.

Chris had forbidden him to even talk about Partridge Security cases from London, so it delighted Quacker to have uncovered a potential case onboard.

Despite Karen's intention to drop the matter he had traced the plate of the black car she'd crumpled in her death-defying swerve. Police had apparently recovered the vehicle thirty miles away from the city.

'But here's the interesting bit.' He leant forward excitedly.' The man who owned the Merc, a property developer, a Mr Paul Honey, died of coronavirus. So Chris is actually quite interested in this one.'

Which hospital did they send him to? Perhaps she might even have treated him? Appetite for the facts whetted, she scratched around herself and turned up a story from a West

London news site relating to his death. Quacker called it up on his own phone.

Chiswick Estate Agent Found Dead in Bed Had Contracted Killer Virus.

'I remember reading this,' said Karen.

'Look, there's a picture.' The photo showed an ambulance, police car, and small white van parked together in front of a house in Bedford Park. Standing by their vehicles, two men clad head-to-toe in personal protective equipment were talking to one another. The caption, *The Pandemic Multi-Agency Response Team attended to confirm the death and identity of the deceased before taking him to the mortuary.*

'Would you believe a third of suspected Covid-19 deaths during those early months, happened outside hospitals,' said Quacker as coffee arrived for the three of them.

'Is that so?'

'And listen. A police colleague of mine told me on WhatsApp the word is that it's not a straightforward matter. Maybe not even the virus at all.' He leant forward to impart his insider gen. 'In fact, his fellow workers speculated he committed suicide. Had business debts amounting to several million and his wife had to sell the house to cover unpaid salaries stretching back months. And I doubt your bashing into him brightened his mood too much either.'

'But it wasn't a him.' Karen remembered just how empty the property looked when she revisited it that day.

'Then who was it?'

'It was the woman who sat at our table.'

'Not a man?'

'No. Definitely a female. I can assure you.'

Quacker and Chris grasped it all then well enough, even if belatedly. So the charming passenger with whom they'd had dinner, and who'd done the disappearing act halfway through, was the wife in question. How weird was that?

Two Americans the Partridges had chatted with at breakfast substantiated this too. 'They met the attractive young widow just after boarding the Hyacinth. They gave her back the credit card she had dropped. Marty, the younger of the couple, remembered the name on it. Honey Estates. It must have been her for sure.'

Chris Partridge had only worked one shift with her at the hospital. But she reckoned it had been enough to form a bond. And right then the retired nursing sister was square-searching the ocean liner to invite her to join them all at a pub quiz.

'You're both coming, I assume?' asked Quacker. 'My wife thought you would like advance warning. That's in case you wanted to avoid any awkwardness over the insurance.'

Karen thanked him for the information and concocted a plausible excuse about the competition. They went off to explore the boat and enjoy the sunshine.

'I need to get rid of my bike, sweetheart. I've been considering it for some time. Lost my nerve a bit after the collision. Perhaps I'm being silly.'

Quacker and Chris made no further mention of unexpected visits to 4101. Plus, the security footage plan had come to zilch. So they both agreed to remove the cameras before the Partridges came across them.

'The conference will be our best shot at locating Ned,' said Haruto. They wandered around the pool and Spa area on the lookout for him. The weather had improved, but the quoits and paddle tennis courts remained deserted.

Having stressed over who amongst the hundreds of passengers could be their target, they relaxed with a drink in the jacuzzi on Deck 8. The hot tub enjoyed a commanding view over the aft of the ship, as the giant propellers churned up the blue waters behind them.

They watched the sun go down, soaking and chilling. A perfect moment. Haruto leant over and kissed her. As the sky darkened, the ship's wake sparkled with a phosphorescent light in the deepening blackness of the ocean. It was the most romantic part of the trip so far. They pushed aside all their troubles, contented and happy.

Returning to their cabin, they dressed for dinner. It felt delightfully naughty to dine alone. The canniest move they'd made was to tip the Maitre d'Hotel and jag a table for two. It ensured a dramatic window placing. It looked unlikely they would come across the ethereal spy for China at this rate if indeed he was onboard, anyway.

'Let's just enjoy being here on the crossing,' Karen whispered, her hand resting on Haruto's inner leg.

That evening aboard the Princess Hyacinth went better than she could ever have hoped. Secure and close together at their table, the howling wind outside the portholes doubled the sense of intimate abandonment. And added an extra sensuality to the occasion.

The Maitre d'Hotel slid the sizzling ribeyes on to their plates and topped up their glasses with the excellent Cab Sav, before discreetly withdrawing. Mellow and excited, a common urge overtook them. To hurry back to their cabin and the promise of the unrestrained sex which lay ahead.

For the first time since boarding, they were on their own together. No Quacker and Chris, no Helen Honey, no anybody.

The message which lit up Tomio's old phone read, 'Meet me in the casino.'

Chapter Forty

With the jigsaw puzzle safely back in the cupboard, Yoyo Chen said to Wang. 'Tell me about your wife.'

'What do you want to know?'

'Where did you meet?'

'Why are you interested?'

'I met Li two years ago. Shall I say where?' She patted down the sides of the blonde wig.

'No, not really. You think about him too often as it is.'

'At the National Congress.'

'Now that surprises me.' So much for Colonel Li's showbiz image. Wang had expected him to have picked up Yoyo at one of the glamorous hotspots, not the annual conference of the Socialist Youth League of China.

'Don't you believe me?'

'Yes, in fact I do.' It made sense. Unreserved love and pride for the State was the sweeping trend amongst the young. Ever since the anti-government protests in Hong Kong, the beautiful set including K-pop stars swore their loyalty to Beijing. As a Twitter and Weibo fan, it was natural for Yoyo to go along with the current vogue.

228

'Was your wife a good communist?'

'I don't want to discuss her.'

'Then what can we talk about?'

'Whatever you like, but I prefer not to bring my her into the conversation.'

'Li says Chairman Mao was seventy per cent perfect. What do you think?'

Li, Li, Li.

'I thought so, as a boy. But then he became power-mad. He cost the lives of tens of millions of Chinese.'

'You shouldn't say that.'

'His cult following was a bad thing. Not a good thing.'

'Why? I believe he was an outstanding man in every way.'

'Back then they arrested you for uttering the word mao in conversation, even though all you were doing was talking about your cat. They took it as if you were belittling the Great Leader. All because cat and mao sound the same in Mandarin. That was over the top. Don't you think so, Yoyo?'

'I love Chairman Mao's ideas. But I prefer Xi Jinping Thought. It is an inspiring work.'

Since the unanimous vote to enshrine the leader's ideology into the CCP constitution, they now deem any challenge to him a threat to communist party rule in general.

'My father told me a story about the little town where he grew up. The chief of the local workers' union nicknamed him

Chairman Mao. He loved to answer to that. But he became a target during the revolution. He protested. I cannot help what name they give me! But they used to say they can call you whatever, but you should not have answered them. That's how people behaved back then.'

She glared, daring him to go on.

'But I don't want to talk politics with you.' He felt hemmed in again.

'Why not? It is fascinating. What's the matter with you?' She followed on in a wingeing, babyish way. 'We never have any fun.'

Entertainment available aboard the Princess Hyacinth was extensive. It included song and dance routines devoted to the songs of Abba, a cinema featuring the film Marigold Hotel and even a variety show where passengers could spend the week training up for the end of cruise performance.

The only production which brought a flicker of interest from Yoyo was a tiresome martial arts display. But Professor Wang needed to circulate anyway, hoping to spot Tomio Nakamura amongst the thousand-odd aboard. That was why he reluctantly agreed to sit through the tedious ordeal of a kick boxing exhibition. And why he spent more time checking out the spectators than watching the fight.

The star of the show, a young Asian whose taut body rippled with highly toned muscles, couldn't take his eyes off Yoyo from the moment they entered. Had he met her before somewhere, or was he simply stunned by her beauty? He'd seen the performer earlier wandering the deck and assumed he was one of the hosts given free passage and meals just to dance with the guests.

'You know him?'

'No, never.'

But she seemed transfixed by his performance. Wang made a quick excuse to leave for the blackjack table. He promised to return before the end of the show. Once out of the auditorium, he sent a text message to Tomio's phone and hurried to the casino.

The place was full of Americans. One group of Chinese, who favoured the roulette tables, herded together talking at maximum volume in their home dialect. At the same table four others, identically dressed in grey suits, stood stoney faced, taking everything in.

Secret service from Beijing posing as tourists. Wang recognised the types immediately.

Spies, part of the long reach of the state. Along with students, the agents made up an army of unofficial information gatherers, nationals who could photograph buildings in restricted areas without arousing suspicion. All elements in an all encompassing campaign to monitor the behaviour of their own citizens when abroad.

However, he doubted the spooks would be any the wiser about DX21. Units worked to their own agendas with specific objectives, didn't they, Wang assured himself?

He found a seat at one of the roulette tables. It had an excellent vantage point and he could watch what was going on. Alongside a couple who looked like they'd been there for hours had accumulated a substantial pile of high value chips. Next to them, an attractive blonde followed the betting closely.

At that moment Yoyo arrived in a full strop. She'd checked out the casino and found him in two nanoseconds.

Wang propped his head on an elbow in despair. Would he ever free himself from this nightmare? Worse than a ball and chain, Li's rejected mistress, his clingy companion. 'What are you doing in here? Weren't you enjoying the show?'

'No.'

'The kickboxer is handsome and so athletic.'

Yoyo gave him a sideways look which would have cracked the hardest stone. 'But we are together.'

'He is more your age.' After midnight the ship had a nightclub which pulled in a frantic young crowd and Wang had bargained on the Princess Hyacinth's very own Bruce Lee taking her there after his performance. That would have solved all his problems.

Yoyo wasn't playing the game. 'You shouldn't stay in here without me.'

'Why not?'

'Because you will gamble away all your money.'

She hit him on the leg with all the confidence of a wife secure of her ground.

No sign of Tomio here.

She tugged at his jacket.

'Don't do that, please. It's very annoying.'

'Come on.'

Her antics caught the attention of the Chinese Mafia, and others. Everyone, for that matter.

Still no Nakamura.

But Yoyo enjoyed the limelight and played up to it. She had attracted quite an audience. It seemed the more she could irritate him in public, the happier she was.

'Ple - e - ease can we go?'

They also aroused the curiosity of a couple dressed like something straight out of the movie Casino Royal.

The blonde across the table gave a half smile of encouragement to Yoyo, egging her on. Wang had a talent for summing people up quickly, took a pride in it. He presumed the young woman was just there for the atmosphere. Or to pick up a wealthy man.

From her lack of play, it was clear she was eking out her remaining chips, enjoying the sideshow. The eye contact and the knowing glances between her and Yoyo were sufficient for them to strike up a rapport. Within minutes they were both deep in conversation about the merits of Yoyo's waist length wig.

To encourage the patter and stall things, Wang bought a bottle of Dom Perignon Rose and pretended to be enjoying himself.

But where was Tomio?

Chapter Forty One

Karen Andersen snuggled into the warm arms of Haruto Fraser. It was day three of the crossing.

Last night's visit to the casino had produced no more leads on the Tomio Nakamura's elusive contact from Beijing.

There'd been plenty of Chinese there. But they got nothing back from any of them but blank stares and quizzical looks when they slipped the code word Miasma into the conversation.

And then there was the blackjack. Haruto, normally lucky, ran into a five-session run of bad variance. Although he pulled out when the losses were merely sad and not catastrophic, it had still been a financial disaster.

So they rose late morning. The front had passed through during the early hours, and the wind dropped, giving way to a clear sunny day. The Hyacinth carved a path through the perfectly calm sea. There was every sign the rough weather was behind them. So they lazed about in the warmer corners of the ship.

They wrote the text message off as a hoax, a childish prank, an unfunny practical joke sent by whoever had stuck a cock and balls gif on Tomio Nakamura's Facebook page. They toyed with the idea of responding, but dismissed it as a waste of cruising time. Plenty of fun things to do.

Both Haruto and Karen had got their sea legs. And so now enjoyed the ride on the entrancingly beautiful ocean. And they were also getting used to the rhythms of the crossing. Passengers headed towards the restaurants as regular as clockwork, unable to believe the huge servings on offer. Quacker and Chris, out to get their full value from the cruise, never missed a meal, and were always in the Britannia Restaurant, explaining it was all part of their generous, inclusive package.

Therefore, it was a surprise to see them for once in the Princess Grill.

'I'd lost ten kilos on a fasting diet. Now I've put it all back,' said Chris. She relished all the fuss being made of her, as she tucked into her crepe suzette.

Quacker had the day's entertainment schedule in hand. The crew delivered them daily to the cabins. 'Overwhelming, isn't it? Listen to this.'

He read out loud the list. Lectures, films, recitals, musical productions, church services, water colour classes, AA meetings, planetarium shows, wine tastings, pilates sessions, whist socials. Despite that, he'd circled only one for later on. Drinks in the Commodore Club, below the ship's bridge.

'This bar has an entire cocktail menu devoted to gin and tonics. Should be right up your alley, Karen.'

'Is that all you are planning today?'

'There's a great temptation to sample everything, but I'm just enjoying the cruising part,' he said. 'Did you know this ship is longer than the Chrysler Building is tall? I enjoy the idea of climbing that horizontally.'

'And books.' Chris held up a copy of a medical thriller she'd found in the library. 'I got this for my husband to get him to unplug from the Wi-Fi, but now I'm reading it.'

'Yes, I suppose it's healthy to cut off for a while. You learn nothing about world events from this,' Quacker said, waving the ship's slim newspaper. 'But then, like us, most of the crowd onboard don't care. Happy to forget their troubles. Or start a fresh lot by meeting another life partner. Just as our young friend from England seems to have in mind.'

It couldn't be more obvious Helen was distancing from their group. She snubbed Karen at the roulette table the night before, which was convenient. And several other times in passing.

Chris Partridge didn't take too kindly to being deliberately ignored. There'd been one incident in the lift. Another in the bookshop. Hospital Helen had pointedly turned her back on her. The more she dwelt on the rebuff, the angrier she became.

'What have I done to deserve that?'

'Well, you can only try, dear,' said Quacker. 'And we aren't too certain of her circumstances, are we? If her husband was a spender who left her with a load of debts. You have to feel some sympathy.'

'A player?' Chris shuffled in her chair.

'Sounds like he could have been. She's most likely after number two and doesn't want us to queer her pitch.'

Leaving the Partridges to their coffee and mints, Karen and Haruto disengaged. They wandered off to check out some sepia-tinted photos lining the lobby walls of real playboys of the past.

Chris's fascination with the medical thriller she was halfway through prompted Karen to pay a visit to the library area. Because most were outside enjoying the fresh sea air, the room was empty apart from three others, two playing chess together and a lone passenger bent low over a game of solitaire.

'This is bliss,' said Karen, plucking a copy of David Copperfield from the shelves and settling into a leather armchair. 'I could live on here with you forever. I'm so happy.'

They spent the next couple of hours enjoying the peace of the moment, feet just touching and exchanging small smiles. On the point of leaving, she noticed the bookplate inside the front cover stamped 'ex-libris of The Atlantic Library'.

She handed it to Haruto.' Have you seen this? Look.'

His normally easy-going expression clouded over.

'Maybe this is the place. The one we've been looking for all along? The message saying "Meet you in the Atlantic" wasn't a typo, perhaps?'

'The problem with that? This room is the Princess Library.'

'Are you sure?'

He pointed to the sign on the wall. 'We checked it out, remember?'

Haruto was right. Karen pulled another book from the shelf and the sticker inside also read 'ex-libris of The Princess Library' with the ship's logo stamped underneath.

'Most of the books have Princess Hyacinth printed on them.'

'But this one doesn't.' They went up to a crew member busy directing a passenger to the lecture hall who told them, 'If you want to remove a book, that's fine with us. But you have to let the Purser's office know. They will sign it out for you.'

'Right.'

'Oh, and if you haven't already seen it, there's a section where people donate paperbacks once they've finished them. Not many at the moment. It fills up more later in the voyage.'

'Why does the inscription say The Atlantic?'

'That was the name of the library. Before refurbishment.'

Chapter Forty Two

What a relief! Helen followed the distinctive lemon-coloured tote bag until it got swept away in the ship's wake. She couldn't risk being caught with it under any circumstances.

The bloody fuss about petty theft aboard the liner was building up, with rumours and exaggeration rife. So she'd tossed it over the railing and watched it slowly drift down before landing on the surface of the ocean where it decided to float instead of sink.

Helen glanced around to check if anyone had noticed her get rid of the tote. And there she was. That bloody Partridge woman again. Always, always after her. What is it now?

Keep smiling, don't engage and be oh so careful, baby.

Am I imagining it, or is that Chris creature really following me? Wherever I turn, she's there.

Helen Rogers viewed the overweight NHS sister in the same critical manner as once they judged her in the hospital. Reverse roles.

The woman swivelled her face around. It reminded her of a snake. The Death's Head adder she'd seen in the zoo as a child. Always slithering about. She was like a serpent too.

You don't have a clue I'm keeping a close eye on you, do you?

That makes a change, doesn't it, Chris?

Instead of the other way round.

From what she had picked up earlier, the stupid woman still bought her cover story. That she was Paul Honey's widow. To think that her henpecked husband, who waddled around like a pregnant duck, was a legitimate security analyst. So much for the detailed investigations and identity protection he did. What a joke!

Helen gazed out over the sparkling seas. Oh God. How I'd love to push the bloody creature over the side. Into the briny. Gone. Vanished forever. What a wonderful solution.

She quickly ran over exactly what she would say beforehand:

To start: Listen, you stuck-up simpleton. Don't you know how you made me feel on the ward? Like a piece of crap. And that is one reason I'm here. The very type the sloppy NHS needs. I left because of you. Nobody paid me, unlike you, who clearly pocketed so much in overtime you can afford to swan about as if you own the entire ship.

The next bit: No, I don't wish to join you and Quack Quack, or whatever he's called, for a game of Monopoly. Or sign up for the bloody Trivia Quiz in the sodding pub. Everyone else on board knows I'm a star. Why don't you? I am not yet rolling in it, but I will be tooty-sweety. And I'll be in a penthouse duplex. Just like my new Chinese billionaire friends. And I won't have to set eyes on your ugly face ever again.

Then: And if you are wondering? Yes, I put a plastic bag over his head. Because he wanted me too. Otherwise we would both be here together. Understand? And I would not have to rush around this pitching ship of fools nicking their stuff. So degrading. Nor would I have to live with your sanctimonious patronising. All because I am travelling alone. Now, do you get it?

Helen saw herself taking her Hermes headscarf off and wrapping it round the snake's slippery neck. Knotting it tightly. Cutting off her air supply. As she'd done with Paul.

Chris Partridge had decided on Deck 9 for her usual constitutional. It was less crowded, which made for a brisk, fast-paced power walk. Striding past the lifeboat duvets, she spotted the NHS volunteer and newly widowed passenger immediately. What to do?

Confronted with an awkward choice, she hesitated. Either barge up and say hello or try to slip away unnoticed. She wanted to invite her to the pub quiz. Perhaps this wasn't the ideal moment.

Helen went for a 'I'm Not Here' strategy. She pressed herself hard against the bulkhead to become as invisible as possible. Closing her eyes, she threw her head back as if engaging in a private time on the deck, taking in the sun and the fresh tangy breeze, and raised her chin sunward, as if she was asleep on her feet.

Confident that she had got away with it, she opened them to find Chris right there in front of her, wearing a huge grin.

'Hello, Helen. What a lovely surprise.'

Quelle fucking surprise. 'Fancy seeing you here.'

'Enjoying the outdoors?'

'The view is absolutely mesmeric, isn't it?'

'Wonderful?'

'Brilliant.'

'I would love to have one like this forever.'

'And such a magnificent day too.' Helen untied and took off her scarf, which flapped crazily. The hair style got blown to pieces in seconds.

'Careful. You don't want to lose it.' Chris Partridge had to raise her voice to be heard. 'I can see it taking off. You're not hiding out here on your own, are you?' She pitched up even more to compete with the whistling wind.

'I'm just happy to be on my own,' Helen screamed back. 'Sorry. It's getting cold too. I'll have to go.'

She needed to prepare for the adventure to come. To restyle. Remind herself how to connect with genuine people. Not waste precious time with peasants.

She took the elevator down to her private cabin and laughed her head off. Helen Rogers had hoodwinked everyone on the Princess Hyacinth. It felt terrific. She'd never experienced a feeling of such intense pleasure before. Just as

Paul described his orgasm. Euphoric. Floating in that space between consciousness and unconsciousness. Transported to a new dimension.

And it gave her a surge of powerful self belief.

244

Chapter Forty Three

Early evening Karen suggested Haruto challenge Quacker to darts. They missed the pub quiz the night before. So such a gesture would pacify the Partridges and keep them happy.

The arrangement would serve a second purpose. Allow her to make an excuse to check out the Atlantic Room. Having concluded it was a likely contact point for Ned to show himself, they'd been back and forth several times during the day hoping to connect.

Chris Partridge was an authority on Honey Rogers by now and had grown almost obsessed with her strangeness. Despite Chris's big-hearted gesture at inviting her to link up with them all, the hospital volunteer had yet again given her the brushoff. In seemed as if their widow had a merrier deal on offer.

Not an hour ago, she'd seen her go into Toby's, the most upscale restaurant on the ship with the same Chinese couple Karen and Haruto had spotted her with at the casino.

'How did she muscle in on them?' asked Chris. 'Odd set up there. The girl looks young enough to be his daughter. Disgusting, really.'

'My friend Alan Tucker, who used to work with me in the CID, got a two-year basing in Beijing. Has heaps of interesting tales to tell,' said Quacker, as he gripped the barrel of his dart before firing it in the general direction of triple nineteen. 'His colleague put him and his missus in an uncomfortable position when he took his mistress on holiday with them. They had to sit with lips sealed about the situation when they had dinner with him and his official wife the following week.'

'You'd love that, wouldn't you dear?'

Quacker pretended not to hear that as he concentrated on lining up the next dart. 'He housed his girlfriend in the same compound. The very same building in Beijing. On another floor, of course. But she never picked it up.'

'Or didn't want to,' said Karen.

Bounding up to the board, Haruto deftly plucked out the darts.

'Well, time was money to him. He'd tell his spouse he was off to the gym or office. He never left the apartment block. Exited the elevator before it hit ground floor.'

'Maybe his colleague's wife was up to the same? Have you considered that possibility?' Chris dropped her bit into the conversation.

'Perhaps she was,' said Quacker, 'but I doubt if she was paying for the bloke. Still, you never know in life.'

With Haruto well ahead in the match, and the temperature rising between the Partridges, Karen excused herself temporarily and ducked back on the double to the Princess Hyacinth library.

As Tomio's contact was likely to be there at some point, she hung around for a further ten minutes. Any longer might have raised questions about her whereabouts with the others.

She was about to leave when Helen walked in with her newfound friends from the casino, fishing out her phone for a selfie with them. However, the young Chinese woman wouldn't join in. It was obvious what was going on. A touch of jealousy.

Karen wondered how long it would be before the cosy threesome fell out. 'Let me. I'll ping it to you,' she suggested, taking a shot of the three of them on her iPhone before the man edged away, more interested in the library itself than either woman. Unsurprisingly. He wanted to check out each nook and cranny of one of the ship's major architectural landmarks.

'Take it on mine too.' Both women held out their phones at once.

Half an hour later, back in the pub, new players had commandeered the dart board.

'He won,' Quacker waved a disappointed hand in Haruto's general direction.

'It was close — *ish*.' Haruto raised an eyebrow at Karen.

She realised something significant had happened between the three of them while away. Nothing to do with the victory. Chris sat with her hands in her lap, deep in serious thought.

'We're headed out to Toby's tomorrow night.' Quacker creaked his chair. 'We were just talking about it. Wondered if you two would like to join us.'

'It's very good. From what I've heard.' His wife rubbed her fingers against one another in the money sign. 'The best on the ship, apparently.'

'Our treat. I wasn't aware until today when she told me. How Haruto gifted our tickets.'

There was a brief silence.

'He winkled it out of me, eventually.' Chris radiated relief. 'Didn't you, dear? Just so it's all straight. The girls at the hospital insisted I use them. It was not my idea to keep them. Not include them in the fundraiser.'

'Fine, as far as I'm concerned.' Haruto added, trying to put her at ease,

'You told me it was for frontline workers.'

'Yes,' He seemed content with the explanation. 'My uncle used the NHS a lot.'

'It was the right decision to hold on to them, Chris,' said Karen. 'Otherwise they'd have got buried in the great mountain of auction stuff.'

'And we'd have had to bid a fortune for them! Thank you very much. So thoughtful.' He fidgeted in his seat. 'Which is why I let you beat me at darts.'

The Partridges gathered up their belongings, ready to go.

Quacker parked his chair neatly under the table. 'Oh, I've an idea. What about one for the road? Back at ours.'

Karen gave the nod to Haruto. 'We'd love to if it's not too late for you.'

After a final check of the ship's library, they went on deck to take in the fresh air and sparkling stars. Then took the elevator down to the companionway leading to cabin 4101.

Clad in a towelling wrap and looking every bit the overweight cage fighter, Quacker ushered them in.

'What are you having? Choice is great. If you like gin and rum. White wine for Karen?'

'Yes, that's good for her, I think,' Haruto replied. 'and a Bacardi and coke for me, thank you.'

The retired inspector busied himself with the drinks as Chris brought out the snacks.

'There you are. There's your drink and here is your CCTV equipment. I assume they belong to you, don't they?' He plonked the cameras down in a small heap in front of them.

For a long ten seconds, the couple sat silent. Lost for words and speechless with embarrassment.

Haruto kept his composure sufficiently to come up with a quick answer.

'Oh yes, they're mine all right. We heard cleaners were nicking jewellery and stuff from the rooms. Didn't want that to happen. I would feel responsible as the trip was my gift. Should have told you. But if nothing happened, I wouldn't have looked at the footage, of course. Sorry. Never meant to invade your privacy.'

'No problem at all,' said Quacker. 'I brought my own along, anyway. See. There it is. Concealed rather well, if I say so myself.' He had integrated the miniature CCTV into a reading lamp and it was completely undetectable to a cursory glance. 'Always carry it, don't we, dear? Once a copper and all that.'

Holding the floor, Quaker got down to a subject that really interested him. Haruto and Karen were off the hook.

'Look, now we can talk in private. There's something very odd about the death of Mr Honey to me. I have a nose for these things, believe me.' Quacker leant forward as he warmed to the topic.

'I've been on this awfully expensive ship's internet digging in to the background of his widow. We'll have to re-mortgage the house to pay the charges when we get home, won't we dear. Ha ha. Anyway, turns out that Helen wasn't his wife at all! So who the hell is she?' Quacker asked rhetorically. 'Possibly someone who worked for his company. And now putting herself about like she's Amphitrite, Neptune's other half.'

'She was a proper diva at work. Unbearable,' Chris put in, excited by the unexpected turn of events. 'Ordering the doctors around as if she was the administrator. Had some sort of special authority. Completely delusional nutcase. Why the nurses had to bring me in to deal with her.'

'What was she doing there anyway,' Karen asked?

'The job I gave her was to dispose of the Covid waste from the ward. If she had contact with Paul Honey, she could easily have passed the virus on to him. That's what killed him.'

'But you don't die straight away from just handling infected stuff, do you?'

'She'd been working at the hospital for some weeks.'

'He never raised the issue with his GP or anyone that he might have contracted it before, dear.'

'Covid can take you faster than you think.'

'But not that quick, surely? And suddenly she left the ward, didn't she?'

Chris had checked her diary to see when she had been in. 'But the day she carried out errands for me fits with Karen's date.'

'Mine?'

'She dropped out at Northwick Park the same Friday you hit her car, Karen.'

'It wasn't her's, actually,' his wife reminded him.

'She was clearing a house, perhaps.'

'How did you come up with that, Karen?' Quacker loosened the belt of his dressing gown and re-tightened it. 'That's a bit random.'

'You'll show us everything in a minute, if you're not careful, dear,' said Chris, rolling her eyes.

'Because she loaded it up with black bin bags and bits of furniture.'

'And borrowed Paul Honey's vehicle to move her stuff from his house?'

'Or *his*,' Haruto chipped in.

'So, Mr Honey was alive then, wasn't he?'

'Why do you say that, Karen?' Quacker leant back on the bed and stretched his legs.

'To ask to borrow the car?' Karen's face was still pink from the embarrassment surrounding the discovery of the cameras earlier. 'Or she took it without asking. Which explains the rush to leave and why she didn't bother to write down my details.'

'Or Paul Honey was already dead. In which case she wouldn't have needed his permission at all, would she?' Chris's eyes were alive and shining with excitement.

Haruto said, 'Or *she* killed him.'

Chris did a double take at that. 'It's possible. By using infected flannels from the hospital. Put one over his face. All to make the police believe he'd succumbed to Covid?' Her wry expression changed, became more serious and thoughtful. 'Bloody hell.'

Quacker gave his wife a look of respect mixed with wonder. It was a jaw-dropper. 'I think you've hit on something, Chris.'

It was getting late. What to do here and now?

'Well, nothing more to do tonight,' he said, looking at his watch. 'But before we go further with this, Karen, it might be worth establishing for certain if she was in fact the one driving the car you smashed into.'

It was the least she could do. Atone for the intrusion into their privacy.

Chapter Forty Four

Helen Rogers might not have noticed Ned Wang at all had it not been for his companion Yoyo. She first saw the young Chinese girl hanging off the arm of the professor as they walked the deck on day one. Who was he?

When she accidentally bumped into them in the casino, it was an opportunity to strike up a conversation and ended with an invitation to join them for dinner in Toby's. What a treat. They chinked glasses filled with the best champagne against a tinkling background of discreet late-night piano jazz. And when the elderly professor traipsed off to the toilet on one of his fifty visits, Yoyo told her more about him.

Wang didn't do it for her. 'I don't want to be that old dog's vagina,' she whispered. 'He's stinking rich but gross. And makes me do things I hate. And he doesn't even compliment me on my looks. I'm beautiful. Why does he not say so?'

Helen kept digging. 'Where did you meet?'

'My long-time lover set me up. It was a smokescreen in case his wife found out how much he loves me. We are just pretending it's all over.'

'Do you think you'll get back with your Colonel Li?'

'Oh yes. He adores me. Far more than her. Know what?' She tittered into her napkin. 'Being with Ned is making him jealous now.'

'Really? How can you tell?'

'Because he says so when he calls. He wants to meet me in New York. We will be together again. I have to be patient.'

She had small, very white teeth and giggled when Wang wasn't around. 'Where is he anyway? Perhaps stuck in the toilet!'

Helen liked the way Yoyo never delved too much. The fact she didn't fancy Ned. Sensed a whiff of opportunity there.

'And if Colonel Li is not in New York and wants to finish with me, at least I'm given a million Yuan from the agency his wife is using. You know what? In China, big business. Getting rid of mistresses. Wives scared of us.' Yoyo sighed a shallow sigh before brightening up. 'I think I get a puppy. What we call puppy. Young man, strong, who looks after me and does everything I need.'

'I've never heard of that one,' Helen gasped, mouth round in astonishment.

'I will ask him to keep a notebook. Write all the things he does to make me angry. That way he won't do them again. He must cook for me too. And tell me he loves me every day, be there whenever I want.'

On the next toilet break, they talked about the New York property market. The best buildings and the top areas of the city. What sort of place the colonel had promised her. The budget was so huge it made Helen's eyes pop.

This could be a win win.

What better? She'd find them a bargain apartment, take a commission, and then maybe move in on Ned Wang herself. A perfect plan formed in her head.

When the three of them left Toby's they dropped by the Princess Hyacinth library. It'd been Ned's suggestion. Helen caught his eye just long enough to convey a sexual interest. She knew the professor had picked up on it too.

The problem was, Yoyo had also.

It was two thirty. Helen Rogers sat alone on a sofa in the Reverie Room minding her own business. The plan was sound. But she needed a quiet place to work out exactly how to implement it.

A familiar voice broke into her reflections.

'Hello. Having a good day, there?'

'Well, I was.' Perfectly contented to sit by herself until then. Dreaming the hours away, planning her moves and looking forward to the evening ahead. Yet another invite to Toby's with her new friends. They dined out at the most expensive restaurant on an almost daily basis.

'It's so relaxing on this ship, isn't it?'

'I enjoy the peace and freedom.' *Take the hint. Butt out.*

'You do, do you?'

This Andersen woman was obviously pretty thick. She doubted she could find her own way home, let alone people who'd gone missing.

So she asked. 'Who on God's earth are you two looking for, anyway? Is that how you security wannabes spend your time scanning the crowd on the lookout for bad guys who might attack your client? Like in that Whitney Houston film. What was it called? The Bodyguard.'

Karen Andersen's voice wavered. 'There's a lot more than that to it, actually.'

'I'm quite observant. Maybe I could do your job. If you told me who you were after, then perhaps I could help you.'

'I doubt it, but thank you anyway.'

'Don't you have to be butch like your boyfriend for detective work?' Andersen was slender and a bit of a short arse as well.

'It's all about applying your brain, not about physical strength.'

'I'm serious, actually. Personal security is a vast business, isn't it?'

'It can be.'

'I think I'd make a good bodyguard. Do you hire women in your company for that?'

'You'd have to speak to Quacker.'

Who in their right minds would sign up for them, Helen said to herself? They were all so small time. Dumb and petty minded. She'd heard that high wealth individuals pay a million a year for security, which would be much more her style.

'Partridge? That woman follows me everywhere I bloody go. Can you tell me why's she doing that?'

'She thought you could do with company, that's all. What with you being newly widowed.' Karen put emphasis on the last word.

Disrespectful bitch. 'I'm serious about taking up a job in the security business.'

'Yes. That might suit you, perhaps.'

'Some celebrity types take on a bodyguard. They don't need one. Just as a status symbol.'

'I've heard that. You're quite right.'

'So? Is there a kind of boot camp where you train? Where they teach you about stalkers and so on?'

'There is actually,' said Karen. 'But you learn mostly about crowd control.'

'Good. Put me down for it with your boss.'

'It could be up your street.'

'You think so?'

'Using social media to verify identities. That sort of thing.'

258

Yes, Helen knew more than anyone in Partridge Securities about faking bloody profiles. But Andersen had obviously been snooping. No doubt about it.

'It sounds the perfect job for me.'

'I sent you a friend request on Weibo and you agreed it.'

'That was you, was it?' She stretched her legs out. *Thanks for the heads up.* She'd accepted the invitation from a Betty Zhou without checking or thinking. As soon as she was on Wi-Fi, she would delete it next thing.

'I quite fancy being a close protection agent.'

'A bodyguard is supposed to look out for someone so they stay *alive*. It's a 24/7 job. Think you could handle that?'

'Of course I could.'

What do you want me to say, clever dick? He had sex fetishes. I obliged. But he died because of it.

Both women were in some sort of staring match, which Helen knew she'd win. But she didn't have to play Andersen's little games. Was she completely braindead?

She looked out over the ocean, tired of the silliness. 'OK. So when do I start?'

'Well, as I said earlier, you have to talk to Quacker, but I can mention it to him. It's a competitive business. You must bring the clients in first.'

'That's the way the security industry works, is it?'

'Yes, it is like that. Have any potentials in mind?'

Helen's phone went off with a text just as the Andersen idiot perched herself on the arm of the settee alongside. Much too close for comfort.

'I'll approach my Chinese friends Ned and Yoyo. Wang's a billionaire and a scientist. That's one of them, for starters. I'm seeing them for dinner later.'

Karen barely covered her gasp of shock and surprise. 'Ned?' she stammered.

Helen fumed. *Yes. We're on a first name basis already. And no, I won't be giving out my other contacts so easily in the future.* 'Ned's lovely. Yoyo's in love with someone called Colonel Li. What more do you need to know at present?'

Must get away.

Why do people always underestimate me? It was becoming beyond rude.

She needed to be on her own. Time to think things through. A fresh idea began forming. The New York property scene might not be the smartest plan on the planet. After all, she had tried. None of the passengers showed the slightest interest when she approached them. Her investment proposals had sparked no response. So maybe she'd get involved in the security business instead. Perhaps the wealthy Chinese couple knew people who'd use her. What a brilliant scheme!

But first things first. The text. Yoyo wanted to come over to Helen's cabin. She had a beautiful long dress. She thought it might be right for her to wear that evening. How exciting. A girlie bonding session appealed too. There'd been a complete lack of that in her life, for whatever reason.

Helen headed for the exit, but Karen called out after her.

'Why were you driving Paul Honey's car the night I collided with you? You were not his wife, were you? Just an employee?'

She pretended not to hear and hurried back to her stateroom. But the fear the questions evoked shook her to the very core.

Helen checked twice to make sure she wasn't being followed. But the Andersen woman hadn't bothered.

Even if Partridge Securities worked out she was involved in Paul Honey's death, there was little evidence to prove it.

She blinked her fears away of arrest, and the possibility of prison. Everything rested solely on her future with Ned Wang. She would find a way. Somehow, build a relationship. But she had to be careful with his scatterbrain mistress. For a while she thought she'd blown it with Yoyo Chen big time. The clumsy attempt to flirt in the Princess Hyacinth library had been a mistake. Too much, and too obvious.

So seeing the girl alone would give her the chance to reestablish the friendship.

Otherwise, the personal security business was still there as a backup.

***

It was approaching seven o'clock and Helen Rogers felt a little better. The nausea which had struck her just after Yoyo had left her cabin was finally abating.

What was wrong with her?

Perhaps caught a chill from spending too much time on deck. At least she did the wise thing and went straight to bed. The nasal stuffiness, twinges of pain in her right leg, and overwhelming sleepiness meant she slept for over three hours.

Even the tickle in her throat seemed to have disappeared. Thankfully. She didn't want to be coughing into her soup all evening in Toby's.

Try the dress on again.

She stepped into the red ankle length Valentino number Yoyo gave her. Checked herself out in the mirror. What a paragon of style.

The Chinese girl was so unpredictable. As changeable as the weather. What was with the sudden soft-soap and charm? She'd been so brazen at the restaurant. Hunched over her plate, elbows on the table, and blocked the banter between them. At the time, she thought it a case of sour grapes.

The old saying. 'A woman may turn off a man. But that doesn't mean she wants anyone else to have him.'

But Helen had got it wrong. Sorry - ee.

Maybe Yoyo realised there was no contest.

Anyway, she was all over her now. Helen this, Helen that. Then given her the one and only dress poor Ned bought her for the trip.

'It is too old for me. You wear it. His favourite look, his favourite colour. Who knows? He might marry yo-o-o-ou instead!'

Me? Old? You flatter yourself, Yoyo. But, OK, I can take that.

Professor Wang had told her they'd booked at Trump Tower for the duration of his conference.

Where do I have to stay? Some two bit dive on the lower east side. If I play my cards right, it'll be Fifth Avenue all that week, which would be so exciting.

Another thing. He would be a buffer against the Partridge Security creeps. No hurry to fly back straightaway to the UK. If ever. Her thoughts ran on. Crazy not to take this opportunity. Something handed to her on a plate.

Helen Rogers had one ability in the struggle for survival. She could always smell the strong perfume of a lucky break heading her way. As obvious as the cheap essence Yoyo sprayed on Helen's wrists.

She undressed and laid the stunning red outfit out on the bed. Alongside, she lined up the other of Yoyo's cast offs. The Dior earrings, gold bag, designer toiletries.

Amazing. What was with this girl's generosity?

Her new friend had seen her cramped cabin bathroom and scoffed at the size. Hers had a built-in flat screen, a heated floor, and a shower bench.

She ran the bath, adding drops of the coconut oil which the Chinese girl had given her. Helen slid her long naked body slowly into the near boiling tub. The emulsified water soothed and relaxed her. She no longer had much feeling in her legs. They had ached like mad for the past hour. It was as if she was floating on air, inhaling the exotic aroma.

Not only her legs and arms, but her whole frame felt a creeping numbness take over. What was going on? How could she haul herself out of the deep tub? Panic took hold.

I'm so groggy and weak for some reason.

The water was too hot. Helen turned the plug with her right foot. As the bath drained, she gripped the side in fear. Tried in vain to pull herself up. But her fingers didn't seem to work properly, and her arms felt completely useless.

Why am I sliding around getting nowhere?

Perhaps I'll just lie here for a bit. Feel so dopey and limp. Been in here too long. That must be it. Can't even think straight.

It's only flu. This will pass.

God. I can hardly breathe now.

What is happening to me?

Helen rolled from side to side. It was no use.

Something very strange is going on.

Through blurred vision she saw her hands slowly turning blue. *How could that be? My imagination?*

Helen's thoughts became confused, and the room darkened as she drifted off into unconsciousness.

Chapter Forty Five

Day four aboard the Princes Hyacinth. It turned into the longest one of the cruise.

When Karen met up with Haruto after his hourly session in the gym at a quarter to five, she couldn't wait to tell him the news.

'I know two hundred per cent who this Ned guy is. And he's onboard the ship right now.'

Back in their cabin, he collapsed onto the bed. 'What's wrong with us?' He buried his head in his hands. 'How come we've taken so long to pick him out?'

'Simple.' Karen replied. 'Because we weren't expecting him to look like he does. Tall and trim. Or that he would travel with a nutty mistress half his age.'

'He was in the casino after he sent the text,' said Haruto. 'It fits.'

'And last night Ned was checking out the Atlantic Library. I even took his photo.'

'He's been searching for Tomio all the time.'

'No good trying to contact him in Toby's this evening. From what Helen Rogers told me, they'll be together, the three of them, and we need to talk to him privately.'

They toured the ship once again, hoping to come across the couple. Or, even better, Ned Wang by himself. But it was a long shot.

'I think the best opportunity will be in the restaurant later. We'll approach him on some excuse or other,' said Haruto.

'It now makes sense that he warned Tomio he would not be alone.'

'Karen. Today I am completely convinced that my uncle was engaged in espionage for China. I didn't want to believe it. Any more than I really believed that Ned ever existed. To actually meet him in person was the last thing I expected.'

'I appreciate that. Nor did I, for that matter. But there's always the possibility Tomio was a newspaper clipping man.'

'Meaning?'

'You sell some press stories to a foreign power which have no value in themselves. But then they've caught you in their web and you can never escape.'

'He was surely not that naïve!'

'But you raised a question mark over his mental stability, didn't you?'

'That was before I learnt about The Miasma Project.'

'Then we have to know, Haruto. All this is freaking me out. Because of my stupid bike prang, we tracked him down.'

'True. But we would have done so eventually, wouldn't we?'

Karen nodded, but inwardly had her doubts. The conference would need a full security clearance to gain access.

'They'll not be overly happy when they learn Tomio has been dead all this time,' Haruto wondered.

'Do we have to tell them? If someone is pretending he is still alive, why not let them believe it?'

'Tempting. But we both know we can't leave things as they are.' Disappointment at this reality hung in the air.

There was no turning back now.

Chapter Forty Six

Professor Wang stood on his private balcony, nostrils flared wide and took in the clean smell of the ocean breeze. How wonderful! Beijing with its perma-smog was never like this, he reflected before turning his thoughts to the previous evening.

There'd been that English girl there, the one with the odd name. Always has a sort of permanent grin on her face.

He wasn't that taken with her. She was shallow and full of shit. He'd noticed how she worked the ship, similar to the bar girls in Shanghai, honing in on their clients. Same operation. Heaps of false charm, friendly to all, particularly the wealthy old ladies she targeted. It was successful too. They plied her with champagne and listened sympathetically to her stories.

No, he didn't like her at all, but he needed help in solving the girlfriend problem. She drove him nuts. Sat and sulked for hours. Only came to life when texting friends. While surly and distant towards him in private, she wouldn't let him out of her sight in public. But the night they went to the casino, Yoyo was all over him, one arm around his neck, her tiny white teeth set in a perfect smile. She leant forward repeatedly to gather in the chips, showing off her barely covered neat breasts to the other gamblers.

The professor sighed and sucked in another lungful of the Atlantic air. All well and good. But the moods were too much. No. She had to go. It was a mega move to build a friendship with the Honey woman. And invite her to dinner.

The effect was dramatic. Gobsmacked in amazement. Competition sprang up immediately between the two women. Yoyo became animated very quickly. And he played up to the English girl when he saw it working.

'Honey? That's your surname, isn't it? Like from the bees?'

'Yes,' she'd beamed back.

'Well, they call me Ned. Neddy if you prefer.'

'Hi Ned.'

'Kiss me, honey, honey, kiss me. You know the song?' He did a take-off of Colonel Li's appalling Texan accent.

Another hit.

'You should live in the land of milk and honey.'

'Where's that?'

'America. Noo Yawk.'

'You talk rubbish,' Yoyo snapped at him.

What a load of bullshit she came out with at Toby's. That she'd been at the London Book Fair for the launch of *Governance of China*. Since when?

'It sold millions. A best seller in the category. Even Mark Zuckerberg has read it.' Wang had laughed out loud. 'That's because he wants to get his company Facebook into Beijing.' It was the only fact he could contribute to the frivolous talk between the two lightweights. Despite their initial clash, both women were social media mad and started exchanging contacts on Weibo like lifelong friends.

So Wang decided to invite Helen to join them again the following night.

That had been a terrible idea. No sooner had they returned to their duplex than Yoyo flew into a rage. Began mimicking her rival's American-style smile and then shut herself up in her room.

Amazingly, she'd not taken the bait over the kickboxer. And he knew she was still in touch with Colonel Li. So Wang felt flirting with Helen was a fair deal. Play Yoyo at her own game. Plus, he wondered if her jealous antics were just another one of her many charades.

Exhausted, the professor went back inside and decided he needed a nap.

How to control and the art of vague accusation.

Psychologists say that clarity serves best to curb a specific behaviour. Let people know clearly what is right. Is it OK or not? If you want to stop them behaving in a certain way. When an individual knows *exactly* what is wrong, such as exceeding the speed limit or failing to submit a tax return on time, then they relax, happy they are living within the rules.

When the intention of an administration is to intimidate, then vagueness works best.

If the authorities make an arrest, for no official reason, it creates an atmosphere of fear. Could you be the next one without knowing what you've done wrong? Classic Kafkaesque situation. Result? You live in a permanent state of confused anxiety.

That's a principle China understands well and one it uses to control its vast population.

A vague accusation pressures an individual to curtail a far wider range of activities than a detailed one.

'If I don't know exactly why I am in the wrong, I'm inclined to pay more attention to all the State's strictures in every respect.' Professor Wang had had many a debate on the issue.

He reflected on it further as he changed into silk pyjamas for an afternoon nap.

How you behave is up to you. What you do, who you meet. Your choice. If you exceed the boundaries, there are consequences. You can lose your job, go to prison and, in some cultures, end up with a bullet in your skull. And if you live overseas and get it wrong, you risk never seeing your friends and homeland again.

Extreme punishment such as this is rare. Even so, the public live in constant dread of them. The ever-present threat alone reminds them who's the ultimate boss. The State.

Self-censorship began in literary and social campaigns in the nineteen fifties. Chinese authorities used blackmail as one of their tools to control the radical elements of the population.

It became part of a dull, entrenched wariness for those who grew up under the system.

Yoyo was no exception and brilliant herself at the art of vague accusation.

She kept Professor Wang on edge, wondering just how she would play up next time in public. To embarrass him. Throw a fit, act drunk. He never knew.

He tried to sleep, but couldn't get her out of his head.

Yoyo, Yoyo, Yoyo.

He had the uncomfortable feeling she was a complete psychic and could read his thoughts. Or a manic-depressive with mood swings. Why did she always do the opposite? Every single time. For example, where was she now? She'd disappeared without a word.

All women knew ways to keep their men on edge, a sort of psychological control system built into the sex. Perhaps Yoyo was simply following her genes.

Also annoying, he began to find her extremely sexy. Her complexity turned him on in a nebulous way. He dwelt on their first abortive night, as she lay under him, how the lustrous black hair partly covered one of her perfectly shaped breasts, the red lips parted, the soft moans as he drove inside her.

Pushing aside the memory, Wang felt *Meng Yan*, the ghost of sleep, pressing down on him. His phone went off with the reply to his former text from Tomio's number.

'Let's play chess. Miasma in the Atlantic. 11pm.' The Atlantic. Code for the Princess Hyacinth Library.

But would he show this time? What was going on? Why had Tomio failed him so many times? Maybe a simple explanation.

Having the English woman along as extra company would make it easier for him to slip away to the meeting point.

Keep Yoyo on her toes, as well!

Toby's was bustling. Seated at the table and waiting for their other guest, Yoyo seemed more composed than normal. Even a trifle ill at ease, Wang noticed. He downed the sweet apéritif which the waiter had set down seconds earlier. Apprehensive, on guard, unsure of herself for once.

She'd also made a major effort in getting ready, taking an age with her makeup.

'You are as jumpy as a cat on a hot tin roof,' said the professor, wondering about the change in her personality. 'A right nervous Nellie tonight.'

'I am not Nellie.' Yoyo glanced towards the entrance on the lookout for their guest. She looked down at her phone, checking for messages. 'Just a little pussy cat. Is that how you see me?' Other than that, she didn't bite.

The English woman failed to show, so the couple ate dinner together in relative silence.

'You look sleepy.' Wang touched her cheek. 'Ready to go?'

'Yes, I'm tired.' She yawned.

'And I want to play chess later with someone.'

'I don't enjoy watching,' she said. 'You know that.'

'I do. It is boring.'

'I'll walk around the boat on my own. You do whatever you like.'

Yoyo was unexpectedly agreeable. It freed the professor to check out the Atlantic Library without her in tow. He wished her good night and planted a peck on her cheek.

Pleased as punch, Wang left the restaurant, his mind on solely what the meeting ahead would entail. So much so, he never checked over his shoulder.

Chapter Forty Seven

Haruto got a text back within minutes.

'What do you make of that, Karen?' he asked, showing her the two-word message he'd just received on Tomio's phone. *Will try.*

'I think he's letting you know he has company and not on his own. Has to give that girl the slip, probably.'

Their Google search around the New York conference listed Professor Wang of Hinling Pharmaceuticals as a panellist.

Some further drilling down gave details about his corporation, their turnover, latest share price, last quarter's profits as a manufacturer of branded wigs.

'Well, that's it, isn't it? That long blonde hair piece his mistress wears might be one of his.' Karen swung a triumphant glance in Haruto's direction.

'And Helen Rogers called him Ned, didn't she? I think we have finally nailed Tomio's contact. Let's hope he's in the library.'

They needed time to plan their tactics urgently. He would be unaware they had booked into Toby's. They could pick up clues about him before their rendezvous at eleven that night.

It was out of the question to approach him in the restaurant.

Quacker and Chris had already settled in when Karen and Haruto arrived a little after eight. Having some neutral topics of conversations prepared made for an amiable and amusing evening. Both of them found the long-winded stories about cock-ups in Quacker's early career highly entertaining. The cuisine was cordon bleu level. Expensive and above the quality in the other restaurants.

Ned Wang and his girlfriend turned up around eight thirty. They took a table set for three in the corner.

Chris Partridge glanced over in their direction repeatedly. So did Karen and Haruto. But for entirely different reasons. Helen Rogers was notably absent and never showed at all. Eventually the waiter discreetly removed the vacant setting.

For once, disengaging from Quacker's generous dinner treat proved easier than expected. Chris planned to watch the late variety show available in the theatre. Then drag Quacker on to the dance floor. She wanted a few selfies to record the event. Haruto and Karen took the opportunity to make their excuses and head off, the sweetish flavour of the dessert lingering on their taste buds. With a weather eye on Wang, busy demolishing a giant ice-cream sundae, they headed to the library and commandeered a table tucked away in the corner.

Ten minutes passed and right on eleven the professor entered alone. He looked around, trying to pick them out. Haruto jumped to his feet and gave him an identifying wave. He ambled over, extending a Covid friendly elbow in greeting.

'Ahh, so nice to meet you at last. This is my colleague and very close friend, Karen Andersen.'

'Good evening. Call me Ned. Everyone does who knows me. I expected to see Professor Nakamura here!'

'That's a long story. Please sit down. And your young companion?'

'She went on to a show.' He glanced from one to the other rather warily.

'Let me start, if I may, by explaining the connection with my uncle.'

Haruto ran through the family history with the minimum of irrelevant detail.

'So, you are my friend's nephew. Why isn't he here in person? Why am I talking to you instead?'

'I'll explain all about it over a game of chess. What do you think? To make it interesting, let's have a bet. If you win, I will pay you 20,000 dollars cash. If you lose, you must tell me everything. The background to my uncle's work.'

'You seem very confident,' said his opponent.

'The information is important to me.'

'Any other condition?'

'I play white.'

The other passengers respected the game underway. They kept a distance so the men could concentrate in peace.

A fair amount of adrenalin mainlined into Karen's veins. Haruto's penchant for winner-take-all gambling had the same effect on her as his wild driving.

The professor eyed his opponent's opening warily, as he slid his King's Pawn forward two squares; a common early move.

'I hope you've got that twenty grand handy, Mr Fraser,' he said, mirroring the gambit.

Haruto guided his KB left through the gap created from F1 to C4.

Wang acknowledged the slight threat to his King's Bishop's Pawn. So what? He advanced his Queen's Knight decisively.

Haruto's turn. He moved the Queen four squares diagonally in the opposite direction to the previous move. A key moment.

The two men eyeballed one another. The minutes seem to stretch out. Haruto knew he'd left his Queen open to attack. It was all up to Wang. How much did he know about chess? How would he respond?

The professor picked up his Knight, moving it back to a protected square. Not completely confident, he kept a finger on the piece for some seconds before confirming the move.

After a respectful moment, Haruto responded by advancing his Queen into a space two squares diagonally on to F7.

'Check mate.'

Wang sat flabbergasted. Stunned and angry at himself at the obvious blunder.

'No way.'

'Yes, I'm afraid so.' There was no escape. The King was doomed.

The defeated player grinned broadly. 'Let's order some champagne and play again.'

'We will drink after we talk. That was the deal.'

'You are a reckless man.'

'True. I love to gamble. One of my weaknesses.'

'OK. Anything I know should be between myself and Tomio. It's up to him to discuss our relationship.'

'My uncle died of Covid nearly six months ago, wasn't it, Karen?'

'Died? You say he has died? But I've had several texts from him. He can't be dead.' Ned Wang shook his head in disbelief.

'I swear to you on the grave of my grandparents that sadly he has passed on. It sounds as though you have been the victim of some sort of intervention.'

'With all due respect, Mr Fraser, I do not believe you. He may not be here on board. But he'll find a way to the USA somehow. I'm sure of that.'

'You won't see him in New York or anywhere else.' Haruto pursed his lips.

'But the texts I got from him?'

Haruto took out Tomio's old phone and handed it over.

The Chinese professor raised both eyebrows and stared him hard in the face. 'He has other phones, maybe.'

'As I said, Tomio Nakamura was my uncle. I buried him in Derby many months ago.'

Wang drew in a sharp breath. 'He must have been killed then.'

'No. He died of Covid-19.'

'I still can't believe it.'

'Look! I have his death certificate here on my phone.' Haruto showed him the document clearly displayed on the screen.

They established the family tie easily enough. What proved difficult was getting Ned around to discussing the report.

'I don't know what you're talking about. What is this "Miasma"?' Wang's face clouded over, concerned. 'Then we must talk.'

The library filled up. People wanted reading matter to take back to their cabins.

He stood up as though to leave. 'Not here. It's too dangerous.'

Chapter Forty Eight

The promenade deck, bleak and black, was an ideal place to guarantee a private conversation. The deteriorating conditions sent the passengers down to the nearest bar. Or back to their cabins for a movie on the ship's streaming service.

Karen shivered and sheltered against Haruto from the cold northerly. He pulled her closer to protect her a bit as another gust hit.

'Sorry about this,' said Ned, 'but we can't be too careful. I know there are several operatives on board who are working actively for the Chinese State. They mustn't see us together. If you hadn't told me that Tomio died of Covid, I would have assumed my government had eliminated him.' Professor Wang braced himself against the ship's rail.

'Six months ago someone broke into my uncle's house? Did you hear about it?' Haruto raised his voice above the noise of the gathering gale.

'No, nothing at all.'

'Well, my uncle fought him off himself. Amazing at his age.'

Ned smiled, his features creased in admiration. 'He was crazy. Crazy brilliant.'

'Yes. Absolutely, but they think he caught Covid from a student who tested positive. And sadly, Tomio died a couple of weeks later. Rumours are he was behind the zoombombing of an online class, and that he was quite anti-Chinese.'

'No.' Ned shook his head. 'He would never have done that. I've known him for years.'

'You must have heard about the sexual assault stories though?'

'Yes. But they never happened, I'm sure of that.' He didn't offer much more.

'Karen, you're shivering,' said Haruto.

'It's fine,' she lied, wriggling even closer.

'And by the way, the young woman, you know Yoyo, knows nothing about my plan otherwise we could carry this on in my stateroom. But we must be brief for now. Your wife is bitter with cold and my companion will look for me shortly. Tomorrow I'll come over to your cabin. Then we can discuss all this in greater detail.'

'How do you expect to do that?' asked Karen, her teeth chattering.

'She has a spa appointment at six.'

'We need to know something. It's important.' Haruto's voice edged with irritation. At last they had Ned Wang on his own. Would he show tomorrow at the next meeting?

'Likely Beijing arranged things to discredit him. We Chinese invented fake news. You understand that, surely?'

Karen caught a brief view of the full moon through a gap in the clouds.

She'd been right all along.

They'd stitched Haruto's uncle up by the sound of it.

'Why would they do that to him? What motive would they have?' She asked. 'He worked for your bioweapons department, didn't he?'

'Tomio was a researcher. That's all. But he knew too much, perhaps.'

'After I left his house back in April, someone tried to set fire to it,' Haruto said. 'Why do you think that was? What motivation?'

'To destroy any awkward documents, he might have had there.'

'But why would they bother with him in particular?'

'He had learnt that China was developing a bioweapon.'

'The DX21?'

'Yes. The state began development in Jiangmen some years ago. In a special high-security compound. All countries run these projects. Someone, still unidentified, broke into the lab and stole a flask, filled with the new virus. Despite all the safety measures, these things happen. Beijing covered it up. On the open market, money talks. Tomio believed, from his own inside sources, cultivated over a lifetime, that an active terrorist cell was behind it.'

The wind strengthened to Gale Force 9, and even the massive ship rolled as the mounting swell set in. 'It's the deadliest weapon yet known. Compared to that, Covid-19 is as harmless as a light cold.'

'Tomio raised the issue with the Chinese academics, but they did nothing. Why would they? There are radicals on the extreme right wing of the military who'd be perfectly happy to deploy DX21 tomorrow. They see it as a defensive necessity. Consider. A mere two milligrams is enough to destroy the population of an entire city.'

'How do you, as a simple manufacturer, fit into all this Ned?'

'Well, they often employ my company as a cover for intelligence operations, because our profile is not suspicious. When I discovered they had the DX21 programme underway, I felt I had no choice. I had to do something. So your uncle and myself decided to work together for a common goal. To prevent its use in future hostilities.'

Karen sensed the relief as Haruto absorbed the news. A bitter wind cut through her thin dress and she shivered uncontrollably. How she longed for the jacket back in their cabin.

'He produced The Miasma Report. He intended it for a scientific publisher in America. I agreed to supply evidence about the DX21 programme.'

'How did you get special access to the information?'

'I had to convince a faction of the Communist Party I was supportive of affirmative action. Otherwise they would never have trusted me. And naturally on the clear understanding I would deliver a sample to their CCP agent in New York. As proof, Tomio and I resolved to pass on everything we knew to counter terrorism. The West could then protect itself and start development of a vaccination programme.'

'And you planned to meet up at the conference?'

'Earlier than that. After the seminar would be too late. We agreed to travel by ship together and coordinated the dates. The Chinese Military must be behind the fake news. All intended to make it appear he is still alive. They have succeeded too.'

'So what about the sample?'

'I have it with me.'

'On the Hyacinth you mean?'

'Exactly.'

'When you don't deliver the vial, won't they come after you?'

'I've no reason to return to China now my wife has died. And I'm sure the Americans will give me sanctuary and a new identity.'

'Tomio thought some students in Liverpool work in collaboration with the Chinese Secret Service.'

'Does anyone else know you have the DX21 with you?' she asked.

'Only yourselves. But it is essential I get a copy of Tomio's report. Which is why I'm telling you all this. I assume you have it with you?'

Haruto and Karen looked at each other. The same doubts in mind. They needed proof Ned Wang was genuine. If so, it was significant. Professor Nakamura was a moral man, not a monster. He spent all his energy on trying to save the species, not to destroy it.

Chapter Forty Nine

Thawing out, back in their cabin, curiosity got the better of Karen. 'I'm amazed at the amount you bet in that game. Why so much? Do you have twenty thousand, anyway?'

He gave a sheepish grin. 'Well, no. I don't actually, but I was confident I wouldn't lose.'

'You could have.'

'It was a gamble, I must admit, but from their correspondence, I learnt Wang was keen but inexperienced. It takes a while before you come across the Scholar's Mate four point move and so I chanced it.'

'God knows what we would have done if you'd lost.'

'Don't think about it. My mind's certainly on something else right now.' He grinned and drew her to him.

Later, lying in the tangled sheets, replete, relaxed and happy, Karen couldn't completely redirect her thoughts from the reality of what was happening aboard the ship.

'Darling, how is it you can commission a killing for less than it costs to design a website, for example?'

'They're mostly scams, or catch points for the police to nail would be killers. Before they act.'

'It's cheaper to hire hackers if you want to destroy someone's reputation and ruin their career. Drive them to suicide.'

'Perhaps that's what happened to my uncle. You never stopped believing in him, did you?'

Karen looked into Haruto's dark brown eyes. 'We're not there yet. But getting closer.'

Haruto took her into his arms and cradled her affectionately. His voice was rich with emotion.'Thank you.'

'When you trust someone, you believe the best of their relatives too by association.'

She never had much trouble imagining the depths terrorists could plumb in the name of their cause.

The 1995 Tokyo Metro atrocity where Sarin was used to kill twelve people.

Poisonous substances were portable and easily concealed.

The 2017 assassination of North Korean Kim Jong-nam with VX in Kuala Lumpur Airport.

The 2018 Skripal incident in Salisbury in the UK.

But it was still hard to believe the deadly DX21 was on the ship. 'Tell me. What are the chances he has it with him?'

'In my opinion, he's using it as bait. He wants to get his hands on the Miasma Report.'

'Reckon he'll show tomorrow?'

'Well, if he doesn't, we'll know what he told us earlier is pure bullshit.'

However, if Wang was on the level, they'd have to divulge everything to Quacker, MI6 and the American Secret Service.

With the gale at full intensity, the ship shook as she ploughed on through the heavy seas, emphasising the warmth and intimacy of the cosy cabin. They had never been so close, dreaming of a shared life together filled with love, sex, and happiness.

Part Four

DEATH AND LOVE

Part Four

DEATH AND LOVE

Chapter Fifty

D ay five started big.

Quacker arrived for breakfast later than usual. When he saw Karen at the coffee machine, he rushed straight over.

'Good morning, my dear.' He lowered his voice to a near whisper. 'I've got some rather terrible news about our friend Helen. Cleaners went into her cabin earlier and found her dead in the bath. Awful. I suggest you two join us so I can tell you what I know about it.'

Karen shuddered and felt a ripple of fear.

Knowing he would pick up that she'd changed seating arrangements for good reason, she followed Quacker back to where the Partridge's were sitting.

'It appears she died in her bath last night.' He continued the moment they sat down.

Chris's outfit that morning was a little more low key than her usual marine-themed cruise wear. Brown loose slacks and a white shirt. Something more in keeping with the sombre news.

'How did you hear about this?'

'Richard, the skipper, knocked on our door just before breakfast. Told us all about it. Shocking.'

Quacker's edge over fierce competition in the security industry came from his non-stop networking efforts. Hence he and the Captain of the Princess Hyacinth were already on first-name terms.

'The crew member who discovered her is pretty cut up about it. As you can imagine. He's taken ill himself. It'd be the impact. It's not what you expect, is it? A body in the bath right at the beginning of your shift.'

'Do we know what happened?'

'No. The Captain said he will order an autopsy when we berth.'

Quacker rubbed his hands together in his thoughtful manner as Chris sat absorbing the news. She nodded her head in disbelief at the turn of events. 'Most likely she took her own life. Not sure at this stage. They've taken the body to the morgue. They have one on the ship, apparently. There's pretty much nothing more they will know until we reach New York.'

'Suicide? In a bath? That sounds very odd.'

'Yes. Death by intentional drowning is most unusual. People who do so usually weigh themselves down or tie their hands and feet. That wasn't the case here as far as I'm aware.'

'You can drown yourself in two inches of water if you're set on killing yourself.' Chis had worked in psychiatry for a period in her nursing career.

'Yes, but there are normally other signs they've tried before. Old scars on the wrist, for example,' said Quacker.

'I realised she had serious mental health problems,' Chris remarked. 'I spotted her up on deck the other day and it looked to me she was ready to throw herself overboard. That was one reason I wanted her to join our party. It can't be much fun doing a cruise on your own, can it?'

'She did not have a monopoly on travelling alone. Listen,' said Quacker. 'There are dozens of ladies here doing just that.'

'But most of the single women are in their seventies, dear. Not quite the same thing.'

'Why would she take her own life?' Karen asked.

'Who knows? Depression, whatever. On a cruise liner? Could be worse.' He paused for breath. 'I know it often happens in the top hotels such as The Ritz and The Dorchester. And there's another possibility, too. I think she cottoned on that she was a person of interest in the death of her boss. The extra factor to tip her over the edge.'

'We have no hard evidence of that,' Karen pointed out. 'I only spoke to her yesterday, and she seemed fine. In great spirits, actually.'

He gave her a quizzical look, head cocked to one side. 'Really? That's interesting.'

She shrank down further into the chair, deep in thought.

The retired inspector banged on about various forensic options. Meanwhile, a theory shaped up in the back of Karen's mind. They had pried into Helen's private life. Perhaps that had been the catalyst.

What I did pushed her too far.

But she had only done so because Quacker had twisted her arm. His nagging about settling the damage, reporting the collision. Harping on about trivialities everyone involved would rather forget.

'It could just be a tragic accident. That's how the singer died in Los Angeles. What was her name again?' A frown of concentration creased his brow.

'Wilfred Somerville? I remember that,' said Chris. 'At the Hilton in Beverly Hills. Not too dissimilar from this. What happened here on the Hyacinth. The official cause of death was *accidental* drowning. Athelosclerotic disease combined with excessive cocaine use.'

'Helen didn't strike me as a drug user though,' Karen commented.

'No, nor I. With the singer they also detected traces of Benadryl and Xanax. And marijuana, too. That brought on the heart attack, according to the coroner.'

Chris Partridge took a deep sip from her cooling coffee. 'I reckon they expected her at the Chinese table last night. I noticed there was a spare chair and wondered about it.'

'Why do you think that, dear?' Quacker crossed his arms. He glanced over to check on Haruto. Why was he taking such an age at the buffet?

'Because she was hanging out with that wealthy couple the previous evening, too. I told you that.'

The conversation moved in the Ned Wang direction. The last thing Karen Andersen wanted.

'Surely they expected another person to join them because of the extra place setting. The waiter removed it. Don't you remember?'

Quacker tapped his fingers on the table. 'All very sad. And what about the other aspect?'

'Oh yes, I'd forgotten that.' Chris exchanged a glance with her husband and raised her left eyebrow.

'What other matter?' Karen wanted to know. But he wouldn't elaborate.

'Might tell you later.'

Carrying a fully charged tray, Haruto arrived to hear the whole story again from start to finish.

After breakfast, the four of them went up on to the promenade deck together. Quacker lent forward against the rail and gazed reflectively across the shining sea, which seemed to stretch out to the horizon and beyond.

'The crew members found lots of stolen goods in her cabin. Security knew about the spate of robberies. They started on the day of departure. What they discovered matched the missing items. She focussed on little old ladies in particular, their handbags, that sort of thing. The constant risk of being caught would have contributed to her mental anxiety. Which brings me to you, Karen.' He bent in closer to make himself heard.

'You mentioned that when you hit the car that time, the back of it was full of bits and pieces, black sacks of stuff.'

'That's right.'

'You said it looked as if she was moving home. Which makes sense for her not to want to hang around if she'd just cleaned the place out, especially as Mr Honey lay dead inside the property.'

'It's a possibility. Yes.'

'More than that. Anyway, nothing to do at the moment,' he wound up and pushed himself back from the railing. 'But we must submit a proper report when we return to the UK.'

'It all happened quite a while ago now, Quacker.'

'Only fair to his real wife. Which means you making a full statement about the prang essentially to make everything right.'

Karen wished she'd never taken the Kawasaki out that night. The Helen Rogers and Paul Honey mess would go on for years. Endless loose ends to tidy up. And none of it would bring either of them back to life.

Chapter Fifty One

Rumours ran riot throughout the Princess Hyacinth. By lunchtime, news that Helen Rogers had been found dead in her cabin was the one topic of conversation on board. Which raised question marks about the cause of death, whether suicide or perhaps something else. It only intensified the speculation. And Chris was the source best qualified to provide the answers.

Set against the nobler side of the human condition lie more fundamental instincts linked to directing our survival as a species. A simple example is the powerful urge to be part of a group. It's a tribal thing. Helen sat at the Partridge table on the first night. Therefore, everyone assumed she was in their party. So one by one, passengers approached them that morning for the latest gossip.

What they all heard confirmed Chris's opinion. The woman had been a pathological liar. She put about she was a qualified NHS doctor who worked in an intensive care unit throughout the coronavirus pandemic. And, extraordinarily, that she was also a cousin of the Duchess of Cambridge. All along she milked the poor young widow scenario for all its worth.

Her tissue of lies had taken many in. One elderly lady passenger, whose shaky hand had obviously administered an overdose of Chanel Number 5, absolutely refused to believe the official suicide story. She showed Chris a selfie with Helen. 'She was an heiress. All that money and so gifted. What a loss.'

To one of her victims, she was just a total con woman who'd taken several of them for a ride. Aside from availing herself of any free champagne on offer, she borrowed some particularly sentimental jewellery on the excuse that she needed it to go with a certain dress, and then the following day pretended to have lost it overboard.

'Ask her a direct question and there was always some great long story attached. Not that I wished her dead, though. No one deserves that.'

'Mythomania. Pseudologia fantastica. But it's a known mental disorder, isn't it?' Karen knew a lot about it. They all picked at their lunch together, going over the whole thing. Amazed how compulsive liars invent such complex scenarios.

'It is interesting how they can deliver a bald-faced lie without pausing for breath.' Quacker reckoned he'd met more than his share of them in his career.

'They're natural performers,' said Karen. 'It's almost certain that the Cartier purse she showed me was anything but a gift.'

'This is a floating city completely outside any police jurisdiction.' Chris remarked. 'No surprise to me you get opportunistic theft on board.'

Quacker stood up and marched off in the direction of the bridge. Ever ready to offer his services to the Captain. All related to the stolen goods found in Helen's cabin. Essential he return everything to their rightful owners and he welcomed the challenge. Chris headed off to her kickboxing class.

Karen and Haruto spent the rest of the afternoon touring the boat. A visit to the hairdressers confirmed Ned Wang's assertion that his companion Yoyo had booked an appointment for six. All signs looked good. Every chance Wang would turn up as promised. But only time would tell.

Out on deck, thick clouds appeared overhead and some sharp showers broke out. The waves became crested with whitecaps as the wind reached twenty knots.

As the hours dragged on Karen and Haruto counted down to the meeting.

It was important to remain calm at all costs. Ahead lay a potentially hostile and uncertain situation. After all, Wang had alerted them to the possibility that Chinese secret service operatives might be on board. And anyway, could they trust the learned professor himself? Many unknowns remained before them.

Haruto and Karen spent the time rigging an elaborate system of CCTV cameras which Quacker had returned to them. They added a further couple of hidden microphones for extra security.

While she listened out for any sound of approaching footsteps tapping on the hardwood floor of the corridor outside, her boyfriend kept a wary eye on his iPhone. They waited in silence, having scaled the potential outcomes down to just two.

The good one: Professor Ned Wang would turn up on time. And repeat word for word what he told them the night before. How a rogue laboratory had developed a deadly bioweapon called DX21, intended for a terrorist attack on the unsuspecting citizens of New York. The official Chinese plan was for him to pass the vial on to their agents when they berthed. Instead, he would defect and hand it to the FBI, claiming political asylum. All of which could only take place if Haruto handed him a copy of Professor's Nakamura's last report detailing the scientific background.

The bad one: A no show. Proving that both Wang and Rogers were peas in a pod. Both inveterate liars.

Six turned to seven. The minutes dragged by. No Ned. No encouraging footsteps, not a tap. By the half hour, they reluctantly accepted the obvious. Another non-appearance and all that implied.

'But why? It has added up so far. This doesn't make sense. I was certain we'd see him tonight.'

'I agree Karen.' Haruto studied his nails in a distant and contemplative manner before continuing. 'I can't work it out either. Look. Leave it for now. Let's go to Toby's for an early supper. I'm starving.'

In the restaurant, both searched for answers in their different ways.

Chapter Fifty Two

Pow! Day six of the cruise. The death of Helen Rogers had shocked them all. But the following morning further dramas unfolded on board the Princess Hyacinth.

Everyone in the breakfast buffet had heard a new rumour. A passenger was missing. Quacker, breathless from the stairs, caught up with Karen who was taking in the sun on Deck 6.

'I'm helping Richard with the investigation. Thought to have gone overboard.' He was so proud of his intimate social relationship with the Captain. 'I was one of the first to hear of it. I've become a sort of semi-official chief of police on board now because of my work on the Rogers matter. So, as I was saying, they've brought me in to help.' Quacker leant back in his chair for effect.

'Do we know who?' Karen asked.

'I'm coming to that. There was an alert on the ship's system two nights ago. The Princess Hyacinth has a man overboard detection technology which sends automated alerts to the bridge. Also holds ten seconds of CCTV footage where it triggered.'

'Why wasn't something done then?'

'If you remember, Karen. That night we were going through a Force Nine gale. Rain was bucketing down. Chris and I got thrown around like wet washing in a tumble dryer. The alarm sounded in the early hours. The duty ship's officer on the bridge at the time assumed it was a false signal caused by the thunderstorms. That happens quite often.'

'I can see that. Anything electronically based wouldn't work well in those conditions. All the rain. That would be the Achilles Heel,' Karen responded. 'It was far worse than the forecast.'

'And the Purser's office has only just received notice there's someone missing. Too late now, unfortunately. Normally a ship would execute a three sixty, a full circle, hoping to pick them up, but in this case we have sailed on nearly a thousand miles.'

'How awful. Poor somebody.' Karen shook her head.

'You asked who it was earlier, didn't you?' said Quacker.

'Yes. Just natural curiosity.'

'It's a Professor Wang.'

This got her attention.

She stared him in the face, shocked at the unexpected news. 'What?'

'Well, you'd recognise him to look at. The interesting part is who he is. A prominent Chinese scientist on his way to a conference in New York.'

305

When he failed to show, it never occurred to Karen and Haruto he might have had some sort of accident. Or that an even more sinister factor had kept him from the meeting.

'I know him.'

'Yes, I thought you did. He's the one with the young girlfriend,' he said helpfully, 'and she lodged the missing person's form at the Purser's office. Also that he could have gone over thirty-six hours ago.'

Karen adjusted her sunglasses, giving herself space to work out what to do.

It sounded like the moment to bring Quacker up to date with everything. But it was Haruto's decision whether or not to raise the Miasma Report. And right then he was lifting twenty kilo dumbbell weights in the ship's gymnasium.

The retired inspector wore his 'take no prisoners' official face.

'Wouldn't they want to search the ship for him first?'

'That is one plan. A muster and head count to confirm. No doubt you'll hear the announcement over the Tannoy if they do that.'

'Why did the girlfriend wait so long to report him missing?'

'The time lag is not that unusual. You can go several hours without seeing someone. Easy enough on a large vessel like this. Helps understand why only a quarter of man overboard alarms result in a rescue.'

She'd heard this before. 'My worst nightmare, that. Falling over the side.'

'The word "falling" is a misnomer,' said Quacker. 'Passengers don't just fall overboard.' He shook his head in amazement. 'They jump often enough, mind you, for all sorts of personal reasons. Depression and so on.'

'It has happened. People have fallen over the railing, though. Pissed or high on drugs. I've heard that myself.'

'And some are pushed. I'm sure of that too. Or thrown.'

'What you are describing there is a deliberate act of murder, isn't it?'

'Yes, of course. Did you by any chance see Professor Wang and his lady friend around the ship yesterday? I might need your head on this.'

Karen raced down to the gym. The tannoy crackled into life. The captain confirmed the news officially. They were going to do a full cabin search for a missing person.

With the ship's multiple decks and warren like structure, he warned the check could take a while. A second announcement advised that the crew now had conclusive evidence the man had gone overboard.

All around the Princess Hyacinth, the passengers buzzed with speculation. The elderly tourists kept well back from the railing. Eager not to meet a similar fate. How long can you survive in the sea in waters at sixteen degrees? Minutes or hours? Theories abounded. Google consulted. All reminded each other of the dangers the beautiful but pitiless ocean held.

The Captain gave one further reassuring announcement to the effect that he had notified the US and Canadian Coast Guard and they would undertake a full air and sea search in the area most likely to result in a recovery.

Nerves settled, the passengers went back to enjoying the multi-talented and distractionary entertainment on offer. No longer a topic of interest, the missing person was soon history. But not to Karen and Haruto. The mystery had thickened, become even more opaque.

It seemed Professor Wang had disappeared on the same night Helen Rogers died, the same evening he met them up on Deck 7.

The couple agreed they had to bring Quacker in on the whole thing. The DX21 implications were too enormous to risk. But they couldn't find him anywhere. Chris didn't know either. Wherever he had his copper's hat on, he was after more information out of Yoyo and fast.

Chapter Fifty Three

The US Coast Guard called off the air and sea search for Professor Wang at three in the afternoon. Yoyo Chen told security that she thought it was a murder suicide involving 'that woman'. A classic love triangle. As Quacker was an expert in homicide investigations, the Captain requested his help.

Karen and Haruto's arrangement was to meet in 4101 to exchange ideas on where they were with it all. He burst through the door twenty minutes later, a wad of notes tucked under his arm.

Because the inspector preferred the printed word, the printout of a section of the Miasma Report lay ready on the bed. Quacker spread his own bits of A4 on every available surface around the stateroom, so the normally neat cabin resembled a paper hanger's nightmare. 'It's all needed, and makes easier reading than on screen,' he said. 'I've always done it this way. Shall we get on with it? The captain has just spoken to me, actually. Explained the damage to the company unless we resolve everything quickly. So, let's start with Miss Chen.'

'She told us, the security people and myself of course, that she thought Professor Wang had fallen for the widow. I've got it all down here. Basically, she was jealous. He was flirting with Helen Rogers at dinner and paying her too much attention. They had a tremendous fight over it, but he persuaded her it was all in her imagination. That he didn't fancy the woman. Was just being social. So Yoyo agreed to allow her to join them again that evening.

'But she never showed. Professor Wang seemed disappointed. After dinner he told Miss Chen he wanted to play chess before turning in. She took him at his word and went for a walk on her own. But he never returned. She thought he'd gone to Helen's cabin and stayed there. She claimed she cried all the following day, waiting for him to come back. Waited in vain. Now we know why.

'The next morning she started packing her clothes ready for the disembarkation in New York and noticed some items missing. Where was her long dress? And where was the jewellery he'd bought her? She reckoned he must have taken it from her cupboard and given it to the other woman. All because she'd never worn it. Been keeping it for a special occasion.

'She went to security and reported it stolen to exact revenge. They told her it was impossible Helen was guilty because they'd found her dead in her cabin the previous day. Yoyo claims this was the first she heard about it. Hadn't left her own stateroom for thirty-six hours.

'She looked shocked. Her view is that Professor Wang must have killed Miss Rogers when she knocked him back. And he committed suicide by throwing himself overboard.' Quacker paused for breath after his lengthy litany. 'Security confirmed they found Yoyo's red dress on her bed and the jewellery as she described. So there's a possibility her scenario is right.'

310

A call on Quacker's iPhone broke the narrative. Before he could respond, a code alpha crew alert sounded. A medical emergency.

'Excuse me,' said Quacker, 'I'll just answer this. It's from Richard, the Captain.'

Karen noticed his face pale as he took in the latest. He rang off abruptly.

'Oh, my God. This is getting serious, you two. The member of staff who found the body of Helen Rogers has died suddenly. Unexplained. His crew mate, who helped take her to the ship's morgue, has collapsed as well.'

'You'd better hear this.' Karen rushed out her words describing the conversation they'd had on deck with Wang. How and why he intended to claim asylum in the US on arrival.

This time Quacker was all ears.

'Can't be Covid, can it? Impossible.' Haruto glanced from one to the other. 'The incubation period is far too short.' They all agreed.

'It looks as though he was telling the truth all along,' he added.

'He told us Yoyo knew nothing about his mission,' said Karen.

'But could he have used DX21 on Helen Rogers?' Quacker scratched his head reflectively. 'He could have taken it over the side with him.' His mouth set to a tight line.

'Or it'll still be in his cabin,' Haruto suggested.

'If so, we could have a major biohazard on our hands.'

When the ship's security team unlocked the door to Professor Wang's stateroom, there was no sign of Yoyo Chen.

The luxury duplex epitomised the opulence for which cruise liners are renowned. But a bio-protected posse of medical staff gave the cabin a brutal contrast to the carefully created atmosphere. An oasis of cultivated indulgence. The Partridge Security team wore full on protective garments, hooded Tyvek coveralls, rubber boots, N95 half-face disposable respirators, wrap around googles, shields, and double pairs of nitrile gloves.

Professor Wang's bedroom, all purple, and fine linen, looked immaculate and untouched. The cleaner confirmed what Yoyo told them. The bed hadn't been slept in for two nights. Ned's clothes hung neatly in the wardrobe. An array of wigs on styrofoam stands sat in silent watch over a stack of jigsaw puzzles. A thorough search failed to find anything suspicious, let alone a vial full of deadly viruses. His briefcase contained only scientific articles and a passport.

In the middle of the process, Yoyo Chen arrived. She stood stunned at the sight which greeted her. As bewildered as if some alien force in Hazmat suits had landed to transport her off to an orbiting starship. It was all too much. She buried her face in her hands and burst into floods of tears.

Quacker pulled out a chair for her and gently explained the reason for the intrusion. How Professor Wang could have been transporting a toxic material which he may even have used to kill Helen Rogers.

'Miss Chen. What did he tell you he was planning in New York?'

'Nothing much in detail really,' Yoyo replied. 'Only that he was guest speaker at a business conference.'

'Did he at any stage mention anything about having some samples with him?' He bent over to pick up the words uttered through her tears.

'No, no. Never.'

With the initial examination completed, security sealed off Professor Wang's bedroom with yellow tape. Meanwhile, Quacker did his best to convince her that perhaps the massive suite wasn't the right place to complete the crossing on her own because of possible contamination.

'No. I am OK. I want to be here.'

They had found nothing untoward, had they?

Yoyo crossed her arms defiantly. 'And I like it. I will stay.' Five times she shook her head. It was obvious wild horses wouldn't shift her.

Faced with such determination everyone agreed she could remain, and one by one they trouped out.

Karen, Haruto, and Quacker did a quick resume. They decided that even if the DX21 had been onboard, and had a bearing on the poisoning, it was likely Professor Wang had taken the vial with him to his Atlantic grave.

Chapter Fifty Four

Quacker rushed off to change out of his PPE. And tell the Captain the good news. No deadly biological agent found. It was approaching ten o'clock at night.

Karen and Haruto followed one of the medical team back down a deck and along the narrow crew companionway to where they had struggled into their Covid safe equipment. The passage, heavy with the smell of diesel, made her feel queasy as the ship rolled slowly over the mid-Atlantic swell.

She felt relieved to strip off the protective clothing.

'So Quacker likes the idea that Ned Wang murdered Helen Rogers and then committed suicide by going overboard. Right? Do you agree with him?' Haruto unstrapped his perspex face shield and shook out his dark black mane.

'No. Personally I don't although I'm convinced he only learnt of Tomio's death from us, because of how he reacted,' she said, mopping her brow. 'He might have felt alone and isolated without Tomio. Faced with the uncertainties around defection, he decided not to go through with it. Not deliver the substance. Perhaps saw suicide as a way out.'

'We know that both my uncle and Ned hated bioweapons of all description.'

'But why would he kill Helen Rogers?'

315

'A knock back? Seems a bit extreme, to say the least. But why the bath?'

'I think the explanation may be quite different altogether.' She wiped away a light dew. The changing room was unbearably hot as it backed on to the pumping station.

'The Chinese military spread rumours to discredit Tomio because they had learnt he wasn't trustworthy. Ned suspected their operatives were on to him, didn't he? Were behind the muck spreading.'

'Correct,' said Karen, reminding him that had been her take all along. 'I never believed ten per cent of what I read about him online. Maybe afraid he'd go to the Americans. And tell them everything he knew. Become in a way an amateur double agent.'

'Which is why China's intelligence community let Ned Wang think my uncle was still alive and going to be on this ship, bent on following the original plan they worked out together.' Haruto paced up and down the cabin, deep in thought.

'Yes, and the Chinese might have tapped into his conversation with us.' He stared at her, his brain working overtime.

'That fits certainly,' she agreed.

'If so, he didn't kill himself. They murdered him. Or had him eliminated somehow.'

'Which puts paid to the love triangle theory, doesn't it?'

'Karen, we were the only ones on deck to hear what he had to say,' Haruto was struggling to peel off the remaining bits of his protection suit.

'Yes, but remember he worried. Sensed there were Chinese intelligence operatives on the ship. That maybe he was under surveillance. Any of them could have planted a wire on him.'

'Shit.'

'But you need to be physically close. It's hard to put a listening device on someone without them knowing. This is where Helen Rogers came in. What if he did fancy her, as Yoyo suggested? What if he went to her cabin before dinner? Or even after our meeting?'

'What are you getting at?'

'That they blackmailed her into helping the Chinese operatives.'

Chapter Fifty Five

'**D**o you think we ought to have a look at it?' Haruto raised a questioning eyebrow.

'Yes, perhaps we should. And quick smart.'

Karen had only just mentioned that she had a current profile as Betty Zhou on Weibo, and a dozen others on Anglo-Chinese chat rooms.

At half ten in the evening, they rushed back to their cabin to access Karen's social media accounts.

'It used to be a revolutionary forum.' She battled to catch her breath. The distance between one zone and another on the ship could be enormous. 'That was before someone realised that it had massive business potential.' She was hyperventilating. 'Now everyone uses it. Celebrities to promote themselves and so on.'

Haruto arced the mouse of Karen's laptop impatiently as she struggled to remove the extra pair of protective gloves.

'Been going since 2009 when China blocked western platforms and today it's got over six hundred million users. Oh, hold on a second. My phone.'

'Sorry it's so late. I'm with the Captain now, and he wants to know exactly why you want an extended lockdown of Professor Wang's room.'

'Can it wait half an hour? I need to check out something on social media.'

'In my view, this is more important. Forget that rubbish on Facebook,' Quacker said grumpily, cutting off the call.

'But maybe the rubbish holds the clue.' The Weibo site spread across the screen of her laptop. 'Helen Rogers had an account with this platform too. I remember.'

Haruto followed the gist. 'How did she get involved with Chinese intelligence, anyway?'

'If she did. You said there's big money in this indirectly, pharmaceuticals, neurological developments.'

'You think she hooked up with them before they met on the ship?'

'I am not sure. My instinct tells me there is more. We've not got to it yet.'

'What's her avatar?' Haruto plopped down on the bed. Freed from the zombie suit, he spread his arms and legs wide.

Karen typed in her password, and the forum opened up. She tapped on Helen Rogers, which came up as her last contact.

'That's a selfie from Deck 8. Recognise it? I see she's posted several pictures of herself from the cruise, all glammed up. So let's assume for the moment the Chinese intelligence recruited her. Offered her an appealing sum to rig a wire on Ned Wang.'

Haruto gave a shrug. 'And he found out?'

319

'Possibly.'

'That could work.'

'But.'

'But?'

'Big but. She wasn't there that night. Never turned up at the table. Therefore, it didn't happen at the restaurant. But maybe earlier on in the evening.' Karen jumped up with sudden excitement. 'We might be making the classic error here. Not seeing the wood for the trees. Say, the reason she never showed? She was already dead.'

'Let's assume they gave Helen something,' she continued, 'and it took effect when she had a bath. What killed her we don't yet know. Wait until the autopsy comes out. Anthrax perhaps?'

'That takes five days to incubate. Very unlikely,' said Haruto.

'What did Ned Wang say about DX21? How lethal it was. Within seconds, the toxin attacks the vital organs. It's still possible that he had some and used it on her.'

Karen scrolled through the posts until she came across the photo. 'There's mine. The one I took in the library!' She pointed to it. 'Look at Helen's expression. She's after Ned Wang for sure. And see Yoyo there? She doesn't like it at all. This makes our love triangle hypothesis more likely.'

'Yup. You could be right.'

Karen expanded the image to get more detail. Helen had tagged the Chinese girl in the picture. It linked through to Yoyo's profile, which included support of Mai Xin.

'We must talk to Yoyo about this.'

'Who's Mai Xin?' Haruto looked quite puzzled.

'A feminist who wrote an open letter on social media asking her university to investigate sexual harassment by teachers. Not a great idea in China. All that remains online now is her WeChat account under the nickname of Mulan. She signs off with five sunflower emojis.'

Karen showed Haruto links to a range of other blocked accounts. 'You need anti-surveillance software or VPNs to get into those.'

'What's the relevance?'

'Mai Xin's not that important. But the key player in this is another poster close to her. She goes by the name of China Girl. If you remember, she accused Tomio of sexual harassment back in Liverpool.'

Karen called up the online newspaper *Liver Bird* again with the fake stories directed at Professor Nakamura. 'Here's she is. Born in 1995 when a one-child policy was still in place. Wealthy parents. Went to Beijing University. Terribly difficult entrance exam. Claims staff sexually abused her because of her extreme views. No current photo of her. Just this picture taken when she was about twelve so you can't identify her easily.'

The image was grainy. A young girl in pigtails giving the workers' salute. A clenched fist raised high.

'After Beijing, she left to move to the UK to study. And there's definitely a military link.'

'Do you think Yoyo Chen knows her?'

'It would make for an interesting connection. But of course she may be just a social media contact. Nothing more.'

Comparing common factors, they traced Yoyo's other accounts across the various platforms, including Twitter. She updated regularly in both Chinese and English.

They needed some way to engineer a meeting with her. And the next day the following post provided it.

Yoyo Chen: RIP Ned. I will throw these for you this morning.

Underneath the message, she'd uploaded a photo of a bunch of yellow and white shop-bought chrysanthemums.

Chapter Fifty Six

I'm almost there! Now I can't fail.

Yoyo Chen couldn't help but notice that although the flowers she'd bought were beautiful, they exuded a faint suggestion of manure. It would permeate the entire cabin in no time. The sooner she got rid of them, the better.

She pulled out her phone and posted a second message on Facebook.

'Flower ceremony in memory of Professor Wang at eleven. Deck 8 Station 70. Yoyo Chen.'

They were certain to read that.

She wanted to cry, but that would have spoilt her makeup. And also bad thoughts might flow. At the sight of the yellow sun, still visible despite the advancing front, all such emotions faded. Pushed aside and replaced with excitement at what lay just ahead.

So close to New York, where she would marry Colonel Li. Nearly done.

Keep calm and stay focussed at all costs.

She took a single refreshing swig from a bottle of clear mineral water.

Yoyo had put up with roughly ten days of Professor Wang's boring routines. Everything had been on his old man's terms. Now she had the cabin to herself and could talk to Li whenever she liked. She'd virtually forgotten how the colonel used to make her laugh. How buzzy it was to be involved with a powerful man like him.

She peeled off the ugly yellow tape which had turned the stateroom into a crime scene. She would toss it all into the sea along with his silly jigsaw pieces.

Time to go.

Yoyo left the cabin and wended her way through the by now familiar companionways of the cruise liner en route to Deck 8.

After ten days, the inside of the ship now felt like home. Maybe tomorrow she'd get glimpses of her future one in New York. Or would Li want her to fly straight back with him to China?

It didn't matter.

As long as they were together.

Ever since she left Liverpool behind, Yoyo had lived in Beijing near the Zoo. The apartment had been an unexpected gift from the CCP. Recognition of her recruitment work for them while she was studying at the university. Planting the story about Professor Nakamura had changed her life and prospects.

Walking past one venue at the onboard entertainment complex, she smiled quietly. Think of all the shows she missed when stuck with Ned Wang! He avoided all the fun. Wouldn't go to any late-night attractions with her.

You can. You don't need me, he always said. Didn't even joke around as much as Tomio Nakamura. She quite liked the eccentric professor who'd given the biochemistry lectures at the university. But when Colonel Li broke it to her that Nakamura had been disloyal to China, she turned against him straight away. Hated him, in fact. Japanese. Untrustworthy. Remember the thirties. The rapes, the murders, the whole scale slaughter. *He deserved everything he got.*

So she happily agreed to the party's instruction. Her lover marvelled at just how many students believed the sexual harassment complaint and in return recommended a promotion. As their relationship developed, he told her how they would go to the top rungs of the party together. Yoyo clapped her tiny hands. She was in love. Would die for him.

She was going to become Li's second wife, certain of that from the moment they met at the annual conference. But then his current one found out about their passionate affair and wanted to end it.

Clever Colonel Li.

Resourceful as ever, his plan was super smart and would serve a dual purpose. Monitor Wang's activities and therefore advance his career by serving party objectives. And second, neutralise his wife's plot to separate them by leading her to believe that she and Ned were a number and not a threat to her marriage.

Colonel Li had asked Yoyo the rhetorical question back in Beijing. 'Do you realise what it would mean if Wang betrayed the people of our great nation?'

Of course she did.

Yoyo's task was to monitor all his contacts on the cruise and pass them on to her lover. To accomplish that, she needed to stay in close touch with the professor. Needed to be with him constantly. By his side all the time.

As she stepped into the gleaming lift, she didn't allow memories of Helen to dull her mood. The Green Tea Bitch wanted to move in on Wang and get between them.

She wouldn't give him any further excuse to slip away.

The killing had been easy as pie. All her fault. Always out to take other women's men to satisfy her ego and greed. Typical European. Big feet, small brain, easily fooled. Going back over it, she deceived Helen so effortlessly. Unbelievable. Just a few simple presents. The red dress, a couple of earrings. *That was all it took.* Happy to accept the last gifts she would ever get, the heady, rich perfume laced with the deadly toxin which she had sprayed over her only too willing victim.

Yes. *That's all it had taken.*

By confessing to Li she'd gone off piste and perhaps a step too far in deciding to kill her, Yoyo had showed her loyalty to China, the party, and her love to him.

And the bitch deserved it.

She felt good and ran over everything in her mind. Colonel Li's instructions had been quite explicit. Stay close to Wang at all times. He is a collaborator and a traitor to the state. She hadn't wanted to believe it. But when she had the wire on him, she heard the treachery for herself. He was a conspirator and planned to defect to the United States.

Things had gone well, but that certainly wasn't the case thirty-six hours ago. Yoyo shivered, recalling the fear she felt waiting in their stateroom for the professor to return from his meeting with the western meddlers from Partridge Security. Doubtless he would have revealed the plan to betray his mother country.

She recalled Wang's familiar footsteps coming down the corridor, and the surprise and delight on his face that she was waiting up for him. Remembered vividly the expression. One of a certain lustful expectation of what might be in store. She kissed him lightly and suggested a drink first. A double rum and coke to get in the mood before bed.

Ned had made it all too easy. The acrid taste of the Rohypnol passed unnoticed. Undetected and buried by the sweet flavour of the cocktail. The Dark'n Stormy slid down fast. She played up to him, teasing, implying, stroking as the rape drug took effect. Even the duct tape stuck down firmly over Wang's partly open mouth didn't rouse him from the induced coma. Yoyo held the professor's nostrils together, ignoring the jerking body searching for air. All over in five minutes.

Killing someone is relatively easy, but disposing of them is many degrees more difficult. But the pretty Chinese girl had a good brain and with her looks rarely had to use it. She needed help and who better than faithful Matt, the kickboxer, her long-term boyfriend from her university days in Liverpool? Her puppy dog, as she had always called him. He had two things which mattered. Kickboxing and an enduring infatuation with his first and only love. Yoyo.

Despite his martial arts qualifications, he wasn't that good. No match for Tomio Nakamura the time she had sent him round to kill him. Nor had he found and brought back the Miasma Report that Li wanted.

All he achieved was to give the elderly man Covid-19!

She stripped off the duct tape and called Matt.

He believed every word she told him. That she killed Ned Wang by accident after he tried to rape her in a perverted way. In the struggle, he had a heart attack. She shed a few crocodile tears and begged for help. It worked. Why not put him overboard? No one, certainly not the professor, would know the difference. In the early hours, they simply dragged the heavy body on to the rail of their private balcony and pushed it over. Down and gone, with barely a splash, into the inky blackness of the Atlantic.

At the Purser's office, when she reported Wang's disappearance, she glibly passed off the story about his affair with Helen.

And to complete the mission, all that remained was to persuade Matt, her faithful puppy, into getting the Miasma Report back from Haruto Fraser.

Nearly there.

Status, wealth, love, all lay in her grasp.

Yoyo stepped out onto the open deck at eleven in the morning. It worked! She'd lured the couple out of their cabin and into her trap.

With no pun intended, she messaged Matt to say the coast was clear.

It was approaching eleven o'clock on day six and Karen and Haruto stood waiting by the railing on Deck 8. Compared to the stuffiness in the cabin, the air was clean and pure.

Out on the horizon, she noticed all the warning signs of another cold front heading towards them as the Princess Hyacinth carved her way westwards.

A hundred negative thoughts crowded into her brain. As the frontal system came closer, gusty wind carpeted the sea with dark cresting waves. Salty air stung Karen's cheeks. And she filled with a sudden dread. The power that the ocean held. She gripped the railing and then agoraphobia took over. The primordial fear of heights. She leant towards Haruto, in need of his strength.

'Are you OK?' He put his arm around her. 'You've gone quite pale.'

'Yes, yes, I'm fine, sorry. Just a few silly thoughts.'

The Twitter post showed Yoyo Chen intended to go to where her lover had taken his life and throw a bouquet into the ocean in his memory. Karen and Haruto aimed to be at the same spot. And ask her some crucial questions.

How had she met Wang? What was their relationship? Did she know China Girl?

'This is the exact location he would have gone overboard,' he said. 'Yoyo Chen would have learnt that from the CCTV.'

What had happened to him? Had he been murdered? Or jumped to his death to end it all?

'You think she will come?'

'Well, I hope so. Then she can tell us a lot more about this China Girl.'

Haruto's phone went off, triggered by the security cameras in their cabin.

'Karen. It looks as though there is someone inside our room. It might be a fault. Or the cleaner. But I'd better have a look. I'll be right back.'

Under a greying sky, everything was going nicely to Yoyo's plan for the flower ceremony. With a light rain dampening the deck, few passengers had ventured out.

But then the Japanese guy ran off. As if he'd left a pot on the stove. What was happening now? Yoyo smiled at the young woman standing alone.

'Hello,' she said to her. 'The weather is OK today. Dry at least.'

'It's supposed to bucket down later, they say.' Karen commented lightly.

'Are you here for the flower ritual? To offer your respects to Professor Wang and his ancestors?'

'No. I'm here to find out how you know China Girl?'

'Who's that?'

'You share her posts on Weibo.'

'What I do on social media is no business of yours.'

'She wrote things there about a certain Japanese academic in Liverpool. His name was Tomio Nakamura. And none of them were true.'

'And who the hell are you, anyway?'

Yoyo had to complete the chrysanthemum ceremony. And take photos as proof for Colonel Li.

This woman is stopping me, ruining everything.

She persisted. 'I didn't recognise you with your natural hair. But close up I realise you look exactly like China Girl herself.'

'I've not changed. The same as I looked at twelve.'

'So *you* are China Girl.'

331

'Yes. So what?'

Karen stared at her with narrowed eyes. 'It was you who betrayed Ned Wang.' She stood stubbornly at the rail, mouth open, bristling.

The hated figure obstructing her plan had become a fox. A symbol of cunning in Chinese culture. The animal with a mystical ability to disguise itself in human form.

Yoyo eyed her warily, could almost swear the eyes had turned red. Who was this woman? *Baizuo*. One of the white leftists.

Move out the way. Stand aside. Get back from me.

'He was a traitor to our nation.' She was ready to scratch her face, hurt her. Show what happens to humanoid foxes in her country.

'So you think China can use bioweapons if it suits them?' *She wanted to kill her now, above everything.*

'West is doing the same thing. My government is protecting the people.'

The fox edged towards her.

Li's orders were explicit. *Cast the tribute into the sea and record the event.*

Angry and frustrated, Yoyo slapped her hard across the face. Shocked at the sudden violence, Karen flailed out and grabbed a handful of glossy black hair. Reached with a free hand for Yoyo's eyes. But her willing Puppy Dog had schooled the young Chinese woman in rudimentary martial arts. She doubled up and, despite her slender form, hooked her right shoulder under Karen's near leg, leveraging her over the rail in one smooth movement.

Losing her grip on Yoyo's hair, Karen was all at once weightless, almost peacefully flying thorough space down towards the white waves rolling past the ship.

Chapter Fifty Seven

Haruto kept checking the footage on his phone all the way back to the cabin he shared with Karen. Somebody was turning the place upside down. And for the first time since he fitted the surveillance system, it wasn't one of the cleaning team.

Reaching their deck, he sped down the companionway and threw open the door.

'What the hell do you think you are doing?' he yelled, ducking a high kick, heading in the general direction of his chest but connecting painfully with his left shoulder. Thrown back, Haruto crashed over an occasional table, reducing it to scrap.

In full fighting mode, he sprang into a crouching attack move, landing a heavy strike on the intruder's head, slamming him against the wall. The skill years of qualifying for the coveted black belt required, stood him in good stead.

Haruto closed in for a chop kill punch. But his opponent gave up. Had enough. And raised his hands in surrender.

'Hey you. I know you, don't I? You'd better start talking and quickly. Aren't you Matt Fong?'

He recognised the kickboxer from the Hyacinth's entertainment rota. His lessons were popular with some elderly men who thought they could master the discipline, at least sufficiently to defend themselves from a street attack. And the ladies signed up too attracted by his rippling muscularity.

Peace came quickly between the two capable fighters, both skilled but in different traditions. Haruto from Japan, Fong from China.

'OK. What are you after here?'

'What you stole, that's what I'm after.' Fong's distinctive Liverpudlian accent was obvious from the moment he opened his mouth.

'What's with the Scouse?'

'I went to Uni there.' He gave a defiant stare.

'What can you tell me about a professor Tomio Nakamura? Old guy. Defenceless. Bit of an oddball. He headed up the biochemistry department there.'

'The one who crashed a Zoom class?'

'Who says so?'

'My mother. She was the teacher.'

'Then she lied to you. What exactly were you looking for?'

'Some report or crap like that.'

'You were wasting your time. I've already passed it to MI5, the British secret service.'

'I understand nothing about this shit.'

'So who does?'

'My girlfriend, Yoyo Chen.'

'You broke into my uncle's house, didn't you? The professor?'

'I was acting on her orders.'

'Do you know you gave him Covid-19, which eventually killed him?'

The kickboxer looked genuinely stunned. Almost as shocked as he'd been when he lost his championship title.

'No,' he stuttered and wiped away the perspiration from his forehead.

'Yes.'

'Honestly. I never had any symptoms. Must have been a passive carrier. So sorry, my friend.'

Before Haruto could respond, three piercing blasts from the ship's whistle sounded. The international signal.

Man Overboad!

Chapter Fifty Eight

In that terrifying five second fall from Deck 8, one survival memory popped up, buried away in a remote corner of Karen's brain. 'Go in feet first if you can.'

Someone must have said it in her past. Reduce the impact.

Still, the shock hitting the surface, and the fear as she plunged down into the black waters, seemed detached, unreal. And then a sensation of weightlessness as the descent ended. Followed by the long pull upwards, upwards to air. At no stage did she even hold her breath in a conscious way. Fundamental instincts took control.

Reaching the surface was a second chance at life. All thoughts and emotions normalised with the urge to survive. The big surprise was the distance the ship had travelled. Already the huge outline of the Princess Hyacinth had left her far behind.

Fear of being sucked under by the wake caused by the churning screws, galvanised Karen into action. She swam clumsily away from the boiling waters, but it caught her anyway, drawing her down before throwing her, gasping, to the surface once again.

Time stretched out, as it does in survival situations. All that represented her former existence disappeared with the liner as it headed for the horizon.

They will never find me. Why must I die this way?

A lonely death. What about her plans? Haruto's love? All gone. It was so sudden, unexpected.

Karen shook badly as the shock took hold. Chaotic thoughts tumbled through her mind.

She lifted and fell in rhythm with the swell. The ship was almost out of sight. But now, instead of the odd square shape of a stern view, it appeared normal, like it should. Why? In her befuddled brain, it was all too hard. Over the hiss of the cresting waves, a new sound. *Chuff, chuff, chuff.* Perhaps just in her head. Karen slipped away into unconsciousness.

The H130 helicopter was a recent addition to the Princess Hyacinth. Intended as a luxury add-on for the premier passengers to fly them ashore at transits. That way they avoided the lengthy queues for the shuttle. It would be the first recovery at sea for the chopper crew. A super rapid deployment from the especially designed hanger on board saved Karen, against all the odds.

She came round into the white world of the Princess Hyacinth medical centre, surrounded by figures fully clad in protective clothing.

'How are you, dear?' A kindly face peered through the mask. 'You've been through a lot. How do you feel?'

'Where's Yoyo?' She tried to sit up as the fear kicked in.

'It's all right. You are safe now, thank God.' Quacker said. 'Security has arrested Miss Chen for attempted murder and locked her up in the ship's brig. But there's a biohazard emergency on the ship. Haruto found the DX21 hidden inside a makeup case in Yoyo's cabin.'

Chapter Fifty Nine

The sky was blue and the air rich and salty. Although still frail from the adventures of the previous day, Haruto and Karen rose early. The New York arrival was an experience they wanted to remember all their lives.

They made their way to the forward facing observation post on Deck 11, a perfect spot accessed from 'A' stairway.

She promised herself nothing but happiness and pushed aside all that had happened during the terrifying time in the ocean. Haruto had filled in the gaps, her rescue by the ship's helicopter, the arrest of Yoyo and all the ramifications.

They stood hand in hand together as the bright lights of Long Island came into view. Then, through the early morning mist, the classically beautiful shape of the Verrazano suspension bridge appeared on the bow.

Karen gasped as the Princess Hyacinth aimed at dead centre of the span. The traverse was too low to pass, surely? As they slid cautiously underneath, the magnificent Manhattan skyline opened up before them.

The ship wheeled right and headed into the Brooklyn Cruise Terminal berthing within sight of the iconic Statue of Liberty.

On schedule at exactly six thirty, the Princess Hyacinth nudged alongside the wharf.

Karen turned to go down to their cabin when Haruto stopped her. 'There's something I've wanted to ask all trip. Will you marry me?'

Part Five

THE KNIFE EDGE

Chapter Sixty

A week after Karen Andersen returned from New York, she woke to a knock on the door.

'Can you hear that racket out there?' A small crowd of media people outside her flat in Devonshire Road had made enough noise to disturb her elderly neighbour. Eyes shining, she announced, 'More press for you, dear. You're very much in the news, aren't you?'

'What are reporters doing here?' Karen muttered to herself. But she already knew the answer.

The Agency for Toxic Substances and Disease Registry had tested the vial found on the Princess Hyacinth and confirmed it contained a harmless substance used in hair transplants.

Despite this, Yoyo sang like a canary. She admitted that she stole the flask off Professor Wang because he'd boasted about it being a bioweapon sample. She claimed that her motivation was to protect innocent lives.

Karen saw through the spin straightaway. She knew the young Chinese was a nasty piece of work. But now the newspapers portrayed her as a victim. And that the investigator went overboard simply because of a bitch fight. Everything the media ran with from then on fitted with that angle. For example, her alter ego, China Girl, who planted all the fake

345

stories on the net in order to discredit Professor Nakamura, magically vanished. Every word vacuumed off into artificial intelligence oblivion.

Further, the real reason why she travelled with Ned Wang avoided. Hadn't anyone asked? And what about her involvement with a Colonel Li? No one in the media was the slightest bit interested.

A freelance journalist had an original take. An unprovoked and petty fight broke out onboard between a small time British investigator and a Chinese woman. All over a bunch of flowers. It had ended up an international embarrassment.

A national magazine ran the headline *Chrysanth Wars On Deck of the Hyacinth.*

Leaked insider information on board claimed Karen Andersen had carried out a completely unauthorised investigation on a fellow passenger, a Miss Helen Rogers. He speculated further in the article. The harassment led to not just the poor woman's suicide, but also that of her heartbroken lover.

Another source, unnamed but possibly working for the Chinese military, had caused a ruckus by posting how any suggestion that the esteemed professor had been transporting toxic matter was defamatory and an insult to China. The whole biohazard exercise, having been a false alarm, added to the acceptability of the narrative in the people's mind.

In the meantime, an autopsy showed Helen Rogers had large quantities of cocaine in her system. The drowning most likely accidental. But nobody read *that*. Helen's mother had contacted an investigative journalist to state that she held Karen Andersen responsible for the harassment and death of her only daughter.

Social media went viral. She was a troublemaker and hysterical attention seeker.

Karen knew her own faults, and intense paranoia was not one of them. Criticism of her somewhat maverick approach to life was not new. She had learnt to take it in her stride. But this was different. The papers had taken a simple line on it. Not a word about Professor Tomio Nakamura's research work. Or that she'd nearly drowned in the Atlantic Ocean. It was all unbalanced and unfair.

Karen flung open the front door to the clamouring press. 'What do you want? I've already made a full statement to both the FBI, and the Met. I have nothing more to add.'

She glared at them above her face mask and brushed aside the boom microphone perched rudely in front of her.

'Miss Andersen. A Chinese girl is under investigation in New York because of your allegation that she had a toxic material when in fact it was just a container of hair oil. How does that make you feel? Weren't you concerned about causing unnecessary panic?'

Jack from *The Insider*, angular and aggressive, had wormed his way to the front of the press pack. 'Admit it! That your dive into the sea was an attention seeking stunt after a fight with your boyfriend? Are you an anti-Chinese racist? Don't you owe Yoyo Chen an apology for what you've done?'

As the media continued to bombard her, she flared up.

'No! She tried to kill me. She threw me overboard. I am the victim here, not her. I've got nothing further to say.' Karen spun on her heels and slammed the door.

Ever since getting back home, Karen had been as high as a kite. Filled with love for Haruto. It had yet to sink in. But the unresolved Helen Rogers matter had tempered her happiness. It was driving her a little insane. A loose end, but a big one. *Had the woman killed Paul Honey?*

Too important to ignore. Possibly a major factor in all that had happened. Karen had to resolve it. She contacted Helen's mother, who was more than happy to meet her the following day.

'She was always a worry to us. Right from early on. And never out of trouble.'

Karen's heart went out to the lady who obviously loved her daughter despite the frailties. 'She would bring home things. Pretend she found them or have some other story. The police used to come round. It was awful. It was as if she couldn't help herself.'

'Yes, I understand, but that doesn't make her a killer, Mrs Rogers.'

'Well, no. And she wasn't. She was angry with him when he broke it off. After all, she gave him everything, and it had counted for nothing. He never respected her. Just used her. Like, they only did this sex stuff in his study. The bedroom was forbidden. Or be seen out with him. Several times he tried to get her out of his life. To end it. But she wouldn't. Kept crawling back. She was that crazy about him. That night she got involved in this weird sexual thing with the plastic bag. Just to please him. My daughter told me that when he became unconscious, she panicked and fled. The next day after work, she drove back to check on him.' The mother looked imploringly at Karen. 'She thought it was all behind her. I know because she confided in me.'

'Helen did steal his car, though.'

'No, not really. That was a company vehicle. She used it quite often.'

'Did they argue that night? Did she mention that to you by any chance?'

'No.'

Driving back, all of Karen's worries resurfaced. The realisation she was in the middle of a sort of nightmare. But at least she'd tied up one loose end.

'They only did this sex stuff in his study.'

For all her faults, Helen Rogers had not been a murderess.

Chapter Sixty One

Gary Smith put on his uniform, ready for another shift. The Deliveroo jacket still reeked of stale cheese from the day before. He needed to change his job, but with everyone he knew out of work and up shit creek, that would have to wait.

He had ignored the economic downturn caused by the Covid-19 effect, at least until it affected him in his own pocket. As he continued to dress, half-listening to the local news droning on in the background, he unplugged the gamepad on his PC. Then something caught his attention big time.

'False allegations could have driven a passenger on the Princess Hyacinth to suicide.' They were interviewing some ignoramus from the cruise. She banged on and on about a car accident earlier in the year. The moment she mentioned a collision with a delivery cyclist, Gary recognised the voice. It was the girl in leathers who'd knocked him for a six.

What the fuck? What is she going on about? *Chinese espionage? Ocean liners?*

He sensed trouble. The very last thing he needed. Eviction, bills, debts. Fortunately, he'd kept the ten-hour tape from his Cycliq Fly 12 from that day. Perhaps the investment had been worth it after all. He dug it out and called the police.

Chapter Sixty Two

Jill Honey peered through the darkness at the bright yellow digits on her alarm clock. It was a quarter to five in the morning. Why bother to set it at all? For the preceding three days she woke at the same time restless. Going over things in her mind.

Additional information about the mystery surrounding her husband had come in following the unexplained death of a passenger aboard the cruise ship. It'd made the national press. Sargeant Baring, in charge of the investigative branch, had established a connection and wanted to ask her some questions about Helen Rogers. He wasted no time in taking it further.

At ten in the morning, she drove over to Woking Police for a Zoom interview. While these had become the norm under lockdown rules, Jill found the process disconcerting. The sterile environment alone intimidated her, as did the Station Officer sitting next to her as a formal witness.

'Payment for the crossing between Southampton and New York was on a company card. Can you shed any light on that, Mrs Honey?'

'No idea what goes on in the office,' she stammered.

'Were you aware Miss Rogers was having an affair with your husband?'

'No, but it doesn't surprise me. She wasn't the only one. He had lots of them. I stayed in Surrey and Paul lived in Chiswick. We led largely separate lives.'

'You told us originally you hadn't been to the London property in the week before his death.'

'Yes.'

'But you visited there on a Friday. The twenty-eighth of March, didn't you?'

I lied to the police. They must know I did.

'I can't remember that far back, I'm afraid.'

'You were there the day before we found your husband dead. On the Saturday.'

Jill looked helplessly at the officer sitting silently in his chair. The face covering masked any expression. Sargeant Baring, in charge of the homicide investigation, did not try to hide his suspicions. The claustrophobic room exuded a strong smell of fresh disinfectant. She felt vaguely nauseous.

'A Deliveroo cyclist, who works the patch, has shown us camera footage,' he continued. 'He delivered a pizza to that address at three fifteen on the Friday. Gave it to an unidentified female. Was that you?'

'What's this all about?' She parried weakly.

The Sargeant ignored the question. 'Was your husband there with you that afternoon?'

352

Jill wanted the ground to swallow her up. It seemed pointless to deny it now.

I thought everything to do with Paul was behind me. In the past forever.

She had practised her cover story fifty times, just in case. That it was a spur-of-the-moment, unplanned drive to London. Lockdown or no lockdown. To accept the divorce agreement while it was in the offing.

'My husband's car wasn't there, so I let myself in. Rang his mobile, but it went straight to voicemail. I waited for an hour and got peckish, so I called Deliveroo and ordered a pizza.'

'So what happened then, Mrs Honey?'

'Well, I assumed my husband had gone out. So I decided to pick up some shoes I needed from the master bedroom. And Paul was there. Lying in bed. I thought he was asleep, but his face was extremely pale. Had his mouth open too. It shocked me. I sat on the stairs in a daze.'

'Did it occur to you he might be dead?'

'He seemed very pale. But I couldn't get my head around it.'

'As a widow, you stood to inherit the entire estate. Far more than in the divorce settlement you spoke about.'

'That was not what I was thinking. The last thing on my mind. I was in a panic.'

'So why didn't you call 999?'

'I should have done, I know. Could they have saved him, do you think?' She blew her nose, heart pounding.

'Possibly. Yes.'

The officer paused for a full thirty seconds before continuing with the interview.

'So what did you do next, Mrs Honey?'

'I just left the house in a state of shock.'

'You telephoned Chiswick Police on the Saturday to say he wasn't responding to your calls. Pretending you hadn't been there.'

'No. I phoned a neighbour. They contacted them.'

'And when the officers broke in, they found him?'

'Yes.'

'When did you learn about the extent of his debts?'

'I rang the office, got an email sent out to the staff. The flood gates opened. He owed everyone in town.'

'Thank you for your help. We'll be in touch with you shortly.'

The police summoned her to a second interview the following day. This time Sergeant Baring conducted it under caution and in the presence of a court appointed solicitor.

'Mrs Honey, when you first saw your husband, did he have anything unusual near him? Such as towels? On the bed? Or covering him?'

'He died of the virus, didn't he?'

'How do you know that?'

'The police called me and they said so.'

'We found a towel over his face like he had a temperature and more soiled linen on the sideboard. They were in fact infected waste material from a Covid-19 ward at Northwick Park Hospital.'

'Really? I never noticed. Like I said, I was in shock.'

'But you told me yesterday that when you first saw your husband, his complexion was pale and his mouth open. How did you know that? His face was covered, wasn't it?'

'I can't remember exactly.'

'We believe someone put them there on the Friday evening. Helen Rogers. She was a volunteer assistant at Northwick Park Hospital. What do you make of that?'

'She had a key to the property.'

'From her time at Honey Estates?'

'I assume so. Paul didn't talk much about his staff to me. Management reasons.'

'When we checked on Miss Rogers' movements, we found she worked that afternoon in a Covid ward. Were you aware of that?'

'No.'

'Nor that your husband had fired her?'

'No. News to me.'

'And you were therefore unaware that she'd been stalking him from the moment he sacked her?'

'Well, that doesn't surprise me because I heard she was a bit strange.'

'What do you mean by that?'

'Obsessive.'

'So you knew her then?'

'I met her once.'

'So you weren't aware she was at the property on Thursday night? The day before you went there? Or that they performed an extreme sexual act?'

'No. I wasn't.'

'Which was why he passed out?'

'He liked deviant sex. That was just one reason I split with him.'

'Or that she threatened to kill him if he broke off the affair?'

'Good God.'

'That surprises you?'

'Not really. The woman was nearly as weird as him.'

'You knew, because your husband told you over a phone call. How he came round to find her gone. Hoped he had finally got rid of her. And you both laughed about it together.'

356

Where is this going exactly?

'Helen Rogers believed she left him close to death on the Thursday night. Went back the following day. Found him dead upstairs in the bedroom, not the study. Put the virally infected waste material over his face as a cover for what she thought she'd done. But she hadn't, had she? It was the heroin overdose you administered to him while he was recovering from the near asphyxiation.'

Jill froze as she heard the words from the officer. 'A Post Mortem confirmed the time of death as late Friday. Due to the exceptional level of heroin in his system.'

'The coroner might be wrong.'

'A dead man can't order a pizza. Paul Honey called at quarter to three for a pepperoni. He was alive when you got there. And not when you left. You made sure of that.'

Chapter Sixty Three

At nine thirty on Thursday morning, Haruto Fraser answered a call from Liverpool University. His uncle had left his entire estate to the institution. The Dean planned to hold a memorial service for him. He suggested the summer. The global pandemic would be behind them, surely?

'He contributed hugely to the faculty up here. '

That was the least they could do.

'You got all his books and historical papers?'

'They'll be in pride of place in the library. We are setting up the Professor Nakamura Scholarship for the advancement of research into biotechnology.'

'It would be a consolation to him, I'm sure. It was his entire life's work, after all.'

As recognition spread, public opinion had swung in his uncle's favour. Students who'd known him posted glowing reports about the knowledge they had gained from their time under the professor's tutelage. Many put up photos and slides taken during lectures. Some went back twenty years or more. His quirky and flamboyant style became legendary. The academic fraternity acknowledged the value of earlier work too. *In Memoriam* articles appeared in science magazines and biochemical journals now referred to him as a genius, a pioneering researcher and a great humanitarian worthy of the Nobel prize for biochemistry.

But Professor Nakamura had also been outspoken on socio-political issues and often misunderstood. They mounted a plaque to honour him in the university's hall of fame. And a fellow of the Royal British Society of Sculptors began work on an 'interpretive' statue for the Japanese English exhibition in London.

Each day during the weeks that followed the trip to New York, Haruto fielded one enquiry after another. He filled in, as best he could, the knowledge and information gaps in his uncle's life. Nothing was too much trouble. He had basked in an enduring mood of happiness from the moment Karen said 'I will'.

The news from the publishing arm of the university was quite unexpected. Came totally without warning. Knocked him for six. When he heard, Haruto Fraser gasped in shock.

Tomio Nakamura's 'groundbreaking book' *The Miasma Project* on bioweapons *was about to publish*.

As it was written in collaboration with a professor from Beijing, they planned a joint launch event at the Chinese Embassy in London the following week.

Chapter Sixty Four

Karen left the fitting appointment for her wedding dress. She was running late for the event at the embassy when the phone rang.

'I think you'd better have a listen to this,' Quacker said.

She grinned. He always seemed to demand attention at the most inopportune moments.

But news of Yoyo Chen had just hit the UK tabloids. He'd been first to pick up on it.

'The headline reads, *Chinese Leader's Wife Poisons Love Rival*. It goes on. The wife of a colonel linked to China's intelligence department has been arrested following the murder of her husband's mistress. Police believe the twenty-five-year-old former Liverpool University student was poisoned when she turned up to meet her lover.

'The killing was carried out at The Royal Garden Inn, a boutique hotel in Beijing. The floor manager has confessed. He claimed it was on the orders of Gui Li, wife of Colonel Li, tipped as a rising star in the Chinese Communist Party.

'The military officer held a news conference in which he denounced his wife's evil actions and disassociated himself from her in every way. He sent his condolences to the Chen family. He admitted that there had been a brief relationship between them which ended some time ago.

'It is the second unexplained death at the hotel in the past year. On March 10, Xixi Wang, married to the world renowned trichologist, Professor Wang, collapsed and died in similar circumstances.

'He later went missing on board the Princess Hyacinth en route to New York on November 19. He had been severely depressed. It is believed he committed suicide by throwing himself overboard. His body has never been recovered.'

'By the sound of it, Ned's wife was murdered. And he never suspected it. Thought it was natural causes,' Karen said.

'I wouldn't talk to any reporters at the event.' Quacker took in a deep breath. 'Not until we get the official line on it.'

She agreed and put down the phone, now running somewhat behind for the function. Ten minutes later the bell rang. A car was waiting for a Ms Andersen. As she reached the bottom of the stairs, her neighbour Elspeth Cochrane appeared at the top of the landing.

'I see you're early for a change.'

It was only as she got into the back of the Toyota Prius, Karen realised, in her rush, she hadn't actually rung for the Uber herself. Haruto must have organised it. Worried she would be late, as usual.

Being engaged meant life was looking up. In more ways than one.

Chapter Sixty Five

Haruto took the underground to Portland Place, leaving time to spare. It was the official release of *The Miasma Project* at the Chinese Embassy. He didn't want to be late.

The directions to Room 10 were clear. So he had no difficulty in finding his way in the vast building. Several piles of his uncle's book lay stacked on a green felt-topped table next to the lectern. Haruto picked up a copy and found a spare seat near the door.

The jacket of the publication was impressive: black background, bright red title with a full-page photo of his distinguished uncle on the back cover.

From the superficial evidence, I jumped straight to the wrong conclusion.

It all made sense at the time. The broken windows, the bloodstained carpet, and then finding the cellar. All had pointed to a secret betrayal of the highest order.

Irrelevant now, with Tomio Nakamura's scientific conclusions out in an open forum for all to read. Haruto flipped through the pages, pausing at a picture of the underground 'research' lab. He glanced at his watch. Where was she, for goodness sake?

The book had turned out thinner than expected, but very well illustrated, filled with esoteric data relating to the project, plus many photos from the professor's youth. Old publicity material, party groups and an early one of him, age six, attending primary school, which must have materialised from other sources. Tomio at work and at play. And grainy black and white shots of him hiking in the Delamere Forest with Ned Wang.

But something wasn't quite right. Haruto flicked through the pages again. Where was the section on DX21? Not a mention of it.

He knew the text backwards by now. Been through it a hundred times at least. He made a mental note to double check with the original. Just in case. Using a quick break in the proceedings, he left the room and called Karen, but her phone went to voicemail.

With mounting concern, he tried her nosy neighbour. Mrs Cochrane's quavering voice came on eventually. 'Any idea where she is? I'm rather worried.'

'Don't be. She's definitely on her way. I saw her leave in the car you sent well over an hour ago.'

'Oh good. Although I didn't send it, actually. I thought she would be better off organising that herself.'

Back in the room, the diplomatic entourage was completing its round of the attendees. Haruto wondered if he should go up. Ask outright what had happened to the missing section of the manuscript. Undecided, he hesitated.

Would the ambassador even know someone had excised it?

'There's a bit of a queue to talk to him.' The attractive young publicist held a glass of sparkling wine in her right hand. And a shiny copy of *The Miasma Project* in her left.

Where's Karen? Why isn't she here? What's going on?

They'd dropped their guard. The invitation to the launch should have raised a red flag. It might have been a ruse.

I should have been more wary. Another mistake.

At each stage of the journey back to London from New York, they had expected questioning by MI6. Or or at very least, the police. But nothing. And then news of the unexpected publication took them both by surprise.

'Can I get you a top-up? It's Jane, by the way,' the publicist said, reaching for his glass.

'OK at the moment, thanks. I'm more concerned about my fiancé. She should have arrived an hour ago.'

'Describe her to me? What does she look like? Shortish hair, pretty?'

'Well, yes. But she's missing.' Haruto tried to suppress his irritation.

'That's not who you're looking for, is it?'

Karen, smiling broadly, stood right behind him.

'What happened to you?' He blurted out, wanting to take her in his arms. His eyes searched hers for an explanation.

364

She leant over and whispered, 'Sorry I'm late. I have just had a lecture.'

'How come?'

'In the back of a car. Driving round and round Portland Place and twice down Piccadilly.'

'The publishers have omitted an entire section from the publication.'

'I know,' she said.

'How could you? What are you holding back from me?'

Karen glanced in the ambassador's direction. She didn't reply directly, but Haruto read her expression. *Walls have ears.*

Affecting interest in the Chinese decor and motifs, they wound a path through the guests to a quiet corner.

'They murdered Yoyo Chen. It's all over the papers this evening. Have you picked up on it?' Karen whispered.

'Yes. On the way here. And what about your phone? I left you a message. But you didn't answer.'

'I couldn't. I'll explain later.'

At ten o'clock they exchanged pleasantries with the ambassador. Then they went out into the night. Under a bright moon, the Georgian buildings lining the square gleamed with a pale beauty.

'MI6 sent a car. During the drive here, the intelligence agent asked a load of questions. Sorry. It all took a while,' said Karen. 'He clarified the government's position, unofficially of course.

It's a political thing. They needed to make clear I understood the official view before I came here. He insisted I turn off my phone. That's why I couldn't answer you.'

'And?'

'They know the book is an abridged version. They agreed between intelligence agencies to withhold the technical background on the development work for DX21. That it shouldn't enter the public domain. All the major powers are doing exactly the same. Carrying out R & D on bioweapons to preserve a stalemate. It is much like the nuclear agreements, except it's all unspoken. They didn't want any specifics published. Certainly not as a bestseller. There was talk of changing the title. A way to keep the profile low.'

'I think *The Miasma Project* is suitably obscure.'

'One has to ask. After all we've been through, have we achieved anything positive?' Karen set her lips in a cynical line.

'Hmm. I see what you mean.'

'Well, I suppose we potentially stopped a rogue element getting their hands on knowledge they could use for a terrorist attack. For some specific political aim. Or in a regional war somewhere.'

'And, don't forget, you cleared my uncle's name. Without that, he would never have received the recognition he deserves. And I suppose, being realistic about it, the neutralising effect of a balance of technology of all types between the powers maintains world peace.'

Haruto and Karen walked slowly through the quiet streets. Tomorrow the city would return to lockdown. Tonight they had just one decision. Which bed were they going to sleep in together later and in the future?

As the black cab drove along through the empty roads to Chiswick, they snuggled down in the soft leather seats. All thoughts of the darker side of humanity were easily pushed aside.

The End

AUTHORS NOTE

The Secret War is a work of contemporary fiction written during the global pandemic and under lockdown conditions. The third in my Karen Andersen thriller series, this story combines all the elements of unexplained murders, grand conspiracy, and a terror threat to world peace. To make these threads tie together realistically, I chose the theme of bioweapons.

My earlier books were set against a background of political intrigue and religious extremism.

Because it is difficult to establish whether a lethal virus has been deliberately manufactured and released, as an act of destabilisation as opposed to having developed naturally, the true origin is wide open to conjecture. I had to address spin and propaganda in *The Secret War* in order to write about modern day espionage against a landscape of twenty-first century counter terrorism.

Social media, fake news, and guerrilla journalism all play their part in building or debunking conspiracy theories. You can sleuth the net and see that for yourself as readily as my protagonist Karen Andersen. When the Coronavirus was first identified in Wuhan, the wave of anti-China sentiment online gave me the central idea for the book.

There have been deniers throughout history from those who refuse to believe the world is round to those who think that the holocaust was made up. Chemical and biowarfare is not new and below are some examples of their usage. From history.

600   Solon uses the purgative herb hellebore during the siege of Krissa.

1155   Emperor Barbarossa poisons water wells with human bodies in Tortona, Italy.

1675   German and French forces agree not to use poisoned bullets.

1710   Russian troops catapult human bodies of plague victims into Swedish cities.

1763   British distribute blankets from smallpox patients to native Americans.

1797   Napoleon floods the plains around Mantua, Italy, to accelerate the spread of malaria.

1863   Confederates sell clothing from yellow fever and smallpox patients to Union troops during the US Civil War.

World War I   German and French agents use glanders, anthrax, and mustard gas.

World War II   Japan uses plague, anthrax, and other diseases Several other countries experiment with and develop biological weapon programs.

1980–1988   Iraq uses mustard gas, sarin, and tabun against Iranian and ethnic groups inside Iraq during the Persian Gulf War.

ACKNOWLEDGMENTS

This novel owes much to the research and analysis of others. Grateful thanks to the Mercator Institute for Chinese Studies and the Liverpool China Partnership. I gained background colour from a Chinese friend in Australia who related the terrifying account of her family's life and final escape from China during the Cultural Revolution. I am in debt to those who have advised me on Sino-British affairs and contemporary security issues. My appreciation to The Cruise Ship Wave Network, the International Cruise Victims Association, and Liz Jarvis for the finer details of life aboard a modern cruise ship.

Thank you to my editor Victor John for his painstaking work and everyone at New Century who have helped get this book on the reading circuit. Hamish Brown MBE deserves a shout out as my police advisor and Dr Ivor Burfitt for his medical expertise. As do Simon McQuiggan and Muse Strategy for their design skills and generous help online.

A special love and thanks to friends and family. In particular beloved Arabella, Brooke, Rhys, and granddaughter Dempsie Lee Williams. I should mention my extraordinary husband Donald Burfitt-Dons for his constant support and ability to make me laugh at my foibles. He is my 'first reader', severest critic and, as a retired airline pilot, *The Secret War's* expert advisor on all things relating to aviation, navigation, and meteorology. Also I poached liberally from his experience when knocked overboard into the path of a real cruise liner. He survived and so did our marriage. At the time of writing, we celebrate our thirty-ninth wedding anniversary in November.

CPSIA information can be obtained
at www.ICGtesting.com
Printed in the USA
LVHW041857050721
691875LV00011B/1499